Cold-Blooded Myrtle

Cold-Blooded Myrtle

A MYRTLE HARDCASTLE MYSTERY

Elizabeth C. Bunce

ALGONQUIN YOUNG READERS 2021

Published by Algonquin Young Readers
an imprint of Algonquin Books of Chapel Hill
Post Office Box 2225
Chapel Hill, North Carolina 27515-2225

a division of Workman Publishing
225 Varick Street
New York, New York 10014

LIBRARY OF CONGRESS CATALOGING-IN-PUBLICATION DATA
Names: Bunce, Elizabeth C., author.
Title: Cold-blooded Myrtle / Elizabeth C. Bunce.
Description: First edition. | Chapel Hill, North Carolina : Algonquin
Young Readers, [2021] | Series: A Myrtle Hardcastle mystery ; 3 |
Audience: Ages 10 and up | Audience: Grades 4–6 |
Summary: Twelve-year-old Young Lady of Quality and Victorian
amateur detective Myrtle Hardcastle returns, and now she is on
the trail of a serial killer in her hometown of Swinburne.
Identifiers: LCCN 2021008082 | ISBN 9781616209209 (hardcover) |
ISBN 9781643752266 (ebook)
Subjects: CYAC: Mystery and detective stories. | Murder–Fiction. |
Great Britain–History–Victoria, 1837–1901–Fiction.
Classification: LCC PZ7.B91505 Col 2021 | DDC [Fic]–dc23
LC record available at https://lccn.loc.gov/2021008082

10 9 8 7 6 5 4 3 2 1
First Edition

In loving memory of
Milton L. Bunce, Jr.

❧

a man who never thought about
murder a day in his life
(except when reading his
daughter-in-law's books)

1

THE METROPOLITAN HOLIDAY

As we approach the New Century, our age-old traditions
and celebrations join us in this modern world.

—H. M. Hardcastle, *A Modern Yuletide:*
An Historical & Scientific Discourse on the Christmas
Holiday & Its Most Venerable Traditions, 1893

"Don't blame me if you're disappointed. You've been
warned." Miss Judson, my governess, dipped a gloved
hand into her jacket pocket and withdrew her watch,
frowning slightly. "Your father was nearly inconsol-
able when he heard."

"I just want to read it for myself," I said stoutly.
I'd been waiting for the December issue of the *Strand
Magazine* to come out, for I had yet to read the newest
Sherlock Holmes story, "The Adventure of the Final

Problem." It had been released in America the prior month, which I thought patently unfair, since Holmes was, above all, an English sleuth.

Moments later, a foggy-breathed Caroline Munjal joined us outside Leighton's Mercantile. "Is it here yet?" she asked, shaking snow from her black hair.

We were not the only people awaiting the opening of the shop. A whole crowd had gathered this Saturday morning for the grand unveiling of Leighton's annual Christmas window display. Caroline had been alight with eager speculation for days now over what Mr. Leighton might have chosen to depict.

"Maybe it will be the Redgraves Murder!"

As if on cue, another figure flitted toward us, balancing a stack of magazines—our neighbor, heiress Priscilla Wodehouse. "The latest issue of *Tales from the Red Graves*," she announced. Capitalizing on her home's recent history, she'd opened a small publishing enterprise named for the notorious residence. "Hot off the press and ready to stock Mr. Leighton's newsstand."

"Is there a Mabel Castleton story?" Caroline wanted to know. The new penny dreadful tales were gaining popularity—at least among a small crowd of devoted followers. Priscilla held out high hopes of their worldwide success. I had mixed feelings on the subject.

Priscilla's eyes twinkled. "You'll just have to wait and see."

"I see Dr. Doyle has a rival," Miss Judson Observed.

"We'll read them *both*." Caroline was nothing if not loyal.

I stood on tiptoe, trying to look past the assembled company. Would there be a miniature Redgraves manor, site of my own first triumph as an Investigator?

"Don't get your hopes up," Miss Judson advised. "It has been a busy year for the village."

"Indeed it has." Here came Mrs. Munjal, arms laden with parcels. She wore a sprig of holly pinned to her collar, and the mingled scents of pine and peppermint came with her. "There was the flower show, Lancelot and Elaine's cygnets"—referring to the ill-tempered swans at the park—"and of course we have a Mayor now."

"Don't remind us," Caroline grumbled—but it was too late. The crowd parted, somewhat reluctantly, and a grandly dressed pair of females paraded through like peahens, nearly identical in matching velvet and fur and towering, beribboned hats.

"Good morning, Mrs. Spence-Hastings, LaRue." Miss Judson's voice was as frosty as the morning as she greeted our former neighbors.

"You may address *me* as Mrs. Mayoress," LaRue's mother said. Inaccurately, not that anyone bothered to correct her.

"And me as Miss Spence-Hastings," put in LaRue, her mother's perfect miniature, down to the arrogant angle of their heads as they gazed down their noses at the common folk.

I managed to avoid rolling my eyes, but Caroline was not as successful. LaRue had been putting on airs even more than usual since her father's appointment to the new office of Mayor. It was all part of Swinburne's ongoing Modernization, efforts to secure its status as one of the most progressive villages in England.

"It's sure to be the Mansion House," LaRue declared. "We've entirely refurbished it, you know. Father's found the biggest tree in the county for the Mayor's Christmas Ball."

I ignored the Spence-Hastingses and turned my attention to the rest of the crowd. Despite the cold, throngs had turned out for the big reveal. A Salvation Army band played an enthusiastic medley of "We Three Kings" and "God Rest You Merry, Gentlemen," and Mrs. Munjal wrestled an arm free to drop a shilling into their red bucket.

The shop itself was quiet, its gas off and a green baize curtain closed over the window inscribed, LEIGHTON'S MERCANTILE EMPORIUM: FINE GOODS & WONDERS FROM ACROSS THE EMPIRE. The deep glass windows were usually crammed full of every manner of necessity and luxury, from reels of lace to rows of books to crocks of marmalade and mincemeat.*

---

* Cook turned up her nose at this, saying any self-respecting Englishwoman made her own.

They'd recently showcased an Underwood typewriter, and inside I was hoping to find a new leather brief-bag for Father's Christmas gift. I still had not decided what to get Miss Judson. Despite being my closest companion in the world, she was notoriously difficult to shop for. Her reception of the pocket toxicology analysis set I'd produced for her last year (for testing her food against poison) had been somewhat . . . lackluster.

This being the first Saturday in December, the ordinary goods had been cleared out of the windows to make room for Christmas. One window held the tree, sparkling with silver and red ornaments, paper chains, sweets, and candles, while the other featured the Display: a meticulously crafted scale model of Swinburne, dressed up for the holidays and depicting the year's most notable events in the village. Mr. Leighton worked on it year round, and the shop window had been shrouded for the last two weeks, as he set up the final touches in absolute secrecy.

As the band played and the snow fell and the Spence-Hastingses preened, the rest of us craned our necks, trying to peek round the curtain for a glimpse.

"Are you ready for your first English Christmas, Miss Wodehouse?" Mrs. Munjal's voice was merry and bright. Miss Judson and the two Munjals were all dressed in festive holiday clothes and smart hats that set off their varying shades of brown skin—tan, bronze, and olive. Priscilla was a picture in pink, with blond hair and ivory cheeks tinted with rose. Beside them all, I felt small and pasty and rumpled.

Priscilla did not have a chance to respond, for at that moment, Mrs. Leighton finally arrived, bustling through the assembled crowd with the great brass key to the shop doors in her hands.

"It's so nice to see you all!" She beamed, blue eyes crinkling beneath her frizzy red fringe. "Basil has been working so hard this year—claims it's his best Display ever, and won't let me see a peep of it! Even stayed in the shop last night to make sure everything was perfect. Had to bring him his breakfast, I did." She patted her basket. "Now, wait out here while I rouse Himself to unveil it properly. He'll want to point out all the details."

With a rattle of her key, the shop door opened, emitting a very Christmassy jingle. A moment passed, then another, then at last the green cloth parted, and—with a little tugging and hesitation as the curtains caught on the roof of a model building—a miniature Swinburne Village appeared.

There was a burst of applause. The band struck up "Pat-a-Pan," and there came gasps of appreciation as we all marveled at the perfection of the replica: the exact details of the Town Hall's broken chimney pot and wreaths of evergreen in every window, the red postbox and telephone kiosk at the High Street tram station, the flocked model horses pulling their glossy sleigh across the wool-wadding snow.

This year Mr. Leighton had *not* elected to reproduce Redgraves and the Gilded Slipper lilies, or the change in Swinburne's local governance. Or the swans. Instead, he had expanded the Display to include nearby Schofield College. The streets of the model village were empty, and there was a collective murmur as we realized that the tiny villagers were all clustered round the Campanile, the college's famous belltower. Amid a ring formed by the model people stood two small objects that seemed incongruous: a stone wishing well, painted entirely black, tipped on its side; and a life-size sprig of grapes—no, olives—still on the stem.

"That's not very interesting at all," the Mayoress exclaimed. "What is that supposed to be? People standing about staring at rubbish?"

"It's certainly . . . unusual," offered Miss Judson. "What do you suppose it means? Olives and a well?"

"What? Let me see!" Mrs. Munjal shoved her way forward, barreling through several small children and their mums, who howled in protest. I squeezed aside to make room, but she halted a few feet from the window, staring at the Display. "No," she breathed. "It can't be. Not again." Without further explanation, she seized Caroline by the arm and hauled her away from the shop.

"Mother!" Caroline cried—but whatever had startled Mrs. Munjal was stronger than Caroline's curiosity, and Caroline could not escape her mother's grip. She gave me a look of confused apology as Mrs. Munjal bundled her swiftly into their carriage and rode away.

"What was that about?" Priscilla said.

"I have no idea," I said. But we had no time to wonder further, for at that moment, from inside the shop erupted a bone-rattling scream.

Miss Judson and I exchanged one brief, significant Look before turning on our heels and diving for the shop door. It flew wide under Miss Judson's grasp, onto a peculiar scene. Deep in shadows, in the very back near the stove, sat Mr. Leighton, in a hard kitchen chair with a mug in his hand, looking for all the world like he'd just sat down for tea and dozed off.

Except his eyes were open, staring blindly at nothing.

Mrs. Leighton's white hands clutched her anguished face. "He's *dead*!"

2

GHOST OF CHRISTMAS PAST

> The liturgical season of Advent is a time to prepare for
> the arrival of Christmas with prayers, carols, and celebra-
> tions. A less happy observation involves reflection upon
> the Four Last Things: Death, Judgment, Heaven, and Hell.
>
> —H. M. Hardcastle, *A Modern Yuletide*

Words poured from Mrs. Leighton. "I couldn't find
him, he wasn't here to open the curtains, and everyone
was waiting, so I went ahead, and that's when I saw—"
She waved weakly toward the back rooms, trembling.
"Oh, Lordy, what'll we do?"

Miss Judson swept the shopkeeper into a firm
embrace. "We'll catch our breath, Mrs. Leighton, and
send for the authorities. Myrtle, will you phone Dr.
Belden?"

{9

I nodded, dumbly—but I was staring at Mr. Leighton with the cold, pooling conviction that the person we really needed was Dr. Munjal, the Police Surgeon.

I summoned the police, too. They were right across the street, after all. Constable Carstairs showed up first, unfortunately, instead of Inspector Hardy of the Detective Bureau, who knows my work. I supposed that made sense; we didn't need a detective for an ordinary death. Miss Judson put me in charge of poor Mrs. Leighton so she could impose order on the crowd outside, which gave me very little time to examine the scene.

Of course, it was possible that I'd jumped the gun, so to speak, and Mr. Leighton had simply passed away while having his evening tea. But something about his posture, upright in the chair, cup in hand, made alarm bells clang in my head. A cracker barrel sat at his side, and it looked like he'd been jotting a note, perhaps to Mrs. Leighton.

"Wot's this?" Constable Carstairs peered in closer, prizing the missive from Mr. Leighton's hand. "It's gibberish. Must've been having a stroke or sommat." He waved the scrap of paper in the air, and I caught a glimpse of it.

"No, it's Greek," I said, which roused Mrs. Leighton.

"Greek?" She sniffed tearfully. "But he hasn't done that in years. Not since he retired."

"Eh?"

"He was a professor, at the college." She flicked an absent hand toward the Display in the window.

"May I see that?" I asked politely, as if it were a perfectly normal request. "I read Greek."

"Course ye do." Constable Carstairs started to hand it to me, but I stepped back, hands knotted behind my skirts.

"No, the fewer people who touch it, the better. It may have finger-marks on it." I leaned in instead. "It's—er, it's upside down, Constable."

He rotated it, and I read the words, frown growing. "But that doesn't make any sense."

"What did he say, Myrtle? Is—is it a suicide note?" Mrs. Leighton's voice was frail.

"I don't think so." But that tugged even harder at my brain. Dr. Leighton's Greek was perfectly legible, and the grammar was fine, but it was totally nonsensical. A message with no meaning at all.

"'*We owe a cockerel to Asclepius,*'" I read, first in Greek, then English, more mystified each time.

"I beg yer pardon?" Constable Carstairs's voice was icy and hard.

"That's what the note says. Don't ask me. It doesn't mean anything. Mrs. Leighton?"

She shook her head, hand at her lacy throat. "Why would he write that?"

Maybe he *hadn't* written it. It had been clutched in his fingers, but there was no pen nearby, and the ink was

{11

dry, unsmudged. "You need to keep that for evidence," I advised the constable, who growled his thanks.

The jangle of bells heralded the return of Miss Judson, Dr. Belden in tow. I scurried across to admit them, hiding behind the door. Dr. Belden strode into the shop and examined the scene with a wise, weather eye. An older man with a reassuring stoop and gnarled hands that spoke of decades of competent medical work, he'd kept the High Street surgery for as long as anybody could remember.

All my self-confidence and assurance withered up inside me when he walked into Leighton's Mercantile. Not for any logical reason; he was as skilled and experienced a physician as there was to be found anywhere in England, I was sure. But he'd been Mum's doctor before she died, and even all these years later, I couldn't help the sinking dread I felt whenever I saw him. He still gave me that sad smile, like he wanted to give me something impossible, and it pained him that he couldn't. He didn't make me feel at all like an accomplished Investigator working a case.

I hung back, edge of my thumb in my mouth like a baby, and watched. The doctor frowned into the professor's clouded eyes, clucking his tongue like he was examining a patient who could actually use his help. I wondered if he'd give Mrs. Leighton that sad smile, too. He touched the man's cold, stiff wrist—although there was no chance of a pulse.

"Did you bring your thermometer?" My voice was a pitiful creak, but I was proud of myself for finding it.

He frowned, as if he couldn't quite place me. "Oh, Miss Hardcastle." Unlike the men from the police force, he wasn't accustomed to tripping over me in his work.

"To test the body?" I ventured. "A corpse loses about a degree per hour, depending on conditions." You could estimate the time of death based on body temperature. Dr. Munjal had taught me that. The conditions here, however, were a freezing cold shop in December, which would no doubt affect accuracy.

"I have no intention of taking this man's temperature while you're all standing about," the doctor said sternly. "Even a dead man deserves his privacy."

"Was it his heart?" Mrs. Leighton's voice wandered over to us. Miss Judson had joined her, a reassuring hand on her arm.

Dr. Belden leaned closer, peering at Mr. Leighton's face and hands. "A stroke, more likely," he said. "Poor old chap. My condolences, Mrs. Leighton. Your husband was a fine man."

I swallowed hard. Mr. Leighton had always been kind to me, happily explaining the entire natural history of every object in his shop—waterproof Wellies from Brazilian rubber, cocoa and cinnamon from Ceylon and Java—and sneaking me copies of *Illustrated Police News* when Miss Judson wasn't looking. I'd been eager to hear his take on the latest Sherlock Holmes number, and now I never would.

At that moment, the doorbells jangled, and Dr. Munjal, Police Surgeon and Caroline's father, stepped in, gripping his medical bag and breathing hard.

"Munjal!" Dr. Belden looked taken aback. "What are you doing here? This isn't a police matter."

"This may be a crime scene, Doctor." Miss Judson spoke up before Dr. Munjal–or I–could reply. She was more soothing than I could have managed. I was working on it, Dear Reader, although I rather feared I was turning out more like the constable, better at barking at people to get my way.

Dr. Belden's hawklike eyes narrowed, and the constable grumbled, while Dr. Munjal just stood freezing and frozen in the threshold.

"Awright," Constable Carstairs said. "Ever'one out, then. Mrs. Leighton, is there somewhere–else–we can talk?" When Mrs. Leighton indicated a room above the shop, the constable instructed Miss Judson to take her up there, and clomped up the stairs behind them. Miss Judson's glance plainly indicated that she expected me to accompany them–but I pretended not to notice.

"I'll take over now, Doctor, if you don't mind," Dr. Munjal said, with a deferential nod.

"I most certainly *do* mind. I'm this man's personal physician, and there's nothing here to suggest this is a criminal matter."

What about the cryptic note in his hand? Or the strange items in the Display, which had so upset Mrs. Munjal? It was safer having Dr. Munjal double-check things, just to be sure.

"I'll be the judge of that." Dr. Munjal was a small, neat man, several inches shorter than Dr. Belden, but he stood politely, still in his overcoat, until Dr. Belden stepped aside. I bit my lip and wondered if Dr. Munjal often had to deal with obstructive colleagues.

I wanted to watch Dr. Munjal examine the body, but Dr. Belden was still hovering—and besides, he'd been right. Mr. Leighton *did* deserve his privacy. Dr. Munjal's poking at him clinically, here in his cozy shop where he'd spent so many intimate years, felt like an intrusion.

I backed away, behind the counter, and studied the Display instead. At first it was just to stay out of the way while still listening to what was happening— but the curious tableau drew my attention now. What were the wishing well and the olives doing there among all the Christmas carolers and bell ringers? Perhaps Mr. Leighton had been meaning to set them up some- where when he'd felt unwell, and simply dropped them before he went to sit down.

But that didn't explain Mrs. Munjal's reaction—or why Dr. Munjal had dashed right over here afterward. I hadn't called for him, and I was sure the police hadn't, either. They'd only do that for an obvious crime scene. So how had Dr. Munjal known someone here was dead?

"Hey, now—what are you doing there, man?"

Dr. Belden was understandably startled. Dr. Munjal was bent low, face close to the dead man's mouth and nose, *sniffing* with tremendous concentration. My interest spiked, and I hastened toward him. Was he checking for toxins? Many had distinct odors (as did several diseases, evident on the patient's breath or skin, like diabetes and kidney failure), and a doctor's nose was a significant diagnostic and Investigative tool.

Something on the floor behind the counter distracted me—another object out of place, perhaps something else that had fallen from the Display. A pale, gold-edged corner of paper peeked out from beneath the cabinets, and I had to wriggle it loose with my toe.

It was an old photograph, a cabinet card showing several young men and women dressed for an expedition, posing on a windswept hill. In the center of the group stood a younger Mr. Leighton in a Norfolk jacket and hunting tweeds. I recognized his lean weathered face and sharp curious eyes. I flipped it over, where someone had scrawled *Cornwall, 1873*. I turned it back, and my heart thumped, one hard cold bang right in my throat.

Next to Mr. Leighton was a young woman holding a pickaxe and smiling jauntily for the camera. Her dark eyes stared back at me, for the first time in five years.

It was my mother.

3

In Camera

Time-honored English tradition requires pickling a perfectly good pudding in liquor then setting it afire like a flaming cannonball as the centerpiece of Christmas dinner, no doubt as a sign of intimidation to the Empire's enemies.

—H. M. Hardcastle, *A Modern Yuletide*

All afternoon I kept stealing glances at the photograph of Mum and Mr. Leighton, which I had collected as evidence. Very well, Dear Reader—I'd swiped it. What else could I do? One doesn't find a photograph of one's mother next to a dead man every day, after all. And the feeling in my chest, deep and painful, told me it was not something I should simply wave in the face of Constable Carstairs. Nor could I leave it behind and pretend I'd never seen it. So instead I had carefully tucked it away in my bag, feeling pinched and fluttery, while the doctors and the constable finished their work and took Mr. Leighton's body away.

I'd come home alone. Miss Judson had stayed in town to help Mrs. Leighton get settled. It had been hard walking out of the shop, leaving her looking so alone and lost, and knowing there was nothing I could do to help. Dr. Munjal had concurred with Dr. Belden's diagnosis of a stroke, and had bustled away again without stopping to talk with me and Miss Judson. There was no mystery to solve, no criminal to bring to justice. There was just the sad abrupt finality that Mr. Leighton was there one night, and gone again the next morning. I hated it.

Now Peony and I sat on the stairs, studying the picture. Cook was in the kitchen, making ginger-snaps, and Father was at his morris dancing practice, so we had most of the house to ourselves. How had Mum known Mr. Leighton, and who were the other people in the picture with them? *Cornwall, 1873.* That was years before I was born, a part of her life I knew nothing about—but I was surprised that the Leightons had never mentioned knowing her, before she was Mum. Come to think of it, though, I couldn't remember Mum frequenting Leighton's Mercantile when she was alive. I fingered the edge of the photograph, the layers brittle and starting to separate, and wondered what it all meant—the photograph, the olives and the wishing well, Mrs. Munjal's strange reaction to the Display, and the cryptic note in Mr. Leighton's hand.

"Mrrr?" Peony's grave green eyes held a question.

"You're right. Mr. Leighton might have died of natural causes—but there are still questions here." Maybe answering one of them, at least, would make me feel better. If I could give Mrs. Leighton some kind of reason, perhaps it would help her, too.

But whatever I sought would not be found among the books and laboratory equipment in my schoolroom. I wasn't sure anything of Father's could help, either. But his study was snug and orderly and comforting, and being there always helped me make a little more sense of the world.

It was dim and chilly within, so I lit the gas and turned up the radiator. The room smelled lemony and leathery, a combination of furniture polish, moustache wax, and bookbinding, and I inhaled deeply. Across from Father's desk hung a framed photograph of Mum, from before they married. She didn't look much like the Mum I remembered, with her mischievous grin, chasing me about the nursery in her nightgown, long black hair loose and flying down her back. This young woman was prim and straight, in a stiff frock with a silly bustle, and gazing frankly at the camera, as if daring it to prove her wrong.

I stood a little straighter, looking at that picture. I always did. It had been taken when she was studying to be a doctor. I'd seen others that were more like I remembered her: wearing a cap and gown, in a comical pose with anatomical skeletons. Or on a hill in Cornwall with a pickaxe.

But the woman Father chose to look at every day was her serious side, the one brave and determined enough to defy convention and pick up a bone saw, right next to all those men saying she couldn't do it.

I walked closer to the picture—and noticed something I hadn't seen before. Or perhaps something that I'd always seen, but never Observed.

I touched the glass over the impressed letters on the oval mat. "Schofield Student Union."

"Dear old Schofield," said a soft, cheerful voice behind me, letting in a breath of warm air and an even stronger scent of lemon wax. Father strolled in and put an arm around my shoulders. *"Dear Schofield, how we adored thee, our studious hours in your ivory towers . . ."* he sang, and I turned to gape at him. Father didn't sing.

Peony leaped onto the desk and stretched luxuriantly, knocking Father's letter knife to the floor, where it buried, point-down, in the rug. She paused threateningly before the inkwell, until Father deigned to pick her up so she could attend to his whiskers. He was still in his dancing costume of white trousers, bracers, and beribboned bells strapped to his legs. How had he sneaked up on us?

I ought to have taken the chance to slip out of the room, before Father could lecture me about getting involved in *another* suspicious death—could I help it if I kept stumbling into them whilst doing perfectly innocent and Ordinary things? The Christmas Display Unveiling was *exactly* the sort of activity he was always urging me to do more—"What?"

He shifted back against the desk. "I was just thinking how much you look like your mother."

I let out my breath in a wistful sigh and tugged at my hair. "I do?"

I'd been told I took after Father's aunt Helena,* whom the Reader may recall from my previous adventures. But now I searched the portrait hopefully, looking not for the Mum I remembered but for signs of my own countenance. Maybe I *did* have a bit of that determined set to my jaw. Most people called it stubborn. (Aunt Helena called it impertinent.)

"She used to bite her lip, just like that."

I pressed my lips together neatly and looked at my hands.

"Professor Leighton was one of her favorites," Father said, and I jerked my head up warily.

---

* Regrettably, according to legal and official records, I am technically *Helena* Myrtle Hardcastle. Aunt Helena and I see eye to eye on very few matters, and I have often wished I might have been the namesake of any other relative. Mum's father's name, for instance, was Algernon. And I believe there was a dog called Rusty.

"*Professor* Leighton?" I said, trying to sound innocent. "Mum knew him?"

"Oh, yes. He taught Classics." Father strolled to the bookcase and withdrew an unfamiliar booklet. *Schofield Yearbook, 1874*. Mum's signature was on the overleaf, swoopy and elegant: *Jemima M. Bell*, along with tiny sketches of a bird and a bell. Mum used to leave me notes signed just like this, for Jemima, a name from the Bible that meant "dove."

I sat down and flipped through it, eager for more, but it was all in Latin, no pictures, just boring lists of classes, professors, and students' names.

"Professor Leighton was a great supporter of the female students," Father said.

"I thought Schofield College always took women." Unlike many institutions of higher learning in England. And everywhere.

"They did," he said. "And Basil Leighton was right there from the beginning, helping found the school. He believed that women and men—that *all people*—deserved a quality education if they were to advance in the world. He knew your mum quite well."

I didn't know what I should say to that. It certainly wasn't what came out. "Now they're both dead."

Father sighed. Peony—who had known neither of them, but who was racking up more than her own share of deceased acquaintances—sighed, too. "I'm sorry you saw that," Father said.

"I'm not—" I tried to say, but he held up a hand.

"I know. I know you're not. But someday you might have a daughter of your own, and you'll understand what I mean."

This made me fidget even more. "I'm sorry it happened, too." I was sorry, of course—sorry for Mr. Leighton, and Mrs. Leighton, and all the other people who'd known him. Which reminded me of something. "The Munjals were there. The Display upset Mrs. Munjal for some reason, and Dr. Munjal acted strangely, too." Dr. Munjal had been at medical school with Mum, so perhaps he'd also been acquainted with Mr. Leighton back then. But that still didn't explain how he'd known to come examine the body.

Father listened, arms crossed and head tilted to the side. "Go on," he said—startling the whole story right out of me. He *never* wanted to discuss cases with me! I described the Display, the belltower and the cluster of people gathered round it, concluding with the odd, out-of-place olives and the wishing well.

"What color was the well?"

That was his question? "It was painted all black. Why?"

"Olive, black well." He ran the words together like a name. "*Olive Blackwell*? Why would he put that on display?"

I scooted to the edge of my seat. "That means something to you, too?"

"Not to me personally, no. It happened long before I met your mum. But it's the reason Professor Leighton wasn't a professor anymore." He pushed a hand through his ginger hair. "This would be a prime moment for me to dramatically unfurl a faded newspaper so you could read the sordid details yourself. Olive Blackwell was a student at Schofield, in your mother's class. She disappeared one night. Rumor had it that she fell from the belltower—"

"Like in the Display!" The villagers clustered round the Campanile, as if to witness a spectacle. Except something had been conspicuously missing from that tableau, if Miss Blackwell had fallen. "But—"

Father finished the thought for me. "Her body was never found. As far as anyone could tell, she simply vanished into thin air, never to be heard from again."

Now I well and truly felt a chill, and not the draft from Father's window. "Professor Leighton was involved?"

"I'm not really privy to all the details," Father said. "I don't think your mum even knew exactly what happened. But it caused a scandal, and Professor Leighton was forced to retire."

I nodded slowly. "And Dr. Munjal—well, *Mr.* Munjal, back then—was there, too."

"I suppose he might have been. I'm not sure."

But I was. Mrs. Munjal wouldn't have reacted the way she did about the olives and the well if she hadn't known all about the scandal. Was Dr. Munjal involved somehow? What about Mum? I didn't like that idea much at all. The sharp edges of the photograph I'd taken from the Leightons poked me through my skirt pocket. I squeezed my fingers together to keep from pulling it out and showing it to Father, before I knew more about what had happened and what it meant.

"What else do you know about Professor Leighton?" I asked. "And before you tell me not to get involved in this, I'm *not*. But somebody Mum knew has died."

Father perched on the edge of the desk. "I know. I can't imagine how she'd react to this news."

"I can," I said. "She'd do something about it. She'd bring a hot dish to his wife."

He smiled. "And knit a muffler for her."

"And organize a vigil."

"And take up a collection for his widow and children."

By then we were both smiling. "That was your mum, all right," he said. "You couldn't stop her, once she set her mind to something." He gave me a fond look that made me feel warm and melty inside. "Remind you of anyone else we know?"

He scratched Peony's back thoughtfully. "Describe everything to me again," he urged.

Careful, not wanting to omit a single detail, I laid out the entire scene: Mr. Leighton in his chair, the cup in his hand, the note in Greek beside him. "Mrs.

Leighton couldn't say whether it was his handwriting or not. He probably wrote it, but it doesn't make any sense."

"What did it say?"

I had copied it faithfully into my notebook, but I gave Father my own translation. "We owe Asclepius a chicken."

He turned round. "What? Are you sure? Sorry, yes, of course you're sure."

"Does it mean something?"

"It sounds familiar, somehow. May I see it?"

Since I couldn't possibly have the evidence itself at hand, I felt a flush of pride that he'd known I would have recorded it. I handed him my notebook, then held my tongue and barely fidgeted.

"I *know* this," he said finally, and spun toward the bookcase with a jingle, long fingers sliding down the rows. "I know this, where was it . . ." His hand came to a stop on the spine of an old schoolbook, the leather binding cracked from wear. He flipped through, faster and faster, then came to a stop and jammed his finger down, like he was pointing out particularly egregious evidence to an uncooperative witness.

"Haha! Crito!"

"What?"

He handed me the book, and I read down the Greek text until I found the same letters I'd written out myself. It was a collection of works by Plato, and there indeed, in a passage thousands of years old, the strange, strange words again: *"Crito, we owe a cockerel to Asclepius. Pay it and do not forget."*

"Those were the last words of Socrates." Father's voice rang with intellectual triumph. The air in his study hung with excitement and meaning, like he'd just handed me a puzzle and challenged me to solve it.

I scrunched my nose. "I don't understand."

"I don't either!" Father sounded almost gleeful. "What an odd note to write before you die! I hope I have the presence of mind to leave behind such a mysterious document—have you all puzzled for decades. Like Fermat."*

"Father!"

He pulled his attention back to me. "Sorry. Got a bit carried away, there."

"What does Socrates have to do with Mr. Leighton?"

Father took down another book from the shelf and leafed through it absently (it was upside down). "Well," he said slowly, "Socrates was charged with impiety, and with corrupting the youth of Athens."

Shocked, I blurted out, "What does *that* mean?"

Father made it worse by turning pink, but hastily

---

* Pierre de Fermat's Last Conjecture, a frightfully pointless math problem scrawled in the margins of a book 250 years ago, which no one has since been able to solve, although for some reason people keep trying. (Why couldn't he have left a note about something we wanted to know?)

said, "Encouraging them to think for themselves." After a pause he added, with a smile, "You might relate to that."

I did indeed. Girls, especially, were actively *discouraged* from thinking for ourselves; whole magazines were devoted to the practice, and people like LaRue Spence-Hastings adhered to it like a law.

I swung my feet and considered this. "Why would Mr. Leighton leave that note behind?"

Father looked thoughtful. "Perhaps he was reminiscing about the past. But it does seem strange for him to depict Olive Blackwell's disappearance in his Christmas village."

I thought back to what I knew of the Greek philosopher, and realization stole slowly over me, cold and heavy, creeping toward my heart. "Socrates was *executed*," I said. "Sentenced to drink poison hemlock."

4

TIDINGS OF DISCOMFORT

Medieval lords appointed a "Lord of Misrule" to oversee their lavish Christmas celebrations. During the brief reign of Edward VI, the Lord of Misrule was a lawyer named George Ferrers, whose Christmas pageant of 1552 cost hundreds of pounds and involved music, feasting, masques, and the ever-popular mock beheadings.

-H. M. Hardcastle, *A Modern Yuletide*

Father set the book down, nearly missing the edge of the desk. Peony uttered an affronted burble and darted aside. "How did you say the professor was found? With a cup in his hand? Like he'd sat down, drunk something, and died?"

I scarcely nodded, but my heart had started to bang, fierce and fast. "We need to tell somebody." Father was Swinburne's Prosecuting Solicitor, which meant if there was a murder, he would have to get involved.

"Tell who? Say what? We don't know anything." Even as he spoke the words, I could tell he was starting to regret them.

"Dr. Munjal," I said simply. This was clearly a matter for the Police Surgeon.

"Very well. I'll drop by his office in the morning."

"Now." My voice was firm.

"Wait a minute—"

I was ready for Father's objections, and rose to my feet. Peony rose with me—a United Front. "Dr. Munjal was his student, too. If there's any suspicion that this *wasn't* a natural death"—I was proud of myself for circumventing the word *murder*—"you have to let him know what to look for in the post-mortem. He needs to know." If I'd had to, I'd have stepped pointedly closer to Mum's photograph, but there was no need.

He was looking out the window, at the waning afternoon and restless wind, scattering beech leaves through the pale, pinkening sky. "It does look like a fine day for a walk," he said dryly.

"I'll get my things." I dashed off before he could object.

Peony and I were waiting at the door by the time Father made it down the stairs—changed out of his morris dancing regalia, thank goodness. He merely raised an eyebrow, made no comment, and swung open the door.

"After you."

It turned out to be after Peony, who bolted out the door as if her own message to the Munjals was even more urgent than ours. She disappeared into the neighbors' hedges, but make no mistake, Dear Reader: she was stalking us, like a leopardess in the jungle.

We set off across Gravesend Commons, the park that used to be a graveyard. The December wind whipped through the trees along the edges of the greenway, and more dry leaves skittered in the gutter. A hazy halo glowed round the gas streetlamp as we made our way over the former graves, past the old stone crypt that now housed a picnic table and the equipment for lawn darts and croquet. It was lovely and peaceful, everything dormant beneath the light snow, and we strolled along in companionable silence.

The Munjals' house sat across the park in a lofty circle of brick streets and tall houses with white façades. Set back from the curb, it had a large back garden and a carriage house for Dr. Munjal's Police Morgue. I often wondered how their neighbors liked that, although they'd all moved in next to a former cemetery, so they'd really forfeited the right to complain about the proximity to dead people.

The butler answered the door, but our arrival had

alerted the rest of the household, and Caroline and Dr. Munjal appeared at the top of the stairs.

"Arthur, Myrtle. What brings you by?" Although by the grim set of his dark features, it was plain the doctor knew exactly why we'd come. He descended to the foyer and shook Father's hand. "I'm sorry Neenah's not here to see you."

"I'm afraid it's not a social call, Vikram. Can we speak in your office?"

"Come upstairs." Caroline waved me over. "We got our copy of *The Strand* today." I heard both men sigh with relief as they headed for the morgue.

"But I want to know what they're saying," I protested, as Caroline steered me firmly into her room and shut the door with a surreptitious click.

"Did you really find another dead body?" she exclaimed. "Poor Mr. Leighton! Poor *Mrs.* Leighton!"

"Why did your mother take you away like that this morning?"

"I don't *know.*" She dropped onto the bed—white lace heaped with more white lace. "Mother dragged me back home, but she wouldn't say anything. She marched straight into Father's office—which you know she never does—she hates the morgue!—but he left right after and was gone all day, and no one will tell me *anything.* What happened?"

I felt a surge of fellow feeling and sat beside her. "Have you ever heard about a girl who disappeared when your father and my mother were at Schofield College? Professor Leighton was their teacher. She fell from the belltower—"

"Campanile," Caroline corrected me.

"—and vanished into thin air." I paused for Dramatic Effect. "Her name was Olive Blackwell. Just like the Display."

"How chilling!" Caroline's eyes darted about the room, as if the ghost of Olive Blackwell might leap out from the shadows. Which was, I reflected, more or less what had happened this morning, in the shop. "What could have happened to her?"

I filled her in on everything Father had told me about Olive Blackwell (practically nothing), along with our deductions about the mysterious note and its strange connection to Socrates. Her eyes grew wider and wider, and she twisted a long strand of hair around her fingers.

"Hemlock? Then it was suicide?" She seemed unconvinced. "He was such a nice man. Why would he do something like that?"

"Unless someone did it to him," I said. "That's what they're discussing right now."

"Discussing without us, naturally." She went to her window. "They're still out there."

I joined her. We could see both men's silhouettes against the lit-up window of the carriage house.

"They're taking an awfully long time for my father

to tell your father that he should check for hemlock in the post-mortem," I Observed. "I wish we could hear what they're saying."

"We can," she said. "There's a spot above the stables where you can hear everything that happens in Father's laboratory. Come on."

Have I mentioned that Caroline Munjal might very well be Irrepressible?

ↄ⟋ↄ

Two minutes later, the three of us were tucked into position in the storage loft overlooking the carriage house, hidden behind a tidy stack of file boxes. The warm air was a not entirely unpleasant mixture of horse from one side and embalming chemicals from the other. Light filtered up through a gap where the wall met the floor, and Caroline, Peony, and I had a nearly unobstructed view of Dr. Munjal's laboratory.

I could see the top of Dr. Munjal's head. He was seated at the desk, directly below us. Father's ginger head was brighter; he'd doffed his hat and left it on the desk beside Dr. Munjal's skull (the paperweight, not his own cranium).

"I'm not doing the post-mortem," the doctor was saying. "I had to recuse myself, of course. But Belden's a good man, and I think we know what the results will show."

"Hemlock?" said Father. Dr. Munjal's head bobbed slightly.

"I wish I could say I was more surprised." His hand came up to rub the bridge of his nose. "This whole business—dredging it all up. Neenah's beside herself."

"Should we warn Henry?"

Caroline and I exchanged glances. *Who was Henry?*

"He'll hear soon enough. I'm sorry to say it, Arthur, but I'm glad your Jemima's not here to be dragged into this again."

Now I tensed, gripping Peony so tightly she let out a *brrb* of protest. Thankfully, nobody below seemed to hear. *What* would Mum be dragged into?

"Vikram, if you know anything about Olive Blackwell's disappearance, now is the time to say something. Before this situation gets any more out of hand."

Dr. Munjal's head was bent, his spectacles discarded on the desk. "No, there's nothing. And if I had known something, the time to speak up was twenty years ago."

"Who would want to bring this up again? Why now?"

"I don't know!" Dr. Munjal cried softly. "I was so busy then, with a new wife at home and my studies to see to—I wasn't that involved in collegiate life, and truly, I had to be more careful than anyone else."

Caroline was nodding; it wasn't any easier for an Indian doctor in England than it would have been for a woman—scandal was *always* ready to attach itself to you, even if you had nothing to do with it. If the police had needed a scapegoat* for Olive Blackwell's disappearance, they wouldn't have had to look far to find two suspicious-looking medical students.

"Mr. Leighton must have been killed because it had something to do with Olive's disappearance," Caroline whispered, fiddling with Peony's ears. (Peony showed Exceptional Forbearance in allowing this.) "Do you think he . . . did something to her?"

"They know more than they're saying," I said, indicating our fathers. "We have to get them to tell us."

She gave me a tired look. "Confess secrets they've kept since before we were born, just because we're curious?"

"We're more than curious!" I objected. "We deserve to know." Only—we didn't, really, I supposed. Unless there really was a murderer on the loose, in which case, the more intelligent people hunting for him, the better. It took me only a moment to decide what to say next.

"Your father has a secret file in his office."

She wheeled round to stare at me. "What are you talking about?"

Some months ago, Certain Circumstances had

* a most curious word, whose meaning today doesn't match its origins. It was once an actual goat released into the wilderness to carry away the sins of the people, escaping unharmed (theoretically, anyway)—while another, more unlucky goat was sacrificed.

resulted in my being confined to Dr. Munjal's morgue, alone, for a few hours, during which time I had availed myself of the opportunity to familiarize myself with its layout. And his possessions. Caroline knew this, but we'd never discussed what I'd found that memorable afternoon. I didn't like the idea that the Munjals were keeping secrets from Caroline. Or that there might be something in there about Mum. "There's a file—it says, '*Decapitated?*'"

"*Decapitated?*" she echoed.

"*With* question mark. I think he keeps records in there of cases he still has questions about—suspicious deaths he couldn't prove were murders."

"But Olive Blackwell wasn't his case," Caroline pointed out. "He wasn't even a doctor yet."

"It's a place to start. Unless you think asking him might do the trick."

Caroline leaned against the carriage house's cold brick wall with a sigh. "No," she admitted. "We should get back before *they* get suspicious."

Now I sighed. "Oh, they're suspicious already." Our fathers knew us both too well.

Our progress back to the house was interrupted, however, by a commotion in the dark street outside.

"That's LaRue's carriage," Caroline said, nodding at the glossy conveyance.

As we watched, the coach pulled up not before the Spence-Hastingses' old house next door, but right in front of the Munjals'. Caroline pulled me deeper into the shadows. The carriage door swung open, and a small figure tumbled out in a heap of red velvet robes. Mayor Spence-Hastings put a hand up to straighten the chain of office falling over the fur trim of his Mayoral regalia. An old-fashioned tricorn hat crowned with black feathers dwarfed his head, and his chin vanished in a fluff of white lace cravat.

"What does he want?"

Father and Dr. Munjal at last stepped outside. "Ah, girls, there you are." Dr. Munjal held out his arm, and Caroline scurried to the safety of his embrace—but I could tell both his attention and Father's were on Mayor Spence-Hastings, hastening up the brick walk.

Now I realized *exactly* who "Henry" must be— Henry Fairbush Spence-Hastings, our new Mayor. And LaRue's father.

He was involved in Mr. Leighton's death, too?

5

HOLIDAY SPIRIT

Theologians, historians, and scientists have long attempted to determine the precise date of the first Christmas, based on various Biblical clues. Several candidates have been proposed, including spring, summer, and fall. No agreement being reached, we therefore celebrate in December.

-H. M. Hardcastle, *A Modern Yuletide*

The next day was colder and snowier, "a proper English Christmas," Father declared, tea in hand and gazing out the dining room windows with great satisfaction. Inside, however, Miss Judson looked weary and pensive, and I was fidgeting with all sorts of unspent thoughts and feelings.

"I could do with a proper Guianese Christmas at the moment," she remarked.

"Like Père Fouettard?" I said.

Miss Judson had tried to frighten me with this when

I was younger. "Father Whipper" supposedly trails alongside St. Nicholas, threatening naughty children, as penance for a great crime he committed in life. She'd given up when she realized I was far more interested in the scientific details of how the wicked French butcher had killed and pickled three boys in brine, who were later resuscitated by the saintly Turkish bishop.* Every year, I refined my theory on how the solution had somehow preserved them in a deathlike state, only for them to revive naturally (my latest hypothesis involved electricity and a distillate of mercury), but since no one would allow me to conduct experiments, I suspected that it would remain, at best, unproven.

"I was thinking more like sunshine and temperate weather." She was plainly recalling the balmy tropics of her native French Guiana. I could hardly blame her. Swinburne didn't usually get this much snow, but we certainly put in for more than our share of cold.

Not that that stopped Father. "Humbug," he said. "Christmas isn't Christmas without snow."

"Jesus was probably born in April,"† I said sagely. "Or October."‡

---

* Miss Judson, devout daughter of missionaries, maintains the event was miraculous and therefore beyond scientific scrutiny.

† according to Gospel accounts of shepherds watching over their flocks by night, typically a springtime activity

‡ per theories that the Star of Bethlehem was a sighting of Halley's Comet in the fall of 12 B.C. I had given both of these factors sober consideration. The Bible, frustratingly, fails to specify.

"Don't let Father Christmas hear you say that."

I eyed him levelly. "I'm *twelve*."

"Alas, far too grown up for presents, Christmas crackers, and fruitcake, then."

"*No!*" Peony appeared at the critical moment, voicing her alarm.

"If *I'm* too old for presents, then so are you." Which would save me the effort of finding just the right gift for Miss Judson, at least.

"Well, this standoff could go all month," Miss Judson said mildly. "I hereby declare that *no one* is too old for Christmas, least of all this family's patriarch." Whereupon she whisked a tissue-paper crown from the sideboard and popped it atop Father's head.

"Excellent," he said. "Now I'm ready for court."

After that we sobered. Father didn't have a case pending at the moment,* which left us all plenty of time to brood about what had happened to Mr. Leighton. I knew better than to press him about it—Dr. Belden had barely had time to start the post-mortem—but that didn't mean it was easy. I stirred at my jam with my knife, trying to think of something I could ask. Anything besides, *How was Mum involved in this?* and *What had the Mayor wanted from Dr. Munjal last night?* Father hadn't let us linger long enough to find out, and he'd refused to speculate as we walked home.

* Apparently most of Swinburne's Criminal Element had taken time off for the holidays.

Which meant he'd also refused to countenance *my* speculation on the subject.

Miss Judson came to my rescue. "Since it's Sunday, I offered to help Mrs. Leighton with some things for her husband."

Father remained carefully indifferent to this remark, and for my part I studied her cautiously above the rim of my cup.

"I thought I'd take Myrtle with me."

Dear Reader, it was all I could do not to leap up from my seat and dash for the door. Instead, I tried to look demure, and said—in a ladylike, not-at-all-thinking-of-murder voice—"Perhaps we could take her some gingersnaps?"

Moments later, Miss Judson and I were bundled up and mounted on our bicycles, pedaling through fat, fluffy flakes into town. I had been eager to set out, but as we drew closer, I felt more and more uncertain.

My silence, evidently, was suspicious.

"You're much quieter than usual today." Miss Judson steered close enough for conversation, but I did not respond. All of my thoughts led to the inconceivable—the *unutterable*—notion that Mum was somehow involved in Professor Leighton's death. Not directly, of course, but via some shared incident or secret from their past that must have contributed to his murder.

"I had to ferret the details of Olive Blackwell's

disappearance from your father. What a mystery!" She continued, as if I'd replied to her first statement, "Combined with the curious note, it puts Mr. Leighton's death in rather a different light."

"What are you saying?" I asked carefully. "Dr. Belden and Dr. Munjal said it was probably a stroke."

"And you, of course, believe that."

I ground my teeth before replying. "Why wouldn't I?"

"Oh, perhaps the small matter of you and your father visiting the Police Surgeon to discuss hemlock poisoning? Myrtle, your father told me everything. But it fails to explain why you're so pensive today. If there's a murder afoot, you'd normally be champing at the bit to solve it!" She braked at the tram crossing, propping herself up with one jaunty boot. "Either you're not feeling well—or something about this case has upset you. You know you can tell me anything."

The tram clanged past, churning the snow to bloomer-splattering slush.* It had a garland of evergreen swagged across its roof, and an advert of Father Christmas selling Pears' Soap on the side.

Truly, even I couldn't say why I didn't want to tell Miss Judson about finding Mum's photograph at the shop. It might very well mean nothing—it could be a wild coincidence.

---

* Perhaps she would appreciate a pair of waterproof gaiters.

Just like the Socrates note and the olives in the Display.

"Very well." The tram had passed, and Miss Judson kicked her bicycle back into motion. "If you won't speculate about the case, then I shall have to do it myself. Assuming Mr. Leighton died from hemlock poisoning—"

"Which is not proved." *Her* usual lines popped out of my mouth, entirely unbidden. With a wordless growl, I bit my tongue.

"Fair enough. *If* it was hemlock poisoning, did he poison himself, or was he poisoned by someone else? Mr. Leighton hardly seemed the sort of man to stage his own death right where all the children of the village would have a front-row seat."

"Miss!"

"Secondly. The matter of the Display. Why choose to depict Olive Blackwell's disappearance at all? That's a mystery of its own, and it's not very likely that he'd make that diorama and then *happen* to die on the very same night."

"It took him months to build it. He didn't know he was going to be murdered," I reminded her. Reluctantly. Every point she raised brought us closer to Mum. "Besides," I argued, "I don't think he *was* re-creating Olive's disappearance. He just wanted to build the college. Before Olive and everything, Mr. Leighton *did* have a distinguished career there." I took a breath. "It was the killer who moved all the people to the belltower, and then put the olives there so everyone would know."

"Exactly. Which tells us that someone must have known he was planning to build that display, and chose the most dramatic moment possible to poison him," Miss Judson said. "Our killer—"

"If there *is* a killer—"

"—obviously has a sense of showmanship."

"A gruesome one," I agreed, nose wrinkling.

We had come in sight of Leighton's Mercantile, and for a moment I felt a stab of—what? Not excitement. Not exactly. "I thought we were going to her house."

"Don't be silly. Nobody was murdered at her house."

Miss Judson swung down High Street, hopped her bicycle over the curb, and coasted to an easy stop before the very same incriminating window we'd waited so eagerly for yesterday. The green baize curtains were drawn again, and the shop door had a handwritten placard, proclaiming, CLOSED FOR BUSINESS UNTIL FURTHER NOTICE. I recognized Miss Judson's precise handwriting.

"Come on," she urged—since I hadn't even dismounted yet. "Don't you want to know what happened?"

And that, Dear Reader, was one question I definitely could not answer.

Miss Judson rapped heartily on the door before pulling it open herself. "Good morning, Emily." Her voice was crisp and bright, though not overly cheerful. She glided through the shop and turned up three lamps, filling the space with warm light.

The shop seemed even lonelier than yesterday, too still and cold and quiet. Someone had put away the chair and barrel where Mr. Leighton had died, but the very emptiness of the spot felt ominous. I kept *looking* that way, unable to help myself.

Mrs. Leighton sat in the shadows, hands limp on her knees. She was so motionless that for a moment my heart jolted into my throat in panic. *Not again–!*

"Oh," she said, as if that one word took all the effort she could summon. Her crinkly blue eyes looked blank and glassy.

"Tea," Miss Judson said. "Hot. Strong." With her nudge, I scurried to the back rooms where we'd seen Mrs. Leighton make tea before. I lit the hob and set the kettle on, rummaged about and produced a tin of tea– not their best, I Observed with a sad little pang; if ever there was a time for Really Good Tea, this was it–and found clean cups and saucers. What else? If Cook were here, she and Miss Judson would also find something sweet and bolstering–of course. The gingersnaps. And in the Billy Garrett stories, people were always handing around flasks of brandy in times of crisis.

I decided that was outside my purview. I checked

the progress of the kettle (nil), then peeked back into the store to see that Miss Judson had coaxed Mrs. Leighton out of the draft, found her shawl, and steered her into the warmer, less gloomy, less-recently-occupied-by-dead-husbands kitchen space.

I found myself wishing for Peony. This would be a moment in which she would excel, being a superlative source of comfort. Miss Judson could briskly take charge, Peony could purr and knead and cuddle—and I? I stood here like a ninny, wondering what to do.

Except I *knew* what to do. Or what I should be doing, at any rate. I should tear the little shop apart, tea-tin and coffee barrel, leaving no sugar loaf or butter crock unturned, searching for any clues the police had missed. I should dig into Mr. Leighton's—*Professor* Leighton's—books and papers, to find any notes about Olive Blackwell or Mum.

I should be Investigating.

The teakettle fluted at me, and I wrapped a towel round the handle and toted it to the table. Mrs. Leighton rose to her feet to gently wrest the vessel from my grip and supervise the production of the tea.

I glanced around, still feeling useless, but caught Miss Judson's eye again.

"Emily, have you fed the boiler?"

"I can do it," I volunteered. I didn't hear the rattle-clank of the radiators kicking in, so Miss Judson was right and it was probably out of coal.

Mrs. Leighton started, again. "Oh, Basil always does that—" And then she remembered, and sat back down abruptly, gripping the teapot with white knuckles. "You'll burn yourself, child." The words sounded forced, and I took a halting step toward her, meaning to—what? Tell her everything would be all right?

Miss Judson came to our rescue. "Myrtle is very sensible. We need not worry that she'll get burned." A Significant Tone to her voice suggested other possibilities were likely, but that she was releasing me all the same, and woe betide whatever mischief I might bring upon myself.

"I'll be careful." I was looking at Mrs. Leighton, but she wasn't the one I said that to.

We were getting rather a lot of practice at this— Miss Judson comforting while I Investigated. (I filed that consideration away for later, unsure precisely what to make of it.) She might just be shuffling *me* out of the way, but sending me into the secret-infested cellar of a murder victim with a deep dark past seemed a curious way of accomplishing that. Still, I had questions about Mum, questions there was no way to ask Mrs. Leighton, and answers to be found, perhaps, among Professor Leighton's past. I could only hope he'd stored them neatly in his basement.

The door stuck, and a dry musty smell crept up from the gloom when I yanked hard, revealing a deep cavern of black.

"Take a lamp, Myrtle. There's no gas down there." Mrs. Leighton was on her feet—tea and Miss Judson were a particularly revivifying combination, as I had cause to know well. She lit a small oil lamp, which I balanced precariously in one hand, trying not to topple its glass globe, while hanging on to the railing for dear life.

The stairs were tight, narrow, shallow, backless, and seemed ready to propel me into the black depths of the Leightons' cellar. I edged my way down, steeling myself not to jump and fling the lamp away should a massive shadow abruptly loom before me—a cast-iron boiler or the coal hod.

Or a murderer.

Peony. I should always bring Peony. She would be utterly fearless in such a scenario.

Her ability to see in the dark would not go amiss, either.

Shadows loomed, leaping away from the light, but revealed themselves to be no more alarming than old crates and empty flour barrels. The cellar was as pin-neat as the rest of Leighton's Mercantile, not a speck of dust or cobweb to be seen. The space was lined with shelves and dominated by a massive, improvised worktable, a huge sheet of wood laid across trestles. And on that table, the remains—or the origins—of Mr. Leighton's grand Displays.

I crept closer, mission to the boiler momentarily

abandoned. Pots of paint, crocks of tools, and every manner of miniature building, conveyance, and Swinburnian (including a flock of crows whose slick black paint job had been permanently interrupted) littered the tabletop. The figures were cast from lead in tiny clay molds, then carefully sanded and painted. Buildings were constructed from wood or clay or tiny building-bricks glued together. It even appeared as though he'd been experimenting with miniature electrified streetlamps (an amenity the real Swinburne did not enjoy).

But he'd never had the chance to finish it all. Because someone had finished it for him. Glumly, I pulled out his cracked and stained stool and settled myself on its spinning seat. I set the lamp on the table between a lumberyard of matchstick planks and a woolen snowdrift and, shoulders hunched, studied the scene. Mounted to the table was a sturdy magnifier, through which Mr. Leighton would have done the fine detail work on his miniatures. For some reason, this year, Mr. Leighton had sat here, months on end, deciding to re-create the darkest incident from his own past.

I did not see any clues among the figures and building materials left behind. I picked up a discarded figurine, a Roman soldier in his red cape and brushed helmet (individual strands of horsehair painstakingly affixed). I wondered how he was meant to fit in among the local English villagers dressed up for Christmas.

A rattle from upstairs stirred me from my reverie, and reminded me of my errand. With a sigh, I abandoned Mr. Leighton's workshop, shoveled a scoopful of coal into the furnace, and headed back to the others.

Upstairs, Mrs. Leighton fiddled with the tea service, straightening napkins and spoons, while Miss Judson examined the Display. She had her sketchbook out, recording the scene. The police hadn't made any special efforts to preserve or collect the evidence, and the well and the olives were still in place. I leaned in, trying to make the snowy landscape and brick tower give up some answers. A smudge of black marred the snow beneath the wishing well and wisps of the woolen snow stuck to its brick surface. The killer must have placed it there while the paint was still wet.

"Your husband's workmanship truly was extraordinary," Miss Judson said. "I think he outdid himself this year."

A small, hopeful sniff arose from Mrs. Leighton.

"What made him decide to do the college?" It was remarkable, how Miss Judson managed to ask that tactfully.

"The anniversary," Mrs. Leighton said, a hint of pride in her voice.

I spun round. "Of–?"

"Of Schofield College," she said. "Fifty years since

the founding, you know. Oh, he was so proud, even now." The sniff was less hopeful this time.

Miss Judson slipped back to her. "Had anything been troubling Mr. Leighton recently?" she asked, voice gentle.

"Do—do they think it was suicide?" She'd asked that same question yesterday.

"What would make you think that?" Miss Judson inquired. "Had he been despondent or melancholy?"

Mrs. Leighton shook her head. "No, in fact he was busy with plans for the expansion of the shop. Talked about installing electricity, maybe even a telephone. Bring us into the modern age!" She attempted a choked, experimental chuckle that ended in a sob. "But, that note, and the Display—" Her hand waved vaguely toward the window. "What else can I think?"

I stepped forward, and gingerly suggested, "Perhaps someone wanted to hurt him?"

Mrs. Leighton's gaze wheeled slowly to mine, eyes narrow and considering.

"Did he have any enemies?"

Miss Judson did not forestall me. Mrs. Leighton stirred her tea, stirred and stirred and stirred, like she was never going to answer. Finally, not looking at either of us, she whispered, "I didn't think so. Not anymore. But then the letters started coming."

Miss Judson wheedled the tea from her grasp. "Letters?"

"He burnt them all before I could read them. Not that I could—they were in Latin." She touched a stray springy pale red curl that had escaped her neat cap. She reminded me of an automaton winding down, and I felt I ought to give her key a few solid twists to keep her going. "You'll think it strange, an uneducated woman, married to a man like that."

"Not at all." Miss Judson's voice was soothing. "You're full of common sense and more clever than you let on. You might not have read the letters—but you suspected what they said."

"Yes." Her voice was flat, firm, not lost at all. "They were dragging it all back up again—everything. Olive Blackwell, the society, everything."

"Why didn't you take them to the police?" I couldn't help myself, Dear Reader.

Now she was scornful. "Them? You think *they'd* help us? Probably reveling in our misfortune even now. I begged him to leave, when it all happened—I have people in Lincoln, they need shops there, too—but Basil refused. Said he was Swinburne born and bred, and he'd die here." With yet another sniff, the tears started again.

Miss Judson patted her on the shoulder. I tapped my fingers on the table, pondering these letters.

"Who do you think might have sent them?" I asked. "Could they have had—erm—ill intent?"

"Ill intent?" Mrs. Leighton scoffed. "I know exactly

who sent them. Not that I can prove it, mind. Of course not. Too clever for that, they were."

Miss Judson and I waited, but evidently Mrs. Leighton was expecting us to know as well.

"Those Blackwells, of course!" The words were like a burst of steam from a pressure cooker. "Blamed my Basil for the disappearance of their girl. Weren't enough to ruin his life back when it happened. Now they have to do it all over again."

Miss Judson and I both looked to the Display. We couldn't help it.

"They're the ones who forced him out of Schofield, destroyed his fine career. But there was no proof he'd done anything to that girl." She jabbed the table with her pointed finger. "No. Proof."

Miss Judson waited a few heartbeats before asking, "What *did* happen? What was Miss Blackwell doing in the belltower that night?"

Mrs. Leighton shook her head. "No one knows! Basil wasn't even there."

I reached into my bag and withdrew the photograph of Mum, and slid it slowly across the table. "This—I found this, yesterday. I didn't have a chance to give it back, before."

Miss Judson's habitual equanimity faltered, and she turned to me, wordless questions flooding her face, but Mrs. Leighton almost smiled. "That's Jemima, isn't it? Your own mum? She was a *nice* girl," she affirmed fondly. "Not like the other one, Miss High-and-Mighty Blackwell. Not to speak ill of the dead."

"She's dead, then?" That popped out automatically, like bubbles in boiling water.

Her gaze was lost in the distance. "Disappeared, dead—what does it matter? She's still taking her revenge on us, all these years later."

I studied the upside-down picture. "Is that the Mayor?" I pointed to a youthful fellow in a campaign jacket, wielding a shovel.

"Think themselves so grand, the way they put on airs. As if they don't owe my Basil anything for where they've got to in life. Came by here the other day, lording his new chain of office over us—I wouldn't let him in, I wouldn't. Good riddance to the lot of them, I say."

She rose and bustled about, gathering up the tea, indicating that this conversation was finished. As she lifted the photograph from the table, she gave it one last thoughtful look, then held it out to me.

"You keep that," she said. "He'd want you to have it. Your mum was one of his favorites."

⁓

Clutching the picture as we made our way back out to our bicycles, I realized I'd missed a prime opportunity to Observe Miss Judson's potential holiday gift preferences. We'd been surrounded by the Wonders of the Empire, but all our attention had been on the case. At this rate I'd never come up with anything!

"Poor woman," Miss Judson said.

I whispered fiercely, "We have to help her."

Miss Judson was all agreement, but, "Kindly detail your plans for said assistance."

"Solving the professor's murder, of course."

"Ah."

"What does that mean?" Really, these Socratic arguments, every time we encountered a case, were getting tiresome.

She fixed her hat more firmly upon her head, wrapping her muffler tighter. "She's already been through scandal once. Does she deserve to have that pain dredged up again, along with the grief of losing her husband and the trauma of his murder?"

"The murderer already dredged it up! Wouldn't she find comfort in knowing who killed her husband? And why?"

She glanced back at the shop window, where the Display still showed villagers clustered about the Campanile, forever frozen in that anxious tableau behind the curtains. If the professor's murder wasn't solved, wouldn't that scene continue, again, with a new generation of Swinburnians affected? But I could tell Miss Judson's thoughts had moved beyond the Display, inside, to where Mrs. Leighton sat, worrying her tea.

"It's clear that her husband's past is something

Mrs. Leighton has put behind her, and wants no part of anymore."

I scowled, a mix of feelings stewing inside me. "What are we supposed to do, then? Don't say go home and forget about it. Mum's involved!"

"You don't know that." Miss Judson's voice was gentle, but firm. "The professor had hundreds of students. One picture—while curious and a bit thrilling, I'll grant you!" Her eyes glittered with excitement, which warmed me a bit. "One picture of your mother does not constitute evidence of any connection between your mother's collegiate past, Miss Blackwell's disappearance, and Professor Leighton's murder. That's like saying *you* were involved because you bought your bootlaces there."

She was right. I dug my toes into the hard, cold verge.

"However," she said brightly, "just because we don't want to bother Mrs. Leighton by prying into her husband's past, that doesn't mean we can't go prying into your mother's."

Somehow, she made that sound entirely innocent and appealing, like a lark. My heart lifted, and I couldn't keep the eagerness from my voice. "Can we go to the college?"

"Where else?"

6

DING DONG
WARILY ON HIGH

Sir Isaac Newton, England's greatest scientific mind, was by British reckoning born on Christmas Day 1642—a charming fact until you realize that the rest of the Western world had already adopted the modern Gregorian calendar, according to which Newton's birthday is, in fact, 4 January 1643.

-H. M. Hardcastle, *A Modern Yuletide*

We cycled to the college the following afternoon, braving the bracing air. The tram would have been more efficient (not to mention warm), but they frowned on Young Ladies of Quality hauling their bicycles aboard during rush hour. It was too cold for conversation. It was nearly too cold for *pedaling.* Bloomers might be less apt to get tangled in your bicycle chain, but they aren't anywhere near as toasty as a good three or four flannel petticoats.

I had visited Schofield College on occasion, mostly for scientific lectures and to avail myself of their capacious library. Being here had always made me feel intellectually stimulated and closer to Mum. I had often pictured myself dashing across the grounds one day, in my black academic robes, from lecture hall to examination, taking up my own university education.

Now I looked about with an altogether different (and slightly frozen) eye. The college was a crime scene—the site of an unsolved mystery from decades ago. It sent a thrill through me, much more pleasurable than the frigid December wind. What secrets lurked beneath these venerable grounds?

We heard the Campanile long before coming within sight of it. As we rode along a paved pathway, oddly clean and dry of snow, haunting chimes shivered through the icy air. They sounded like a child's toy made gargantuan. Miss Judson braked sharply, planting a foot against the pavement.

"That's remarkable!" she said. Yelled. "Those aren't ordinary church bells."

The sound had struck me senseless, and I could scarcely nod my agreement. Church bells in town just went *clang* or *bong*. This was a vast, spectral organ reverberating through the sky and deep into our bones, pulling us toward it like a magnet. "Let's go see."

Our route took us among castlelike stone buildings with tall fretwork windows and lead roofs. The Campanile towered over them all, rising over a stand of fir trees and a circle of snowy park. The whole place had a solemn, studious air, but was eerily empty. We hardly saw a soul about—just another young woman in a short blue coat, strolling along the grounds, plaid skirts swishing through the snow. She briefly paused to Observe us, before moving along once more.

"Where are the other students?" Tracks in the snow suggested that they were not long absent.

"Yes, why isn't everyone out enjoying the beautiful weather?" Miss Judson wound her muffler more snugly about her head, leaving a mere slit for visibility. "Here we are."

Here we were, indeed. Gazing upward, taking in the imposing height of the brick Campanile, it was alarming to imagine someone falling from the belfry— and downright impossible to conceive of her simply vanishing into the night. The great bells, just visible through the huge open arches near the roof, had stilled at last, leaving the world feeling hollow and desolate.

"There's no way anyone could survive such a fall," I said with certainty. "It must be a hundred feet high."

"One hundred ten," Miss Judson read, from the bronze plaque. Clad in rosy brickwork, with tiny arrow-slit windows, the rectangular tower soared up to a pointed roof amid a nest of stone spires. It had a fanciful, romantic air, as if it had escaped from a story book and was doing a poor job hiding in Swinburne.

"It's just like the Display." Miss Judson's sketch-book was out, although I had no idea how she thought she might draw with frozen fingers. "Look, there's the belfry, and the clock . . ."

"*How* does somebody fall from there?" I had to bend far backward to see all the way up into the blinding sun; I imagined the view down would be even more dizzying.

"Did she jump? Was she pushed?"

"What was she even doing up there? At night? In December?" *Was Mum there?*

"Was she alone?" My eyes darted to Miss Judson, but she wasn't looking at me. *Surely* she hadn't read my mind. "Very curious."

Miss Judson studied the surrounding landscape. A thick hedge of holly encircled the tower's base (or, rather, *ensquared* it). "Could she have landed here? Maybe the bushes broke her fall."

Glistening with red berries, they were taller than I, and thick enough to hide in. "They'd have been shorter all those years ago, though," I reasoned. "Were there any bushes in the Display?"

Her gloved fingers fumbled to the sketch she'd made at the shop. A neat series of small round plants—not the vast fairytale thicket before us—represented the younger shrubbery.

"They wouldn't have provided much cushion." Certainly not enough to save someone from grievous injury.

"Nor concealment for a body. One might assume that even all those years ago the constables would have thought to search the bushes." Miss Judson's estimation of Historical Constables was not especially great.

"If I dropped my pocket watch from up there, it's the first place I'd look," I agreed. I looked up from the hedge to the belfry arches high above, another thought dawning. "But if I *threw* my watch . . ." Digging my notebook from my satchel, I strode purposefully away from the tower, trying to work out the correct Newtonian calculations. *Inertia, trajectory, mass and acceleration . . .*

Miss Judson followed, crunching deftly through the snow in her tall boots and bloomers. She glanced at my notes with approval. "Physics. Excellent."

"There are too many variables, however." I tapped my pencil against the notebook. "If she fell, she'd have probably gone straight down."

"But if somebody *pushed* her, she'd have landed much farther out." Miss Judson faced away from the Campanile, out into the snowy field. "What do you think? Let's assume she was about my size."

"Nine or ten stone, then?" I jotted that down. "A

hundred and ten feet . . . thirty-two feet per second per second . . ."*

"And was she thrown, or merely pushed?" At my frown of revulsion, she elaborated. "If she was unconscious when she fell, she'd have been a dead weight, going straight down. But if she was pushed while standing—or fleeing—there would have been a greater arc to her trajectory. She could have made it—maybe fifty feet at the outside?" She headed into the field, counting out paces as she went.

"And people call *me* morbid," I muttered, on her heels.

Of course, twenty years on, there was nothing to see and no way to know if our estimations were correct. If it even mattered, since by all accounts Miss Blackwell had never landed at all. It was as if some great hand had reached out and simply plucked her from the sky.

In the fading day, the Campanile's shadow was long and wide and gloomy, and I shivered with more than cold. "I want to get up there."

"Naturally." If Miss Judson sighed, I was too far ahead to hear.

The base of the Campanile was a spacious open portico framed by pointed Gothic arches and miniature guard towers (decorative only, no room for

* Acceleration due to gravity is a most convenient mathematical constant.

a lurking attacker *or* a hidden victim). An arched wooden door in the same medieval style was set into one corner. Disappointingly, however, it was locked.

"A sensible precaution," Miss Judson remarked. "Considering." A notice board hung inside the brick walls, protected from the elements, and she strode over for a look. "*Christmas Carillon Recital,*" she read aloud, as I was still tugging fruitlessly at the door and gazing upward into the depths of the buttressed ceiling. "*Saturday, ninth of December, featuring the music—*" She started to lift the edge of the notice covering that one, when a sweet voice piped up behind us.

"Are you coming to my concert?"

I whirled about to see a slight young woman about Miss Judson's age in the archway, with pale hair whipped free of its knot, wearing a voluminous dolman that matched her blue eyes. It was made for a much taller woman, and its wooly fringe brushed the snow. "I'm the carillonist," she said, joining us. "Are you coming to my recital? It's free and open to the public."

Miss Judson replied smoothly, "It sounds lovely. Was that you just now, ringing the clock?"

The young woman smiled shyly. "No, that's automated. But I was just about to go up and practice. Would you like to come? Visitors are welcome to see the bells. They're even more impressive up close."

"If it's not too much trouble," I put in eagerly, before Miss Judson could decline the offer.

She led us into a dark closet of a space, tiny arrow-loop windows casting faint illumination over an iron staircase. "It gets easier after this first bit." The first narrow flight spiraled through the tower's cramped stone footing, but then the stairs widened to fill the entire square tower, where light poured down from the belfry arches. It was gloriously warm inside, and Miss Judson unwrapped her muffler.

"There's the motor that runs the bells unless I'm playing." The carillonist indicated an intricate mass of machinery mounted on a platform, hammers and pipes and gears waiting for their cue.

"What powers it?" I asked.

"Steam. We're atop a network of steam tunnels that heat and supply power to the whole college. It's very modern."

That explained the surprisingly cozy atmosphere. I pictured a great pipe organ inside the tower. "Like a calliope?"

Her smile grew. "Not quite. In that case, the steam actually makes the music. Here it just powers that motor you saw. The system was devised by quite brilliant architects and engineers. Here we are!" We had reached a landing a little more than halfway up, and the carillonist shook out a ring of keys. "The clavier is in here. That's the keyboard."

I had not thought through the logistics of the instrument, but it made sense that the bell-ringer must be some distance away from the great bells, if she wished to preserve her hearing. The carillonist admitted us into a small room that housed what looked, at first, like a huge weaving loom—or, I realized, the insides of a vast piano: a spare wooden frame hung with dozens of weighted wires, attached to a series of plain wooden handles, jutting out like teeth. It was quite impossible to make out what any of them would do—but somehow this device produced the oversized chiming of those monstrous bells. For a moment I stood there, mesmerized by the mechanics of it all. It was so beautifully precise and systematic, and yet something otherworldly came out of it.

"Do you want to try?" The carillonist had Observed my awestruck gawking and slid over, making room on the bench. "Here, I'll teach you 'Westminster Quarters.'"*

Dear Reader, for the next few minutes, I forgot all about Olive Blackwell and Mr. Leighton, about Mum and secrets and mysterious deaths. The carillonist—"You must call me Leah"—was a splendid teacher, almost as enthusiastic as Miss Judson. She showed me how to depress the huge foot pedals that rang some of the bells, and thwack my fists against the large wooden handles—the keys—that rang the others. It was done with great energy, not to mention *noise*—not at

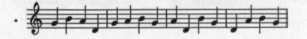

all the sort of delicate activity typically expected of Young Ladies of Quality.

Leah was tiny, scarcely bigger than I, and we had to constantly shift up and down along the bench to reach all the keys we needed. The long blue fringe on her sleeves swung and danced as her hands flew along the keyboard. I was flushed and breathless when we finished.

When the final reverberations had died away, Miss Judson broke into spirited applause. "Brava!" she cried. "That's marvelous. You'll be giving up Investigation for bell-ringing now."

I gave *that* the response it deserved, but I offered my thanks to Leah, who seemed pleased as well.

"You must come up to the belfry," she said. "The tour's not complete until you've seen the bells themselves."

Whereupon Miss Judson and I recalled the purpose of our errand. Leah did not appear to notice our awkward silence, but led us from the clavier chamber back to the stairwell.

"It's up this way, past the clock." She said this gravely, as if there were anywhere *else* they might have stashed thirty tons of bronze bells. After the ringing of the bells, the silence was crushing, pressing in all around us, but thin fresh air rushed in from every direction, including below. We Ladies of Quality instinctively held our hands to our skirts to keep them from inflating and carrying us off.

"Are you a student here?" Miss Judson inquired as we climbed, but Leah shook her head.

"No, I just play the bells. My father was a lecturer—Divinity—and we still live on the grounds. You can see our building from the tower."

"How long have you been playing?" asked Miss Judson.

"It feels like all my life," she confessed. "But really just the past few months. My mother was the carillonist before me."

"What a lovely legacy," Miss Judson said.

"There hadn't been a carillonist for years since Mother retired after—well, for several years, anyway."

"Since what happened to Olive Blackwell?" I said that unintentionally. My excuse, Dear Reader, is that I was dizzy and breathless from the climb, and not nearly enough oxygen was feeding my brain cells for things like etiquette.

Leah—clearly accustomed to the exertion—tilted her head and regarded me with those unsettlingly pale eyes. "Exactly. That's why you came, isn't it?"

I flushed, and Miss Judson looked chagrined. "We didn't mean to pry," she lied politely.

"It's why everyone comes." Leah's voice was kind. "If I'm honest, it might even be why I come. You can't help but be curious. It happened up here." Voice hushed, she indicated the space right above us. There was no doorway, just the abrupt end to the stairs as they reached the belfry. She held out an inviting arm. "Watch where you step."

If the irony was intended, Dear Reader, it was impossible to say.

The belfry was like being atop a huge chimney. The icy wind whooshed through the stone arches to buffet us, but merely whistled among the forest of bells, not strong enough to budge them. They hung in marshaled rows, largest to smallest at the top. Miss Judson and I could have fit together inside one of the largest bells, suspended in the emptiness below our feet; those nearest the ceiling were no bigger than my head. And in between, dozens more of every graduated size.

"There's hardly anywhere to step," I said. Only a precarious wooden catwalk hugged the perimeter to permit maintenance of the bells. But it was all too easy to see how one *misstep* could cause catastrophe.

One thing was certain: this was not a place anyone would bother to carry an unconscious or dead victim. It was too cumbersome, too inaccessible, when there were perfectly good ditches and sewers available. Whatever had brought Olive Blackwell to this belltower that frigid winter night, she had come of her own volition.

"What was she *doing* up here?" I hadn't—really—meant to ask that aloud.

I wasn't expecting Leah to answer. "There was some sort of ritual," she said, voice soft as a whisper.

I jerked my head around, to see Miss Judson staring at her as well.

"A group of students gathered here for a secret ceremony." She laid a pensive hand upon a curve of bronze. "And it all went horribly wrong."

7

Sharp as Any Thorn

The common holly, *Ilex aquifolium*, one of England's few native evergreens, is the source of several toxic chemical compounds, including alkaloids, caffeine, theobromine, and saponins.

-H. M. Hardcastle, *A Modern Yuletide*

The wake of the carillonist's words was as heavy and resonant as the silence after the bells. I could do no more than stare at her, and from what I could tell, Miss Judson felt the same. She'd braced a steadying hand against the wall, and another upon my arm, as if to hold me here in case I suddenly took it into my head to dash for the edge.

Leah's serene smile never wavered, as she squeezed onto the catwalk, strolling between bricks and bells. Her footfalls on the narrow planks were creaky and echoing, and I felt an anxious jolt with every step she took. Her cape rustled and swung, and I was convinced it would snag on a bell or tangle in the ropes and send Leah plunging to her death as well. But she was seemingly unafraid.

"Olive Blackwell was a member of a secret society here at the college. Look, you can still see where they left their mark." She pointed out a shadowy shape on the wall—remnants of old graffiti scrawled on the bricks: the profile of a Roman soldier in a brushed helmet.

Leah's voice was low and dramatic, like she was declaiming a ghost story. "Disbanded now, of course. So they claim." *Creak, creak, creak*—she had made it halfway round the tower, and her soft words echoed from the brickwork, thanks to the exceptional acoustics. "Late one winter's night, the members of the society gathered here to initiate their new brethren. Six went up, but only five came down."

That chill, Dear Reader, had nothing at all to do with the weather.

"It was this archway." Leah beckoned us closer, and I would have gone, against my will—if Miss Judson's grip on my shoulder hadn't clamped me like a vise. Thank goodness. "They were blindfolded," she continued. "The two new initiates, Olive Blackwell and another girl called Jemima Bell."

I could not tell if that sharp intake of breath was

Miss Judson's or my own. I strained forward, as if I could pull the scene up along with Leah's words, envision Mum up here, blindfolded, in the dark.

"No one ever explained what happened. No one saw her fall. The other students all ran down to see what had happened, but they never found her body." Leah looked down through the archway. "There was freshly fallen snow—indeed, it was snowing all that night—and there were no tracks, or impressions from where she would have landed. She simply . . . disappeared."

"What do you think happened?" I could only whisper—what if Mum had fallen, instead? What if Mum had pushed her? I felt dizzy, and I wasn't even near the edge.

Leah turned back and spread her hands. "A terrible accident? It shook everyone, and for years the Campanile was closed, the bells silenced, even the clock stopped at the moment Olive fell. Eleven fifty-two." She brightened. "Until the college governors decided that enough time had passed, and everyone had forgotten, and it was time to get the bells ringing again. I couldn't wait to come back up here, where Mother had spent so much happy time."

"Not everyone forgot," Miss Judson said gently.

Leah's hands were hooked at her waist. "No, of course not. But it was so long ago. It's time to put those sad memories to rest."

"But doesn't it bother you," I said, "coming up

here, where—" There was no possible way to finish that sentence.

"Where she died?" She was thoughtful a moment. "It should, I suppose. But no one *really* knows what happened to Olive. Perhaps she didn't fall after all, and she merely ran away to a new life. I like to think so, anyway."

My heart jolted. "Is that possible?"

"Anything's possible." At that moment, she took a step toward us, her expression faraway. "They're about to chime," she warned. "You might want to step down a few stairs. It gets rather loud."

I could imagine.

No, strike that: I could *not* imagine. Miss Judson and I backed away as advised, but even so, when the gears on the mechanism clicked and the clock hands shifted into position, a cacophonous concert erupted around us, like the heavens crashing open and all the angels singing at the top of their celestial lungs in strange discordant harmony. The simple notes of "Westminster Quarters," the very ones I'd just practiced, jarred out, rattling us to our cores—followed by four slow, ponderous tones from the largest bell: *Bong. Bong. Bonnnnng. Bonnnnnggggggg.*

I gripped hard to Miss Judson and the railing to keep from toppling down the stairs—but I wanted to laugh. Or cry. Or something. I was shaky and exhilarated by the time the last notes faded, my bones still vibrating. I'd be feeling that for weeks.

We left Leah to her practice with a promise to return for her concert Saturday night.

"There are two performances," she said. "Twilight and midnight—the midnight Christmas concert on the last day of term is a Schofield tradition! It will be especially grand this year, because of the fiftieth anniversary."

"And the first concert since Olive," I said. Leah's light eyes glittered with anticipation.

Miss Judson and I made our somber way back down and outside (by the customary fashion, naturally). I went through everything the carillonist had told us, trying to make sense of what we'd learned. A secret society with arcane rituals? What did that have to do with Professor Leighton? Or Socrates? How had Olive fallen, and what had happened to her after that? What had my mum known? What had my mum done?

Daylight had faded while we'd been up there, and the twilit air blasted our bare cheeks and sucked our breath away. The Campanile was a looming shadow against the pink sky. The clock face had lit up—"Steam, again," Miss Judson speculated—glowing like a full moon, soft and pearly. The bells were about to sound again, and we had a long ride home in the cold.

But neither of us could seem to pull ourselves away.

"What happened up there?" I mused aloud. "People don't just disappear into thin air." I didn't share Leah's conviction that Olive had merely run away to a happier life. She must have either jumped or fallen—or been pushed.

I chewed on my glove, trying to work out a theory. "Unless they killed her some other way, some way that wouldn't be easy to cover up in a fall—and they had to hide her body."

"Do you really think your mother could have been involved in something like that?" Miss Judson looked unconvinced—and more: appalled. Defensive. I felt a spike of pride at her loyalty, but I smashed it down with ruthless logic.

"We don't know," I said bitterly. "She could have done anything. She's not here to defend herself."

Miss Judson regarded me steadily. "Exactly," she said. "But there were four other people in that tower that night, too. We need to track them down."

‿

We arrived back at Gravesend Close to find a dim and quiet household, with the exception of Peony (who is seldom quiet), proclaiming to anyone within earshot* that it was well past teatime, and that supper was expected posthaste. We could hear Cook in the kitchen, battling with the hob; their Christmas Truce

* roughly the population of Northern England and some of the Netherlands, depending on wind conditions

was over, and she was back at her perpetual quest to beat it into submission. I had it on Good Authority that Father Christmas would be delivering her a new, huge spanner and a welding torch for the ongoing feud.

Father sat in shadows in the parlor, frowning (or perhaps squinting; see previous reference to inadequate lighting) at some paperwork. When he saw us enter, frosted and rosy-cheeked, he did not even attempt to hide it from us, just waved us closer with a weary smile.

We had to circumnavigate Peony, who was doing her utmost to hobble us (should we perchance be carrying armloads of fresh salmon that might felicitously rain down upon her), to make our way into the mistletoe-bedecked, pine-cone-adorned, paper-chain-festooned parlor. Father had been busy in our absence! In the corner, upon a sturdy table, stood the Christmas tree, a feathery potted evergreen* from the greenhouse next door at Redgraves. Mum's treasured chest of ornaments had been ceremoniously toted down from the attic and sat waiting beside it.

After doffing my wet winter things, I squeezed in alongside Father, trying to catch a glimpse of his

---

* *Pinus sylvestris*, the Scots pine, which had been transplanted as a seedling from its native Yorkshire. I had been helping Mr. Hamm, the gardener at Redgraves, tend it all fall—pruning, watering, and training the branches—in anticipation of its debut. After the festivities, it would move back outside once more, as it did not do well in the stuffy heat of an English parlor.

documents before he could spirit them out of my reach. Miss Judson took the seat opposite.

To my surprise, Father handed the papers right to me. "The Police Surgeon's report?" It was actually Dr. Belden's write-up of his post-mortem findings, but it had been signed and stamped by Dr. Munjal, making it official.

"Mmm," Father affirmed. "As suspected, Mr. Leighton died from hemlock poisoning."

For a moment we were all silent enough to hear the clock ticking on the mantel, and the cheery pop of embers in the fireplace. Finally Miss Judson broached the delicate subject.

"Was it suicide?"

Father's eyes darted between us. "Medical evidence cannot determine how the dose was administered," he said carefully.

I sped through Dr. Belden's findings, trying to focus on the science and not the disheartening fact that it was about kindly Mr. Leighton. "He also found traces of chloroform?"

Was that what Dr. Munjal had been searching for, when he'd smelled the body? Chloroform (so I understood) had a sweet, cloying odor. I eyed Father over the papers. "You wouldn't chloroform *yourself* before also taking hemlock." It would be redundant. But it would make an ideal way to incapacitate a victim whose death you meant to stage in the most dramatic way.

I continued reading.

Cause of Death: Poison (Hemlock)
Manner of Death: Unexplained/Suspicious

My heart *bonged* once, low and heavy. I looked up. "What now?"

He plucked the report from my hands, and I only held on to it a little longer before releasing it. "Now *the police* will investigate," he said—enunciating rather more than necessary. "Were you two able to learn anything new?"

Miss Judson and I exchanged Looks, and for once Father actually noticed.

"And whatever you found out, I expect you to tell me everything," he said.

"Why would you think otherwise?" Miss Judson asked innocently.

In fact, Miss Judson and I had already decided exactly what to share with Father, discussing it fervently during our ride home. We had agreed that Mum should remain out of the story as long as possible. Father, knowing well that Miss Judson is an absolutely immovable witness, turned his steely Prosecution gaze on me. I was far more likely to crack.

"Mr. Leighton had recently received several threatening letters," I reported, "which Mrs. Leighton believes to have been sent by the Blackwell family. He burned them all before she could read them—"

"Although they were in Latin," Miss Judson put in, "so she could not have given up their contents in any case."

Father looked thoughtful. "Perhaps the post-mistress will have some record of these letters. I'll inquire in the morning. Anything else?"

Another exchange of Looks. "We cycled over to the college to see the Campanile for ourselves," I said.

"Really?" His voice was unexpectedly keen. He settled in more comfortably on the settee. "I've only seen it from afar. What was it like?"

"Tall," replied Miss Judson.

"And loud," I contributed.

He gave us a long-suffering Look.

"They've just reopened it after all these years since Olive Blackwell's disappearance," I added. "The new carillonist gave us a tour."

"He didn't happen to seem the threatening-letter sort, I suppose?" he asked.

Miss Judson let out a little clap of laughter. "She. And no. *Nor* the sort to push someone out of a belltower."

"Well, she would have been a little girl at the time," I pointed out.

"I don't know," said Father, "I personally make a

habit to never underestimate what mayhem a young girl is capable of."

"Mayhem!" I exclaimed. "When have I ever caused mayhem?"

"On that note." Miss Judson rose smoothly. "It's been a day. I believe I shall retire before dinner."

"You'll join us, won't you, Miss Judson?" Father had been making this appeal more and more often lately, and Miss Judson was declining with as much frequency. Eventually, I assumed, one of them would have to wear down. Yet again I wished there was some way I might tip the balance in their favor.

"Indeed no," she said with a mild smile. "Cook and I have things to discuss."

"What things?" I demanded.

"Secret Hardcastle Staff Things. Good evening."

Before departing, she paused to regard the swag of greenery in the archway, but said no more. Father's face was set, watching her leave—but when he turned back to me, what he said was, "We need to discuss the mistletoe."

"What about it?"

"It's making Miss Judson uncomfortable."

It seemed to be making *Father* uncomfortable, but I didn't say as much. "Talk to Priscilla. She's the one who brought it all." And no one could prove otherwise. There was certainly no evidence of conspiracy between me and any American neighbor with celebrated gardens, an unnatural interest in romance, and a scheming mind. I knew perfectly well how inappropriate it was for a Young Lady of Quality to interfere in the courtship (or frustrating lack thereof) of her father and her governess.

But there was, so far as my understanding, no such prohibition upon neighbors. There were therefore boughs, wreaths, and balls of the shrub deployed strategically throughout No. 14 Gravesend Close, at places Miss Judson and Father were likely to cross paths: the foyer, the hallway, farther down the hallway, the stairwell, the stairwell landing, the parlor doorway, the dining room, above the front and back doors, and all around the kitchen.

Father sighed. "I cannot go about kissing young women in my employ."

"Who said anything about kissing? It's a toxic parasite. I don't know why anyone should consider that romantic."

"*No*." Peony had returned from her fruitless errand to the kitchen.

Father scooped her up—and *she* made no objections to being kissed beneath the mistletoe, Dear Reader.

Still toting Peony, he turned up the gaslights, filling the parlor with a bloom of golden light. "Shall we trim the tree?"

I suspected this was the true motive for Miss Judson's departure. She'd wished to preserve this as a private family ritual for Father and me. But with her parents in Cayenne, this was *her* Christmas tree, too. And the two of us could certainly use her Artistic Temperament. For an otherwise eminently sensible person, she really had some curious ideas about Propriety.

Whistling "Good King Wenceslas," Father produced the trunk of decorations and removed the lid. "Aha!" He plucked forth a blown-glass ornament, a fat, ugly cherub Aunt Helena had bought at Leighton's. It was part of a set, ordered in from Germany, just like Her Majesty's. Several of them had Mysteriously Broken over the years.

Peony hissed at it, ears pressed flat.

"Mum hated that," I recalled.

Father spun round with a grin. "Yes, it's hideous, isn't it?" He held it aloft, the lamplight flickering off its inefficiently tiny wings and chubby tum. "Guaranteed to terrify even the most mayhem-prone child into good behavior!" A Reasonable Man would have stuffed the ghastly thing back into the box—but Aunt Helena *would* expect to see it on the tree, so he shoved it to the very center of the branches, and turned it away from the light..

I dug about, carefully withdrawing the remainder of the tissue-wrapped ornaments, the tin stars and paper poppets. Peony batted hopefully at the tissue and swiped her cheek and whiskers along the corner of the box. At the very bottom, my searching fingers found something I didn't even realize I'd been looking for—but as soon as I felt the cool metal, I grasped it with purpose.

It was a lead figure, a Roman soldier in a red cape and a helmet crowned with a brush of horsehair. Mum had looped some ribbon through his posed arm so he could hang, awkwardly, because I had enjoyed playing with him when I was small. I had forgotten all about it, but now I blinked at the painted figurine in astonishment. It was a perfect mate to the one I'd seen yesterday in Mr. Leighton's workshop.

"Did Mr. Leighton make this?"

Father held out his hand. "Goodness, I haven't seen that in years."

I handed over the centurion, and Father tipped him downward, to peek at the soles of his strappy sandals. "M-D-C-hmmm, this seems to be a Roman numeral, but I'm not—"

Father was hopeless with Roman numerals, so I snatched it back. *MDCCCLXXIV.* "Eighteen seventy-four," I translated. More letters on his shield spelled out *Cohortis Hadriani.* I had just enough time to work out the English—*Hadrian's Guard*—before Father snapped his fingers.

"It must be from your mum's college days. She'd have been graduating just about then."

"That's the year Olive Blackwell disappeared."

"Well, I doubt there's any connection between this old chap and that sad business." But he sounded uncertain.

This was the moment to speak up—to let Father know that Mum had been involved, somehow, in that sad business, after all. That she and her cohort had been present in the Campanile when Olive Blackwell's fall from the tower had precipitated Professor Leighton's fall from grace, and for some reason, somebody was dredging it all back up again now.

But the moment passed, Father moved on, and then it was too late. "I'm glad you found Octavius, here," he said, prizing the figure from my grip. "He can protect us from the cherub."

"And Père Fouettard," I said, making Father shudder.

"What else is in there?" He leaned his tall frame over the box, and found a crepe-paper clown, its springy limbs bobbing.

"Peony will eat that," I predicted, and Father put it on the highest branch (only making it more tempting). Then we were lost in the merriment of the moment, sad memories set aside.

⁓

Sleep was impossible that night. I lay abed, still feeling the ghostly vibration of the carillon bells in my bones. We were too far away to hear them, but I still strained to catch the faint automated chiming of the hour through the cold night air. It had been such a long few days, from Mr. Leighton's death to the exhilarating and disorienting visit to the Campanile—and the even more disorienting story of Olive's disappearance—to the autopsy report bringing us right back around to who'd killed Professor Leighton.

Olive's disappearance and the Professor's murder were two intertwining mysteries, and if I could just untangle them, perhaps it would solve them both. Whenever I closed my eyes, however, I kept seeing Mum's face—swinging a pickaxe on expedition in Cornwall, boldly facing down the camera in the portrait in Father's office, or focused and intent as she bent over her mending.

With a jolt of revelation, I sat up. Peony grumbled, then stretched out a white paw and tried to go back to sleep, but I nudged her out of the way to free the coverlet. It was a crazy-patch quilt Mum had pieced from scraps of our old clothes. Here was a bit of striped silk from her wedding dress, there a snippet of Father's robes from law school. I could find what I was looking for in the dark, but I pulled it closer to the window and the streetlight outside. In a lopsided trapezoid of dark velvet was an embroidered dove, and Mum's initials: *JBH*. Her signature.

I stroked the sleek stitches of the dove's wing. Mum's portrait had the name of the photography studio stamped on it. Miss Judson's sketches all said

Ada J~ in a neat swoop in the corner. Even Mr. Leighton had signed his own Displays, after a fashion, always including a figurine of himself, somewhere, in the village—bespectacled and be-aproned and holding a paintbrush. But I hadn't seen his miniature there this year, because another artist had signed it instead.

Artwork. That's what had been troubling me about the way Mr. Leighton had been found. He had been killed like Socrates, then artfully (if gruesomely) arranged, posed and placed in a *tableau mort*—a display of the dead.

And the killer had signed her work. Like Mum with her little dove, she'd left her name right there for all the world to see.

Olive Blackwell.

8
WINDOW DRESSING

Although we have Her Majesty and Prince Albert to thank for the popularity of the Christmas tree, the first English tree was the inspiration of an earlier monarch. In 1800, Queen Charlotte, deciding that bedecking her castle with various disparate boughs of greenery was inefficient, opted to have an entire yew tree brought inside instead.

–H. M. Hardcastle, *A Modern Yuletide*

It turned out I was not alone in that insane deduction.

The post-mortem report had been published in the *Police Gazette*, and Tuesday morning, the papers were saturated with rumors and headlines like **MISSING GIRL BACK FROM DEAD TO MURDER LOCAL SHOPKEEPER**. Or simply, **OLIVE BLACKWELL LIVES**!

"It's that Miss Shelley again," Father said. "Peddling her sensationalist rubbish."

Imogen Shelley was the *Swinburne Tribune*'s newest reporter—and their first woman. She'd begun by writing advice and fashion columns, but her diverting and energetic prose had swiftly garnered the admiration of readers, and the respect of her editor. She was now covering the crime beat, and had, on occasion, been sharply critical of the police and the Magistrate's Office. Which included Father.

You could say, Dear Reader, that my father was *not* among Imogen Shelley's most devoted fans. He flung the paper aside and (un)fairly attacked his soft-boiled egg.

Overruling Father's objections, Miss Judson slid the paper closer and read the article aloud.

SHOPKEEPER'S MURDER LINKED TO MYSTERIOUS DISAPPEARANCE: REVENGE FROM BEYOND THE GRAVE?

The shocking murder of former professor Basil Leighton in his High Street shop last weekend appears to be the handiwork of a dead woman, if clues are to be believed. Inspector Hardy of the Swinburne Detective Bureau refuses to offer comment, but sources close to the investigation reveal that evidence recovered from the scene points to one Olive Blackwell as the culprit—the Schofield College student whose baffling disappearance nineteen years ago led to Leighton's retiring in disgrace.

We remind our Readers that Miss Blackwell's

case was never closed. Will Inspector Hardy be so careless this time?

"Careless!" I cried. "Disgrace! How can she say those things about the professor and the Inspector?"

"I don't recall you being so outraged when she criticized *me*," Father noted.

Accompanying the text was a halftone portrait of Olive Blackwell herself, a small, round-faced, fair-haired girl with mischief in her eyes. I had to take a quick gulp of my tea to keep from exclaiming in surprise. She was in the Cornwall photograph with Mum! The look on Miss Judson's face, watching me slobber all over myself, indicated that she had made the same realization.

"It *is* intriguing," she said. "Olive Blackwell, back from the dead? It might be possible."

Father grunted.

"They never found a body," I reminded everyone unnecessarily. "Or any trace of her. And that carillonist thought she just ran away."

"That's entirely different than being 'back from the dead.' That sort of hyperbole serves no purpose."

"It sells newspapers," I pointed out, to a high clear laugh—abruptly cut short—from Miss Judson.

"Well, there is that," she agreed, meticulously buttering her toast while she continued to read.

"You're meeting with the Inspector this morning, right, Father?"

He rubbed the bridge of his nose. "He's not going to love this."

I kicked the legs of my chair. I wished I had something to offer him, that Miss Judson and I had found some evidence that pointed firmly to Mr. Leighton's killer (someone less impossibly dead than Olive). But so far, we knew no more than the police.

Father and I glumly returned to our toast and jam, while Miss Judson crisply turned the newspaper pages. "I don't know why you're still reading that," he grumbled. "She has nothing new to say."

"Hmm," she replied. "Then I suppose you won't be interested in the dedication of the Basil Leighton Gallery at the museum this weekend." With a perfunctory cough, she read:

> The tragedy has thrown a shadow over what was to be a great triumph in Professor Leighton's legacy, but a spokesman for the Antiquities Museum tells the *Tribune* that the upcoming dedication of the new wing devoted to artifacts from Roman Britain, named in Professor Leighton's honor, will continue as planned. The event, held in conjunction with Schofield College's 50th Anniversary celebrations, will be Saturday evening, by

invitation only, featuring Notable Speakers and local dignitaries.

"A ceremony honoring Mr. Leighton? Why wouldn't Mrs. Leighton mention that?" I said.

"I got the feeling that her husband's career brought back painful memories. Perhaps she has no interest in revisiting any part of it. *My* question," Miss Judson continued, "is why your father hasn't mentioned it."

He froze, toast halfway between his plate and his mouth. "Well, er, I'm not—why would you think I knew anything about it?"

"Come now, Mr. Hardcastle. This is the sort of event the best of Swinburne society will be invited to."

"Sadly, the Prosecuting Solicitor is not exactly one of Swinburne's most estimable offices," he said.

"Yes, it is," I objected. Father worked alongside magistrates and police detectives—the highest echelon of criminal justice in the village!

"Be that as it may," Miss Judson interposed, "I was in fact speaking of Aunt Helena. I imagine *she* has received an invitation."

Miss Judson was right. If this was an Exclusive Society Event, Aunt Helena was certain to have wrangled her way onto the guest list, no doubt trampling worthy Local Dignitaries along her way. I bit my lip, silently thought several Inappropriate Words, then said, "Do you think she would take us?"

⌒

I sent Father off to work, still wishing I'd been brave enough to ask him more about the case. I had nagging questions I longed to pose to him—not that he'd answer any of them—yet could not bring myself to voice. What would I ask? How would I explain my interest, or my urgency?

Instead, I mulled over my thoughts in the steamy kitchen with Cook, who was attempting to initiate me into the arcanum of English Christmas Cookery. Today's lesson was the all-critical mincemeat, and I was stoning raisins. I am sorry to say, Dear Reader, this was not some Biblical torture, but simply the removal of their tiny pear-shaped seeds by rubbing them between my fingers, after soaking them (the raisins, not my fingers) in boiling water.

"Raisins are a terrible thing to do to perfectly innocent grapes," I grumbled, as the sticky heap before me grew.

"Hush you, Young Miss. Mincemeat is Himself's favorite, as you well know." She brushed a strand of grey hair from her ruddy forehead with the back of her hand. "But your mum weren't partial to them, neither," she admitted.

I rubbed another raisin nearly to death. "I don't remember that."

Cook was overseeing the boiling syrup in which these raisins would be drowned. "Your mum, rest her soul, was the finickiest eater I ever did meet. Tested even my skills in the kitchen, let me tell you. No onion—"

"*I* hate onion!" I exclaimed.

"No," Cook said with flat disbelief, and went right on with the catalogue of Mum's preferences. "But she did love this mincemeat. Even give the receipt a tweak or two of her own, didn't she?"

"Really?" I tried to peer past Cook to the stained and faded card on which the recipe was recorded—but she artfully blocked my view with her stout shoulder. I was not adept enough to learn all her secrets yet.

"Now chop those fine," she commanded, handing me a wicked-looking knife whose heft and size explained the heft and size of Cook's strong arms. I worked in obedient silence while Cook obliged me with more of her memories of Mum at Christmastime. When I judged the moment right, I gently steered the conversation.

"What would Mum have thought of this 'Olive Blackwell lives' stuff?"

Cook paused only briefly, then resumed her brisk stirring. "Now. What has you asking a thing like that?"

"You have the newspaper in your apron pocket."

Cook's florid face got even redder, and she yanked out the paper and swatted me with it. "It's to wrap chips in for Himself's tea." She gave the boiling fruit a judicious glare, and, evidently satisfied, left it to its own devices and joined me at the table. "But seeing how it's handy, it would be a shame for it to go unread."

Since Cook was responsible for ironing the ink dry on the newsprint, so Father wouldn't accidentally wipe it on his shirt or waistcoat, I knew perfectly well she'd already read every column inch of every story on the subject.

"Now, mind you, your mum never did talk much about her college days. Not to me, anyway. It wouldn't have been proper. But that doesn't mean I didn't pick up a thing or two. She had a couple of school chums she used to get letters from, and Christmas cards, too."

"School chums—like who? Was there anyone in particular? Do you remember their names?" Was there someone she would trust enough to let blindfold her at the top of a tower?

"It's been years, Young Miss. Who could remember all that?"

"You never forget *anything*," I said boldly. "That recipe card's a sham, and we both know it."

"None of your pertness, now." But I could tell she was pleased. "Well, let me think on't. There might be something. I might even still have her correspondence book about somewhere. One of those friends of 'ers was quite the world traveler. Always sending outlandish recipes for cactus leaf tea, or some such nonsense."

"Cook! Thank you!" I surprised her by flinging my arms around her. "I'll even eat the raisins."

ᴄʀꙅ

Cook was not my only Witness to interview that week. I was due to check in with Caroline Munjal about how her own Investigation was proceeding. Mrs. Munjal had recovered somewhat from her shock, and was more than happy to release us for an outing to town to go Christmas shopping. The Munjals were Hindu, but they bedecked their home like a scene from a Christmas card, and because of their position in Swinburne Society, exchanged gifts and tokens with nearly everyone in town. Therefore, Caroline and elder sister Nanette arrived at my house in the family carriage, toting a shopping list as long as Santa Claus's.

I was eager to discuss the case, but Nanette would instantly report back to their parents on any Unladylike Behavior Caroline and I committed. I needn't have worried. The murder was all *anybody* was talking about. I had scarcely clambered aboard the open carriage and said hello to Hobbes, the coachman, before they drew me into their discussion.

"Myrtle's clever, let's see what she thinks." Nanette plunged me right in. She was a plump, pretty girl with glossy black hair caught up in a fashionable winter hat. "Do you think it's true? Olive Blackwell has come back and killed Professor Leighton?"

"Don't be a goose, Poorvi." Caroline's voice was sharp on her sister's nickname. "You heard what Father said at breakfast."

"Yes, but you saw the newspapers," Nanette insisted. "They're saying that Olive Blackwell has been in hiding all these years, and she came back to murder Mr. Leighton. It's right out of *Otranto** or *Udolpho*!"† Nanette shared our taste in sensational fiction, with an extra emphasis on the supernatural and gothic. "Her ghost has returned to seek her revenge! What if she's back to kill off everyone who had a hand in her murder?"

"Maybe you're right." I turned her theory over in my mind as we jangled along the streets. "Well, not about the ghosts, but about the motive. Caroline, were you able to find out—why your mum was so upset?" I stopped myself before asking if she'd charged into her father's private office to search for secret files. "Or what the Mayor wanted the other night?"

Caroline chanced a quick glance at her sister. "Not really," she said carefully. "I thought maybe it had . . . something to do with when they were at college?"

Since that was self-evident, she, too, must've been hedging for Nanette's sake. So I contributed what

---

* Horace Walpole, *The Castle of Otranto*, 1764, a romance about haunted castles, cursed families, and Italian noblemen

† Ann Radcliffe, *The Mysteries of Udolpho*, 1794, another romance about haunted castles, cursed families, and more Italian noblemen

Miss Judson and I had discovered from our visit to the Campanile, filling them both in on the secret society.

"Hadrian's Guard," Nanette supplied unexpectedly. "That's what it was called—that college club Father was in. Well, it was in Latin, um—" She struggled to produce the words, but they were right on the tip of my tongue.

"*Cohortis Hadriani.* My mum had a lead soldier—a *Roman* soldier—with that on it."

Caroline was nodding fervently. "Our father has one, too."

"Does it say 1874 on it?" I asked.

"In Roman numerals?" Nanette clarified. "I don't know what they say, though."*

I sat back, trying to put these pieces together. Were those little soldiers some sort of grim trophy of whatever had befallen Olive Blackwell during a Hadrian's Guard ritual at the Campanile in 1874? "Mr. Leighton had one, too. It was with all his miniatures for the Display."

"We need to find out more about this club! They

---

* Nanette was far cleverer than this account makes her appear—it would have been scientifically improbable for her not to be, with Dr. and Mrs. Munjal as parents—but she had devoted her mental energies to ladylike pursuits, not academic rigors. She played the piano and sang, and did splendid needlework. And her deportment was flawless. If I ever did decide to improve my Young Lady of Quality skills, I should apprentice myself to Nanette Munjal. She made Caroline and me look like a couple of lawless street ruffians.

must be the ones who killed Olive. Mayor Spence-Hastings was in it, too—"

"How do you know that?" Caroline demanded.

"They talk about it all the time whenever they're over for dinner, all that reminiscing about the Good Old Days at Schofield College. Like the other night when he came over."

Caroline and I turned to stare at her.

"What?" she said. "I heard everything. Well, almost everything. I got there late."

Caroline looked shocked. "Listening at doorways? That's not very ladylike."

"Of course it is. How else are women supposed to learn anything about the foolish things men get up to?" Privately, I thought Nanette had a point.

"Are you going to tell us or not?"

Nanette smiled conspiratorially. "Well. I didn't *exactly* catch everything they said, but the Mayor mentioned Olive. He said that Father owes him for something back then, and that he knows Father won't let them down now."

"Who's 'them'?" I asked.

"It must be Hadrian's Guard. Those secret societies are *for life*. You know they make you take blood oaths."

"Poorvi!" Caroline said with exasperation. "*What* does Father owe the Mayor for?"

"I didn't hear that bit."

Caroline and I uttered matching groans. "Maybe

LaRue knows something," Caroline said. "You know how she is—it's always 'my father this,' and 'my father that.'"

"*My father killed Olive Blackwell?*" I said it as a joke—but Caroline and Nanette stared at me in shock, followed by a grim, cool acceptance as the idea slipped in, settled down, and stuck.

త∿

When we finally arrived on High Street, Nanette headed straight for Leighton's Mercantile, Caroline and me trailing behind. "Maybe she's opened back up again. Mother likes that orange chutney she's been carrying, and she asked us to bring back some candied dates for another fruitcake," she said—fooling nobody. Although I gave myself a moment to consider how Miss Judson might like orange chutney.

But at the shop, the doors were locked and the lights off, Miss Judson's neatly lettered sign still in place.

"That's odd, though," Caroline said. "The curtain's open. You can see the Display."

An edge to her voice filled me with alarm, and I hurried to the frost-tinged window. The green baize curtains were spread wide. One oil lamp burned brightly above the model Swinburne—and someone had been rearranging the figures. The miniature crowd had moved on from the scene of Olive Blackwell's tragic fall; indeed, the snowy streets were deserted.

"What's that?" Nanette's voice was shrill, and she pointed one plump brown finger at the window.

A lead figure was posed in the middle of the Display—a scantily clad woman in exotic, drapey clothes that exposed more skin than they covered. Nanette, properly equipped with fully operational Delicate Sensibilities, pressed a hand to her lips as blood flooded her cheeks. But she could not seem to look away.

"Let me see." I squeezed in and took in the scene, and instantly identified the miniature personage: her black hair and elaborate diadem, the gold bracelets stacked upon her arms, the jeweled collar at her neck, the dramatic green paint outlining her eyes. The tiny, richly patterned carpet she was half-wrapped in.

"Wait, isn't that—?" Caroline began—then we all spoke at once.

"It's Cleopatra."

And beside her, bold and striking against the artificial snow, the well and the olives. Olive Blackwell's signature.

Nanette found her voice. "What do you think *now*?"

9
CHRISTMAS CARDS

Of all the flavors and spices we associate with the holiday season, cinnamon, nutmeg, peppermint, &c, the queen
of them all must be the clove, whose pungent oils pair so
readily with everything from citrus to dairy to meats.
This unprepossessing woody spice is in fact the dried
flower bud of a myrtle tree.

-H. M. Hardcastle, *A Modern Yuletide*

We spent the rest of that afternoon not shopping (mission to select Miss Judson's present failed *yet again*), but
at the police station. The other girls convinced me that
delivering the news of the latest vandalism directly
to Dr. Munjal would be preferable to announcing it
to the general constabulary. He received it gravely,
betraying no thoughts, theories, or emotions about the
incident, let alone the rest of the case, and it took every

dram* of my Exceptional Forbearance not to pester him to share more.

But Caroline and Nanette were diffident and obedient, not demanding to see his paperwork or insisting he call in reinforcements, and I did not wish to get them in (even more) trouble. Dr. Munjal often indulged my interest in his work—but now, sitting in his tidy, official office at the police station, beside his proper, pretty, and ladylike daughters, I felt like Morbid Myrtle more than ever. I sat on my hands so I wouldn't chew on my fingers, and didn't say anything.

After we—by which I mean Nanette—told him about the Display, Dr. Munjal held the three of us in a heavy gaze and said, "Wait here," in tones that indicated we were not to move, twitch, or even breathe until he returned.

"He must be going to inform Inspector Hardy," I said.

Nanette and Caroline exchanged nervous glances, but my restless eyes wandered about the office. It had grim green walls hung with Dr. Munjal's medical degrees and framed photographs of Her Majesty and Mr. Gladstone. A new one had been added since last I'd been here—Mayor Spence-Hastings. What

---

* one-eighth of an ounce, or 1.77 grams (or, incidentally, three *scruples*. Take that as you will.)

sort of hold did he have over Dr. Munjal? From what Nanette had told us, it seemed more than likely that Henry Spence-Hastings was one of the people in the Campanile the night Olive disappeared. Was Vikram Munjal another, contrary to what he'd told Father?

The desk was littered with papers, and I *swear* I wasn't snooping, Dear Reader, much less Investigating—but I know how to read, and that isn't something you can just stop yourself from doing. Among the official documents was a folded sheet of creamy letter paper with a deckled edge, and on that creamy paper, a scrawl of bold inky handwriting. In Latin.

Before I quite realized what I was up to, I slid from my seat and crept to the desk, where I used a pen to tease the page from beneath the other papers.

"What are you doing?" Caroline whispered.

"What's this?" I beckoned them over. Nanette refused to budge, but Caroline, glancing furtively over her shoulder, tiptoed to join me. We could not have looked more suspicious if they'd sketched us for the front page of *Illustrated Police News* dressed as bandits in black masks.

Caroline studied the note, sounding out the Latin words. "*Quæstio Repetundarum.* What does that mean?"

For some reason, we looked to Nanette, who shook her head in bewilderment, then waved us back to our seats so we could be timid little church mice when Dr. Munjal returned.

He regarded us again with grim and weary eyes. "I've dispatched a constable to the shop," he said. "And am now dispatching the three of you back home. I don't suppose I need to tell you not to say anything to your mother."

༄

I assumed the injunction did not apply to Father and Miss Judson, who also took the news with perplexity. Father promised to relay the police report to us as soon as it came in—but the newspapers beat him to it.

OLIVE BLACKWELL STRIKES AGAIN! greeted us at breakfast the next morning, along with an Artist's Rendering of the miniature Cleopatra splayed on her rug in the street.

Father folded the newspaper crossly—which I had not realized was possible, until I witnessed his overly crisp snapping of the pages, the tense pinch of the crease, before he slapped it to the tablecloth. I was afraid to draw it toward myself—but could not resist a peek at the author's name. *Imogen Shelley.* Naturally.

"Did the police find any signs of a break-in this time?" I inquired. "The vandal must have some way of getting into the shop undetected."

Father replied with a growl.

"And why Cleopatra?" Miss Judson mused. "This whole thing is so mysterious!"

Father slammed his chair back. "I will not have idle speculation at the breakfast table!" And stormed from the room forthwith.

Miss Judson and I waited a polite moment, then immediately set about Idly Speculating.

"What does *Quæstio Repetundarum* mean?"

My Latin instructor eyed me over the edge of the newspaper. "I don't recall that being in the lesson I prepared for you."

"It was in a note hidden on Dr. Munjal's desk."

An eyebrow lifted. "Hidden?"

Impatiently, I waved that aside. "Mrs. Leighton told us they'd received threatening letters in Latin, remember? It must have something to do with this Hadrian's Guard." I pushed away from my place at the table.

"Where are you off to?"

"Father's study," I said. "I need to do some research."

This being an Investigative Errand Miss Judson could get behind, she joined me. I stood a long time frowning before the shelves, uncertain where to begin. "Perhaps a dictionary?" she suggested.

I found that easily, it being a beloved favorite: Lewis & Short's *Latin Dictionary.**

---

* **Charlton T. Lewis and Charles Short, *A Latin Dictionary Founded on Andrews' Edition of Freund's Latin Dictionary, Revised, Enlarged, and in Great Part Rewritten*, 1879. We typically just called it "The Latin Dictionary."**

I knew *quæstio* meant "question," but started there anyway. "'*A seeking.*'" I drew my finger down the page, performing a *quæstio* of my own: "'*An inquiry.*'" My eyes lifted to Miss Judson's. "An Investigation."

"Go on," she said, voice soft but eager.

Repetundarum was not quite so easily sussed out, but a few more textbooks later, we'd managed a vague (very vague) understanding of the note's contents. The Roman court of *Quæstio Repetundarum** had tried cases of extortion, blackmail, and corruption.

I scowled. "Is it a blackmail letter, then? Shouldn't it make some kind of demand?"

"It's certainly not much to go on. Presumably whoever sent it felt the recipient would recognize the significance."

I sighed. Another question only the dead could answer.

The dead—or Dr. Munjal. I'd probably sooner get an answer out of Mum or Olive Blackwell.

It was not all dead ends, however. That afternoon, Cook triumphantly produced some long-lost correspondence from Mum's "college chum" that had been used to mark a page in *Mrs. Beeton's Book of Household Management*, another gift from Aunt Helena (her tastes ran toward the self-improving). Cook's scornful sniff, when revealing where she'd found it, explained why

---

* or *Quæstio de Repetundis*, depending on the syntax

it had stayed hidden so long. Neither Cook nor Mum had had much enthusiasm for Mrs. Beeton's advice. The letter she'd found was a handmade Christmas card with an engraved desert scene pasted on—camels trailing past ruins of a temple.

"Egypt?" Miss Judson turned it over and back. "The Holy Land? Maybe that's meant to be the Magi."

"There are only two of them." Its envelope was missing, and there was very little other evidence beyond a lazy note scrawled inside:

Dear Columba, Happy Xmas & Congrats on your Nuptials! Love Nora. P.S. Saw David in Italy. All is well.

It didn't tell us much, and there was no date—but it was more than we had before. "Nora and David," I said aloud.

Miss Judson's eyes sparkled. "Nora and David," she replied.

We resumed our excavations of Father's study and retrieved Mum's thin Schofield College annual.

An age later, after poring through endless lists of students' names, I had something. "Carmichael, Mr. David, class of 1874. Carmichael, Miss Nora, sophomore."

"Brother and sister?" Miss Judson speculated.

"It doesn't tell us if they were in this secret society, involved in the ritual at the Campanile, or had anything to do with Miss Blackwell's disappearance."

"They're both listed as reading Classics. That means they were most likely Professor Leighton's students." I leafed through. "Same as Mum. And Olive Blackwell." And just about every other student at the college. I sighed.

Miss Judson was thoughtful. "*Columba* is Latin for 'dove.' That could well be the sort of private nickname you'd share with the closest members of your secret society. How many does that give us? Five? Who do you suppose was Number Six?"

Looking at the booklet, names I recognized leaping off nearly every line, I was afraid I knew. I counted them out on my fingers. "Olive. Mum. Nora. David. Mayor Spence-Hastings. And Dr. Munjal."

Miss Judson reached out and lowered the book. "That's rather an inflammatory statement," she said. "What do you have to back it up?"

That was the problem—nothing but whispers, hearsay, and supposition.

⌒

As we plotted our next move, I tried to sell Miss Judson on my theory of the crime. Or my prime suspect, at any rate. The Mayor had the opportunity to kill Professor Leighton, and there was no way to prove someone didn't have access to hemlock. I couldn't recall if it was one of the regulated poisons you had to sign for,* but it grew all over the English countryside.

"Not in December," she pointed out. "And what is his motive?"

"Covering up the murder of Olive," I said, whereupon she turned to me, chalk in hand, face a mask of skepticism.

"And what was his motive for *that*?"

I jabbed my pencil into my paper. "I'm still working on that," I muttered.

"Without countenancing that theory," Miss Judson said, "what next?"

"We have to go to the carillon concert. Whoever killed Professor Leighton is bound to be there."

"And not at the event being held in his honor across town at the museum at the same time? And for which I spent *an entire afternoon* convincing Aunt Helena to give us her tickets? Kindly explain how you arrived at that conclusion."

I only growled faintly, because of course she was right. Either venue was just as likely to attract the killer. Why couldn't we be in two places at once?

Miss Judson studied the notice for the museum gala in the paper. "The two events overlap somewhat.

---

* the Pharmacy Act of 1868. Hemlock wasn't named specifically, but technically speaking, it should fall under the category of "plant alkaloids." Laws are often not as specific as one might wish. ("That's why we have lawyers," appends Father.)

It would *barely* be possible to squeeze them both in—if we're very efficient about it, and the tram schedule cooperates."

❧

The tram schedule cooperated, but nothing else did. By Saturday afternoon, I was still no closer to solving either case, chiefly because Miss Judson had kept me busy with pointless exercises like conjugating Greek verbs and having a hem let down.*

"I don't think Father's coming," I said, fidgeting by the window. "We're going to be late."

I cast a doleful look toward the street outside. Father had skipped morris dancing practice to go into the office, an indication of just how much pressure everyone was under to solve Mr. Leighton's murder.

"We'll have to go without him," Miss Judson said— and I thought I Detected a note of disappointment in her voice. "Alas. I thought he might enjoy an evening off."

Back at Schofield College, the Campanile glowed against the cool twilit sky like a lonesome candle. In the commons below, a jumble of people jumbled about a jumble of chairs dotting the snow-covered lawns. I spotted a familiar flash of bright pink among them, and waved to Priscilla. She hastened over, pink-and-white skirts swishing like a walking peppermint stick.

---

* I had finally managed to grow an inch, and my best skirt was now too short to be ladylike.

"Isn't this exciting?" She clasped her hands with relish. "A concert at a haunted belltower!"

"It's not haunted," I said, but she just winked at me.

"It will be when it's in *Mabel Castleton and the Secret Society*!"

"Don't you dare," Miss Judson said. "We're already having enough trouble with Imogen Shelley's version of the tale."

Priscilla recognized the name. "She's a firecracker, isn't she? Quite notorious—even among sensation writers! I heard she once went undercover as a dockworker to investigate a smuggling ring in Liverpool, and got herself arrested with them. She was in jail for a *week* before anyone realized she was a woman!"

"Makes you wonder what she's doing in Swinburne," Miss Judson said. "Surely there are bigger stories than our little business here."

"Who can resist an unsolved mystery?" Priscilla gestured to the crowd assembled for the concert, and I saw her point.

"Let's take our seats." Miss Judson balked at the scattered chairs. As did everyone else, milling about trying to make sense of the strange seating arrangement.

"I know I haven't been in England all that long, but is this quite *de rigueur*?" said Priscilla. The chairs, a small army of pretty folding deck chairs with cloth seats, were spread in random clusters across the grounds.

"No," Miss Judson said, frown growing. "It is not." With a sharp glance at me, she withdrew her ubiquitous sketchbook—a small model this time, suitable for hiding in a lady's most impractical bag, the reticule— and swiftly took down the arrangement. I didn't wait to see her drawing emerge. I had a better idea.

I dashed off for the Campanile itself. The bells weren't ringing yet, but I felt their ghostly shudder clanging in my brain.

I had to get past a gentleman standing in the doorway like a train porter, arms crossed. "No admittance, Miss, until after the concert."

"I'm—Miss Leah's assistant," I improvised. "I turn her pages." That sounded vaguely musical, right, Dear Reader?

"Best get on up then." With a look of reproach, he cracked open the medieval door.

It was even darker and stuffier than before, but I pounded my way higher and higher, chest bursting, until I reached the landing for the clavier console. There, one of the small arrow-loop windows overlooked the audience, and I pressed my face to the opening.

"Myrtle? You came!"

I whirled back, heart pounding from the climb, from the surprise—and from the scene on the grounds below. Leah stood in the doorway to the clavier room, in her blue fringed dolman. "What's wrong?" she said.

Breathless, I couldn't get the words out. Instead I just pointed.

Leah slipped past me to peer out the loophole. There wasn't enough room for both of us to look out at once, but I knew exactly what she would see: the crowd of spectators who'd come to hear the Campanile's first concert in nearly twenty years, and the chairs in their peculiar haphazard arrangement in the snow. Only they weren't haphazard at all.

Viewed from high above, they spelled out *O-L-I-V-E*.

10

SATURNALIA

One of Christmas's ancient forebears was the Roman festival of Saturnalia, several days spent in riotous devotion to Saturn, god of agriculture. Celebrations included feasting, gift-giving, the closing of public offices, and the upending of the normal social order: masters served their slaves, folk abandoned their traditional roles and indulged in licentious behaviors rarely tolerated the rest of the year.

–H. M. Hardcastle, *A Modern Yuletide*

Leah stared at the chairs for a long moment, before turning back. "Well," she said, twisting the fringe on her sleeve. "I haven't seen that before."

She wasn't grasping the severity of events. "Someone is trying to threaten you. To stop you from playing, maybe." Or worse.

"Oh, I don't think so. They're just keeping Olive's memory alive. This sort of thing happens all the time. It's a college prank, that's all."

"But Professor Leighton—"

"That poor man." Leah's eyes brimmed with sympathy. "But I'm not scared. Certainly not of Olive's ghost!" Her light laugh sounded strained. "I'd say this calls for a little Bach."

In the clavier room, she flung open a cabinet and whipped out a piece of music. "This wasn't on the program tonight, but it seems appropriate." The score was called *Toccata & Fugue in D Minor.* "Do you want to stay? You really can hear better from down on the grounds."

"I don't think I should leave you—"

"Nonsense. I'm perfectly safe. There are dozens of people around. What could happen to me?"

What had happened to Olive? But I could sense there was no use trying to persuade her. Reluctantly, I made my way back down to the ground. If the man guarding the door wondered at my dereliction of duty, he made no remark.

When I returned to the crowd below, there was no sign of Miss Judson, but I found Priscilla easily. "Ada's gone to fetch a guard," she explained. "But—"

She didn't have a chance to finish. While the audience was still trying to figure out where to sit, a thrilling cascade of sound rained down upon us—startling everyone into a rush to sit down, like a strange variation on Musical Chairs. I ended up next to Priscilla, at the bottom (I thought) of the V.

"No *ghost* did this," I said to her.

Miss Judson slipped in across from me, and waited for a lull in the music to give her report. Leah's chosen song was a riot of Baroque notes that really did sound like she was summoning a ghost—or exorcising one. Members of the audience were alternately enraptured or puzzled. More than one set of lips pursed in confusion at the un-Christmassy aspect of things.

Miss Judson surreptitiously pointed through the throng. A line of people stood right at the Campanile's base, apparently representatives of the college. She whispered to me when Leah finished her *Toccata & Fugue*,* "A woman from the Musical Committee told me that the chairs were put up by the grounds staff this afternoon. But no one checked their work, so she can't say whether *they* did this, or someone else came in after to rearrange them."

"Is Leah in danger?" I demanded.

Miss Judson frowned. "There's only one way in or out of the tower, and there's a man guarding the door. I asked them to have someone walk her home."

"Fat lot of good he'll be," I said. "He let *me* in."

"Did you see anyone suspicious in the crowd?"

"No." I sighed. The Mayor wasn't here, nor was

* a complex sort of musical composition evidently designed to first show off the musician's nimble fingers (the toccata), followed by a section with at least two separate melodies played simultaneously (the fugue), and resulting in many crashing notes happening all at the same time

anyone toting around olive branches and a stack of threatening letters. Everyone looked like ordinary innocent Swinburnians out for a holiday gathering.

"That's what they *want* you to think," put in Priscilla unhelpfully.

The remainder of Leah's concert—what we were able to stay for, anyway—passed uneventfully, and her music was beautiful, chiming through the evening as darkness enclosed the college grounds and a light, damp snow began to fall. It sounded like a spectral sleigh jingling across the sky, conjuring images of snowfall and angels and every kind of holiday wonder. But eventually we grew restless for our next engagement.

"You two go ahead to the museum," Priscilla said. "I'll keep an eye on things here. And I'm coming back for the midnight showing, too."

I couldn't help shivering. Somehow, I felt that's when disaster would most likely strike.

"Don't worry," she promised. "I won't come alone."

We would have to be content with that.

With a final wave to Leah that I knew she could not see, I followed Miss Judson away from the tower, the bells clamoring in our wake.

❧

It was too far to walk, for two Young Ladies of Quality in smart evening dress, at night, in the snow, so we took the tram back into town. The Antiquities Museum sat a few streets over from the courthouse and the police station, looking grim and imposing and not at all the sort of place you'd want your bones to spend Eternity (which was, mostly, just a myth—more people than you'd realize get moved around a bit after they've died). It had dark brick walls and tiny windows, a lead roof that drummed in the rain, and a skinny little flight of stairs that might as well have a DO NOT ENTER sign posted above, just in case anyone found them welcoming enough to scale on anything other than a dare.

Inside, however, was another matter. The building opened into a great hall, vast stone walls hung with Flemish tapestries and Chinese screens—all ten or eleven panels depicting famous emperors and their triumphs in battle—and dinosaur bones unearthed in America. Glass cases marched along the perimeter, each with its own preserved specimen: a Turkish knife, a Greek headdress in a cascade of gold, a marble statuette of a Sphinx—not the one in Egypt, but a winged woman with lion's paws. Peony would appreciate that.

"There's the Mayor," Miss Judson said, gaze skirting the crowd. I searched the assemblage for the remainder of the Spence-Hastings family, but it seemed his womenfolk had shied away from such a stuffy and intellectual gathering. The Munjals hadn't come, either; evidently "appearing at public functions" was not the Hadrian's Guard favor Mayor Spence-Hastings was calling in.

"We should follow him."

"We should *not*."

Nowhere among the men—and one woman—in academic dress, the gentlemen in eveningwear, and ladies in gowns of every description, did I see poor Mrs. Leighton. Indeed, it was difficult to imagine her here—hard to picture her in anything other than her practical cotton day dresses and her endless array of aprons and neat caps. Harder still, in fact, to picture Mr. Leighton here. Although I supposed in their pre–Olive Blackwell days, they must have attended many such functions.

The person I could not stop staring at, however, was not someone I knew at all. A small-boned, black-haired, dark-eyed beauty in a shimmering gold gown and long gloves stood bent before a glass case on a pedestal, admiring the object within. There was some-thing naggingly familiar about her, although I was sure I'd never seen her before.

I found myself drifting away from Miss Judson, toward her, until we stood on opposite sides of the case. Inside was an imposing goblet of hammered bronze, elaborate figures molded into its sloping sides. It was flecked with age, pitted and worn and missing a handle, but no less magnificent. My eyes followed its grand lines, from bowl to base, down to the card on the pedestal:

THE SATURNALIA CHALICE

FOURTH-CENTURY ROMAN BRITAIN.
DISCOVERED IN MAURIER, CORNWALL, 1873.

PRESENTED BY PROF. BASIL LEIGHTON, SCHOFIELD COLLEGE.

"Cornwall!" I said too loudly, too eagerly. The woman met my eyes through the glass, and smiled. She was older than I'd first thought, with lines around her eyes and silver glittering her hair.

"Do you know Saturnalia?" She had a warm, liquidy sort of voice, like treacle. "The Roman midwinter festival of unbridled excess." She slipped around the case and offered her hand. "I am Nora Carmichael." She said it like I was *expected* to know who she was—but I yanked my hand back in surprise.

"You're Mum's friend!" I blurted out, then stumbled through an introduction.

Her striking face lit up like a lantern. "But of course," she purred. "Columba, we called her. Our little dove. You look just like her. And Myrtle. How appropriate."

I wasn't sure what that meant—but I had so many questions, I couldn't find my way to begin. Before I could come up with anything sensible, one of the museum directors came over and got Miss Carmichael's attention.

"I must go. But do come find me later. We have so much to talk about!" Her sphinxlike smile grew as she slinked away.

I wondered what Miss Carmichael thought she was inviting me to.

And whether it was wise to accept.

As she departed, I was swept into the crowd, where a rumbling voice called out a warm greeting.

"Why, if it isn't Miss Myrtle!" I turned to see a tall, bald man in a black coat and tie, brushy black moustache twitching. "Don't recognize me without the uniform, then?"

"Inspector Hardy!" I wanted to hug him, but it wasn't terribly professional. "What are you doing here? Are you working?" I glanced furtively at the crowd. "All the suspects are likely to be here."

He chuckled. "I see you haven't taken the night off."

I felt my cheeks redden. "Would you believe that Father sent us?"

"Ah, never mind me," he said. "I know all too well how a case like this gets under your skin. I remember the night that girl vanished like it was yesterday."

"You worked on Olive Blackwell's disappearance?"

Inspector Hardy's smile was weary. "All old

coppers have an unsolved case that haunts them. That was mine."

"You're not old," I objected. Although, being strictly accurate, his moustache *did* look a little more grey than I recalled. Perhaps police work had that effect. "You must have Investigated my mother, then. She was the other initiate at the ritual."

He started. "That was *your* mum? I'll be."

"Was she ever a suspect?" When he paused too long, I pressed, "You can tell me."

"And I would," he vowed. "But no. She was blindfolded the entire time. Didn't see a thing."

"And you believed her?"

"Of course I did. Miss Myrtle, what has you going on like this? What would make you think your mum—God rest her soul—could have been involved in a thing like that?" With a forced laugh, he said, "Been spending too much time with *old* coppers, if you're beginning to suspect your own mother."

He gave my shoulder a kindly squeeze before moving on—and I *wanted* to believe him. But he hadn't really known her.

Maybe none of us had.

I let the crowd move me along, and eventually found myself at the base of the wide stone steps, near a huge urn overflowing with poinsettias—and in between two of my favorite people in the world.

Miss Judson had slipped up alongside me, and coming down the stairs, looking quite smart in a black coat with tails and a crisp white waistcoat, was our good friend Robert Blakeney.

And on Mr. Blakeney's arm was a young woman in a tight velvet frock and spectacles, her light brown hair looped up carelessly.

"Stephen!" Mr. Blakeney called, meaning me, and fairly tugged his companion headlong down the stairs. She restrained him with a fierce grip of her gloved hand.

Unaccountably, I froze rigid, clinging to Miss Judson's side.

"Mr. Blakeney, how nice to see you." Miss Judson then offered her hand to the lady. "I'm Miss Judson, and this is Myrtle Hardcastle."

Mr. Blakeney's companion had a quick, sharp smile that reminded me of a fox. "How do you do? I'm Imogen Shelley, and I see you know my colleague, Mr. Blakeney."

Mr. Blakeney and I reacted much the same way: with a look of surprise at Miss Shelley. Father's nemesis* from the newspaper!

"Colleagues, is it, *Miss Shelley*?" He sounded wounded.

---

* This beautiful word has come down in the world: Nemesis was the Greek goddess of divine retribution. Nowadays it has a much less lofty meaning, and there was certainly nothing godlike about Miss Shelley.

"Are you a reporter now?" I asked him.

Miss Shelley let out a clap of laughter. "Hardly. We just keep him on for appearances." She pinched his boyish cheek, making it flame red.

"How'd you like 'The Final Problem,' Stephen? I couldn't believe—"

"Stop!" I covered my ears with my hands. "I haven't read it yet!"

"Yes, there's been some distraction," Miss Judson said.

"Oh, don't bother," Miss Shelley said. "It was horrid. You should see the angry letters we're getting at the paper! I had to tell Mother we can't print that sort of language." She shook her head. "Robbie, fetch me a drink while I talk to Miss Judson and Myrtle." There was a note to her voice I found distinctly dangerous. And I had not forgotten her last article about Father.

"Stephen, Miss J., don't go anywhere. I can explain everything. Well, not everything. Well, nothing, actually, so don't ask. But be careful."

"Robbie."

"Drinks! Yes!" Shaking his curly blond head, Mr. Blakeney stalked off.

As soon as he was gone, Miss Shelley turned into a reporter. "You found Professor Leighton's body," she said—breaking every rule of polite behavior. In any other circumstance, I would have admired her. But somehow I couldn't bring myself to.

Miss Judson was studying her, trying to work something out. "Such a sad morning."

"It's a shame Mrs. Leighton couldn't make it tonight." Miss Shelley gazed about the gathering. "But I see the old gang's all here. What's left of them, anyway."

"What do you mean?" I asked.

"Oh, that's right," she said. "You're the daughter of one of them. Miss Bell, right? I don't suppose she's here tonight, either, since you've brought your governess to chaperone you."

"She's dead," I said coldly.

Miss Shelley turned her clear brown gaze on me. "Funny how that happens," she murmured. The words should have been insulting, but instead they sent a shiver up the back of my dress.

"I think you'd best explain that," Miss Judson said.

Miss Shelley was only too happy to fill us in. She counted softly on her gloved fingers (no doubt covering up ink stains). "Olive Blackwell," she said. "Then David Carmichael—oh, yes. A mountaineering accident in the Alps. Then Jemima Bell. Now Professor Leighton. Who's next, do you suppose?"

"Why should anybody be next?" I said with alarm.

"*Olive Blackwell lives,*" she said, echoing her own sensational headline.

"*You* made that up!"

Miss Shelley shook her head. "I just write what

people are saying. The question is, why are they say-ing it?"

And against my will, I had to admit she was right.

I had no chance to ask her more—or, thank good-ness, vice versa—as one of the Distinguished Museum Fellows mounted the steps to begin the presentation.

"Ladies and gentlemen, thank you for braving tonight's weather to pay tribute to one of Swinburne's greatest figures, a man whose unexpected passing last week will be greatly mourned."

A moment of respectful silence followed, Miss Shelley Observing the crowd with intensity. What was she watching for? What did she suspect? She seemed to be waiting for something to happen—just so she could be on hand to witness and record it.

The moment passed, and the Museum Director looked up again with a broad smile. "We will miss our friend and patron, Basil Leighton, both for his con-tributions to scholarship and to the museum, and for his service to the village in his latter years. Everyone here knows Leighton's Mercantile. Best chocolate in town!" He patted his stout belly, earning a laugh from the audience.

"That's what I'd like to hear, and remember, about Basil Leighton," he continued. "The happiness he brought to all of us in Swinburne, stuffy old scholars and schoolchildren alike. In fact, we have one of the people most influenced by the professor's legacy here tonight. She hardly needs any introduction, as her feats as an archæologist are known round the world. Indeed, she was among the discoverers of one of the Antiquities Museum's finest treasures, the Saturnalia Chalice. Please join me in welcoming Miss Nora Carmichael!"

Miss Carmichael mounted the podium, skirt swishing. "Friends," she said, in her molten-gold voice, "you did not come here tonight to listen to me. You came to pay your respects to a man beloved and respected by all who knew him—"

"Not *everyone*." That voice belonged to Miss Shelley.

"—and to whom I owe a debt I can never repay. Professor Leighton was my teacher, my mentor, my inspiration. He taught me how to hold a spade and a brush, how to date bone fragments and potsherds. He opened up the wonders of the past, and showed me the doorway to my own future. None of my own accomplishments—the Meritaten Tablet or the Heliopolis Papyri, or our own Saturnalia Chalice"—she lifted her hands toward the goblet in its case—"which gave me my first thrill of unearthing the past . . . None of it would have happened without him.

"But his legacy as a scholar of our own past is far more than that. Before Professor Leighton, archæology was not the modern science we practice today. It was a field of treasure hunters, plunderers, glory seekers, and frauds. He helped shape the field into a profession, advancing scholarship immeasurably, helping rewrite the history of our island. Ladies and gentlemen, I give you the Basil Leighton Memorial Gallery of Ancient Britain!" She bowed, hands crossed over her chest like a pharaoh, and the room flooded with applause.

Even Miss Shelley was clapping softly, one hand wrapped about a flute of champagne. "She does know how to woo a crowd, doesn't she? Oh—excuse me, I want to catch the Mayor before he slinks away. That man is like an eel."

As the crowd flowed up the stairs to the gallery, I stayed behind. The object I wished to see most was down here, the Roman chalice found in Cornwall. I was certain that it must belong with the photograph of Mum I'd found in the shop. It was taken at an archæological dig, I realized, with a ripple of excitement. Mum, an archæologist?

Miss Carmichael had lingered as well. "Stunning, isn't it?" She placed her gloved palm on the glass. "I will never forget that day. Our last in Cornwall. Everyone said the Romans had very little presence there, that we'd never make a big find—but Professor Leighton knew we'd prove them wrong. Did you know," she continued, "that before we found the cup, he'd nearly lost his post? His detractors were gaining power, claiming his dream of a great Cornish Roman find was just that—a dream." Her hands made a little flourish, like smoke dissipating. "But we proved them wrong. The professor, your mum, David—all of us."

I tried to put all these pieces together. "Mum helped save Professor Leighton's career?"

She gave a wistful sigh. "It didn't last, though."

"Because of Olive."

Something flashed across Miss Carmichael's face—but it was gone too quickly for me to identify. "Poor Olive," she said. "Poor Professor Leighton. Look what's become of us all."

I suddenly wondered what Miss Shelley might say. "It didn't all turn out too badly," I said. "You're famous and successful. And Mr. Spence-Hastings is the Mayor now." I silently unspooled the rest of that thought—he'd been successful even *before* becoming Mayor, with interests in businesses all over Swinburne. I found myself regretting—just a very little bit—not listening more closely to LaRue's bragging over the years.

"All thanks to the Chalice." Miss Carmichael patted the case. "It cemented our reputations and made everything—that whole awful year—worthwhile." She looked lost in the past. "I understand why your mum left, though. Why she had to get away. David couldn't bear it, either—losing Olive that way. He loved her, you know. But he'd already graduated, and I was determined to stick it out. And look where I am." She gazed up at the coffered ceiling, at the tapestry and statues. Then she looked at me, and reached out and—and *petted* my head. It wasn't horrible. "Your mum made a good choice. Look at you. She must have been so happy."

My heart caught and I bit my lip, scarcely able to nod. I *knew* there were questions to ask, a murder to Investigate, an even older mystery to unravel, and I was speaking to one of the key witnesses. But, Dear Reader, all I wanted to do in that moment was stand there and let Nora Carmichael talk to me about my mother.

11

CIRCULUS IN PROBANDO

No British Yuletide tradition is more picturesque than
Wales's Mari Lwyd, in which a skeletal horse—bedecked
with skull and white sheets—is carried from door to door,
while revelers demand entry with a contest of songs. No
one has consulted the horse about this pastime.

-H. M. Hardcastle, *A Modern Yuletide*

When I caught up to Miss Judson again, she was practically arm in arm with Miss Shelley, a disgruntled
Mr. Blakeney lagging behind. I had never seen him in
a bad temper—and if Miss Shelley had put him in one,
it made me dislike her all the more.

"We must run," Miss Shelley said. "I have to meet
a source."

"This late?" Mr. Blakeney frowned at his watch.

"The news never sleeps," she said.

"G'night, Stephen." Mr. Blakeney shook my hand, and we went our separate ways.

"I don't like her," I said as soon as we were out of earshot. (Or perhaps a *bit* earlier.)

"I can't imagine why. I did make some interesting discoveries about Miss Shelley and Mr. Blakeney," she added. "Very interesting ones, indeed."

I gave her a sour look. "And just what *fascinating* facts did you uncover?"

"You're the detective. You figure it out."

And that made me crosser than ever.

As the museum emptied out, Miss Judson and I lingered, admiring the Saturnalia Chalice. Miss Carmichael had not been exaggerating about unbridled excesses. The figures depicted on the goblet were engaged in all sorts of Inappropriate Behaviors, and I was surprised that the museum hadn't hung a black cloth over the thing, to protect the Delicate Sensibilities of its visitors.

Miss Judson did not seem shocked, however. She was now engaged in drawing the goblet, intent on capturing its every detail.*

"Your *mum* found this," she said, when I raised an eyebrow at her unseemly interest. "She held it in her own hands."

---

* *every* detail, Dear Reader

I didn't like that much, either. *Corrupting the youth of Athens.* I knew I was mixing my ancient history, and with a proper, Nanette-approved shudder I abandoned Miss Judson to her Saturnalia revelers and wandered up into the new gallery.

Inside the brick archway stood a vast diorama I had seen on previous visits to the museum. Rolling green hills covered a platform the size of our dining room table, a winding stone rampart snaking its way across. Grey battlements, turrets, and gatehouses were patrolled by miniature Roman centurions—the brothers-in-arms of Mum's and Dr. Munjal's *Cohortis Hadriani* soldiers. Any English schoolchild would recognize the model immediately: Hadrian's Wall stretching across northern England, the border between the Civilized Roman Empire to the south, and the wild barbarian tribes to the north.

And now I recognized something else about it, too. I leaned in to better admire what was so plainly Mr. Leighton's work. Who else would build such an elaborate miniature model of a beloved landscape, populated by tiny villagers—these in finely woven togas, tunics, and polished armor, and those on the other side, with animal furs and homespun plaids over their painted skin? Gazing at the tiny figures in their scrubby artificial grass and meticulously detailed firepits, I could picture Mum's lead soldier right here among them—perched as a lookout on that guard tower, or fetching water from that stream.

No wonder Mrs. Leighton hadn't wanted to come tonight. She probably couldn't bear to see another one of her husband's models defaced by vandals, take the risk that someone had scattered olives and wishing wells across this one, too.

I heard footsteps approaching, and glanced up to see Miss Carmichael. This was my chance to question her properly. I started to step out from behind Hadrian's Wall—but she was trailed by Mayor Spence-Hastings. She half-shoved him into an alcove hidden from view.

Obviously, in the interests of good taste and polite behavior, the proper thing would be to make my presence known—particularly if they intended to engage in some sort of . . . Saturnalian behaviors, right here in public! But instead I froze, concealed behind the vast diorama, as Nora tore through her reticule to wave a folded sheet of paper at the Mayor.

"Is this your idea of a joke?"

The Mayor dropped the note like it had bitten him. "I never sent that."

"Oh, well, it must have been Olive, then." Her voice was thick with sarcasm.

Mayor Spence-Hastings let out a strangled sob. "What are we going to do?" He paced the wide corridor, wringing his hands. His tricorn slipped, and he shoved it back—whereupon it slipped again.

"Pull yourself together!" Miss Carmichael's liquid voice was a throaty snarl. "People will notice."

"But—she can't be back—it can't be her. I thought David took care of her!"

I clamped my jaw down hard to keep from letting out even the *thought* of a sound.

"He did. And then I took care of David. Calm down. Someone is just trying to scare us."

"Someone *murdered* the professor," he said. "I'm not imagining things. If it wasn't Olive, who was it?"

"I don't know. Maybe it was that power-hungry, grasping wife of yours. Did you consider that? Or even that wife of *his*, tired of her humdrum life as a shop-keeper. I'd have killed him ages ago, if he'd resigned me to that fate."

Mayor Spence-Hastings did not look as offended as he ought to have, Miss Carmichael having just insulted his wife (and accused her of murder). Or nearly as offended as *I* felt, on behalf of poor Mrs. Leighton!

He seemed to be churning ideas around in his head. "Or maybe . . . maybe it was Vikram."

Dr. Munjal! How could he say that?

Miss Carmichael's pretty face took on a keen look. "Now, there's an idea. Couldn't show his face here tonight, I see. Still shirking his obligations. It doesn't matter. I'm out of here in the morning, and I'll be happy if I never have to set foot in this frozen little backwater again." She stretched her long fair neck toward an imaginary sun. "Give me the Valley of the Kings any day of the week."

The Mayor grabbed Miss Carmichael's gloved arms. "You can't leave me to deal with this alone again. I have the Christmas Ball coming up."

"*You have the Christmas Ball coming up,*" she mocked, shaking him off. "Chin up, Caesar. You've got everything you ever wanted. Little Olive can't hurt us anymore. Now if you'll excuse me, I'm expected elsewhere. I'm meeting an admirer." And with that, she sashayed down the corridor, slinky train trailing behind her like snakeskin.

I wanted to excavate myself from my tomb beneath Hadrian's Wall, but Mayor Spence-Hastings *wouldn't leave.* He stood in the corridor, shoulders slumped, as my feet started to prickle and I got a cramp in my side. When he finally decided to move along, he came straight for me and the diorama. In an ill-considered moment of panic, I scrunched myself beneath the plinth it stood upon, heart clogging my throat. There was absolutely no defense for what I'd been doing—eavesdropping was bad enough. Eavesdropping on the Mayor, while he and a co-conspirator confessed to a murder plot they'd got away with twenty years before, while *another* murderer was wandering about loose in the village? That wasn't questionable at all.

I was about to be uncovered committing a desperate transgression—but fate intervened, in the form of a glorious and timely apparition in the gallery.

"Mayor Spence-Hastings! I was looking for Myrtle."

The Mayor wiped his eyes and straightened. I heard the rustle of his velvet robes and the clink of his chain of office. "Miss—I, no. I haven't seen her."

But Miss Judson plainly had—she was looking straight at me. I could not tell if I was saved, or if my doom was merely delayed, but for the moment I was suffused with relief. "Oh, dear," she said flatly. "She could be anywhere. You know how young girls like to run off."

Was that a dig? And at me—or Olive Blackwell?

Sometimes with Miss Judson, it's impossible to tell.

"Well, she can't be far. Let's check the Africa Rooms. My daughter used to love the cheetah."* The Mayor seemed relieved to have a problem he could solve, a constituent whose immediate crisis he could smooth over. As they strolled away, I unpeeled myself from my cramped corner and tried to shake some feeling back into my limbs.

I nearly stepped on my next clue. Nearly invisible against the creamy marble flooring was the paper

---

* I knew that cheetah, Dear Reader—a specimen prepared by a taxidermist who had clearly never seen one in the wild. It was stuffed plump as a leopard. LaRue had probably ridiculed it for being stouter than the other cheetahs.

Miss Carmichael had thrust at the Mayor. I picked it up—and was almost not surprised to see what was written on its surface, or the fat, blotchy handwriting.

QUÆSTIO REPETUNDARUM

⌘

We exited the museum onto a scene of Christmassy Wonder. Everyone else had long departed, and the streets were empty, already covered in a flat soft sheet of white. Thick flurries of snow obscured our vision, soaking our clothes in moments.

"We'll have to hurry to make the tram."

One step onto the pavement, and it was clear that we wouldn't reach the tram stand—if the trains were even running. Miss Judson's leg skidded dramatically, showing an unladylike flash of petticoat and stocking, and she fetched herself upright by a last-minute snatch at the lamppost. I grabbed her other arm so she wouldn't slip again, although I wanted to applaud. We regarded each other in consternation.

"Perhaps someone at the museum could call for a cab?" Not that there were any about; this weather was no friendlier to horses than humans. "Or maybe we could reach Father's club?"

Miss Judson came up with a much worse alternative. "No, we shall avail ourselves of Family Hospitality. It is nearly Christmas; she cannot in good conscience turn us away."

She couldn't mean what I suspected.

"We could stay at the museum. There's a Tudor bedstead in the upper gallery."

Miss Judson smothered a laugh. "Come along."

I clung to the iron railing of the depressing museum stairs. "This doorway looks snug," I proposed. "Look— our capes are warm and nearly waterproof. The brick- work makes a windbreak, and it's practically dry inside. There must be a cab along by morning."

She held me in a long, sarcastic gaze, as I tried to sell her on my campsite.

"I have half a mind to take you up on that," she said, "if only because it would be instructive in the matter of Christian charity to the less fortunate. But I don't fancy losing my post because I let the daughter of Swinburne's Prosecuting Solicitor freeze to death in a doorway this close to Christmas."

"How about criminal negligence or reckless endangerment?"

"Exactly why I mean to get you inside posthaste. Move along. She's only the next circle over."

"I *mean*, for letting the daughter of the Prosecuting Solicitor commit—" I fumbled for a word that did not yet exist.* "Amitacide. Auntricide. Some kind of homi- cide, anyway."

* The perfectly felicitous *avunculicide* applies to the murder of an uncle—which could not possibly have come up nearly as often throughout history.

"Don't be silly. You spent an entire week in Aunt Helena's company two months ago."*

Indifferent to my pleas, my threats, and my whining, Miss Judson set off for the second time that week to my great-aunt Helena's house, just as a blast of wind swooped round the corner, carrying with it another armload of snow and flinging it right in our faces.

Aunt Helena's house was distressingly close, but the walk in the worsening conditions seemed to take hours. Miss Judson mushed me onward like a dog-sled driver, and I wondered if the Royal Geographic Society might find a use for her on one of its proposed Antarctic expeditions. The blizzard carried an eerie half-light of its own, and by the time we dragged ourselves up the stone steps of Aunt Helena's town house, frosted as sugarplums, the snow was ankle deep, and we were soaked and silent.

I vaguely recalled that the Mayor's Mansion House was one of her neighbors—just across the circle—but I'd had as much of the Spence-Hastingses as I needed for one night.

Aunt Helena had a terrifying housekeeper called Dawes. She was stiff and upright, and looked with disapproval upon pets, children, foreigners, or anyone who was not sufficiently English (or sufficiently Aunt

* and a lovely week that was. Aunt Helena was in jail for most of it.

Helena) for her taste. If only Peony had been here, our disgrace would have been complete.

Dawes's unwelcoming form materialized silently in the doorway, like the Ghost of Christmas Yet to Come. "The Mistress is Out," she intoned, in a voice like teeth grinding.

Miss Judson just breezed us both right past her, into the cluttered and cavernous foyer. "It's snowing," she said cheerfully. "Myrtle will take the green guest room, and I assume the attic is still available?"

"You can't sleep in the *attic!*" I exclaimed, indignant that she would consider it a possibility, and glaring at Dawes for somehow putting the idea in her head.

They ignored me, facing each other down like two rams preparing to knock each other off a mountaintop. "Myrtle will need a hot bath drawn right away."

"The Mistress gave no instructions."

At that moment, it seemed the blizzard outside really might be less chilly and unwelcoming than Aunt Helena's house, but Miss Judson is a natural phenomenon of her own. Within thirty minutes I was tucked snugly in Aunt Helena's dignified spare bedroom. I changed into a nightie that was ready on the bed, as if it had been awaiting my arrival—which gave me a twinge of some emotion I could not name. Was Aunt Helena expecting us?

A knock at my door answered that question. Miss Judson slipped inside, carrying a lamp with a friendly, flickering flame. She wore a quilted dressing gown that was too fine for the servants, but far too small for Aunt Helena, in an Indian print cotton that looked like the sort of thing Aunt Helena would pick out for Miss Judson.

She stroked its puffy sleeve and piped cuff. "Nice, *non*? It was in the room next door, along with my brand of hair tonic, a sleeping cap, and a bottle of *eau de parfum*." She held out her wrist for me to sniff. "Lily."

"I could almost believe Aunt Helena staged this weather to lure us here and hold us captive." Which sounded like a plot Nanette Munjal would dream up.

"Nonsense. I think she had great fun on our holiday together, and wants to share in the Family Amusements again. It does tend to be catching, you know."

(I remind the reader that Aunt Helena spent the aforementioned holiday *in jail*.)

"Perhaps it unhinged her."

Miss Judson did not dignify that with a response.

My aunt had taken things one step further. On the bedside table were notepads and pencils, fully supplied with leads. It would hardly surprise me to find a set of law books or a blackboard concealed behind those green velvet drapes.

All of which, I grudgingly admitted, made for excellent speculation about the case. "Get in bed," Miss Judson commanded, perching beside me so we could commence. "I certainly hope you have something to show for your skulking about after the Mayor tonight."

"I wasn't skulking! I was already there when they came in, and they started arguing before I could leave." Could I help it if they'd gone on to confess to murder—or almost, anyway—while I was on hand? I called that *luck*, Dear Reader.

Miss Judson regarded me sternly. "You had several choices in that situation, yet you elected to hide beneath a table. I believe that is the very dictionary definition of skulking."

I was the dictionary definition of *something* just then. "Isn't that why we went there tonight? To learn who killed Mr. Leighton or pushed Olive Blackwell out of a tower?"

She crossed her arms. "I suppose now you're going to tell me you discovered both of those things."

"Yes! Well, maybe. Look." I produced the folded note I'd found at the museum. "This is *just like* the one Dr. Munjal had! And there's more." I recounted the conversation I'd overheard between the Mayor and Miss Carmichael. "Don't you think that's suspicious?"

"So, according to Miss Carmichael, her brother killed Miss Blackwell—and then Miss Carmichael killed her own brother?" Her lip twisted in distaste. "I hate to say anything against your mother, but I'm beginning to question her taste in friends."

So was I. Miss Carmichael had been so cool about everything, detached and bored. It was all too possible to picture her pushing Olive Blackwell out a tower window or slicing through her brother's ropes. She'd admitted to being ambitious—and she'd have to be fearless, maybe even ruthless, to turn her back on the life of a Young Lady of Quality to go adventuring as an Egyptologist, poking among the dead. Perhaps murder would come just as easily.

"But neither of them admitted to killing Mr. Leighton," I conceded. "And Miss Carmichael seemed genuinely fond of him." Miss Judson kindly did not point out that they must have seemed genuinely fond of Olive, too, in order to lure her up into the Campanile. "Mr. Spence-Hastings believes the rumors about Olive coming back from the dead."

"Then *he* didn't kill her," Miss Judson mused. "Presumably. Or he didn't do a particularly thorough job."

"Miss!"

She held up a hand. "Let's think through this. They only *alluded* to killing Olive, right?"

I nodded. "They said David Carmichael 'took care of her.'"

Miss Judson pulled her feet onto the bed, tucking them neatly beneath her. "I suppose that could mean a lot of things. Maybe he bribed her—gave her money so she could run away."

"Miss Carmichael said he loved Olive. Maybe they ran away together!"

Miss Judson was nodding. "When I was at school,

girls were always plotting elaborate escapes with imagined beaux. Just like this—" She waved a hand to encompass our surroundings, chatting late into the night. "And we do know at least one couple who eloped," she reminded me.

"But Olive and David didn't go through with it—Olive disappeared, and David died later in the Alps. In a climbing accident. Or not."

Miss Judson had started sketching idly in one of the notebooks. I watched her pencil turn round and round, forming a Pictish spiral on the page. "The ritual in the tower, Olive Blackwell's disappearance, Mr. Leighton's murder. What ties them together?"

I sat up and started from the beginning. "We know that Mr. Leighton's death has something to do with Olive's disappearance."

"Mmm. And we know that *Professor* Leighton's retirement from Schofield College is *also* connected to Olive's disappearance. It caused a scandal that Mrs. Leighton still hasn't recovered from."

Miss Judson's circling pencil hypnotized me into *almost* understanding something. "Why did Olive disappear?"

"We don't know," Miss Judson said. "Oh, I see what you're doing, *Socrates*," she added, with a touch of irony. "Why did Professor Leighton resign?"

"Because Olive Blackwell disappeared. Why did Olive Blackwell disappear?"

"Because Professor Leighton resigned?" Miss Judson's spiral turned and met itself. "We're going round in circles." She flipped to a fresh page. "Professor Leighton resigned because of a scandal." She made a mark, swooping it out into a small spiral of its own.

"Olive Blackwell's disappearance," I supplied.

"Right. But something *precipitated* that disappearance. *One*"–she drew a question mark–"and *two*: Olive Blackwell. And *three*: Professor Leighton." She scribbled a fierce circle around the question mark. "What happened *here*?"

Blood pounded in my ears. "Of course. Corrupting the youth of Athens! The real scandal wasn't Olive's disappearance–it was whatever *led* to Olive's disappearance and Professor Leighton's involvement in *that*." I recalled Nora's chilling words: *Little Olive can't hurt us anymore.* "Olive knew something that the rest of the Hadrian's Guard would kill to keep secret."

"Perhaps it was something that could damage the professor's career or reputation? So she had to disappear."

"But she *did* disappear, and it ruined his career anyway." I groaned. This was circular reasoning at its worst–we just kept treading the same ground and getting nowhere. "All I know is, Mum was involved."

And that, I reasoned–in a perfectly straight line– was cause enough to keep Investigating.

12

ALGOR MORTIS

Even in our modern era, nothing is quite so cheering on
a frigid day as a roaring fire, a hot drink, and convivial
company.

-H. M. Hardcastle, *A Modern Yuletide*

Aunt Helena's guest room was surprisingly cozy, and
the snow we'd trudged through made me feel snug and
sleepy. After Miss Judson retired, I drifted off to curiously pleasant dreams about being served cocoa in
bed by a sweet and subservient Dawes.

What *actually* woke me was a shrill whistle, shatter-
ing the predawn. Police whistles! Throwing aside the
bed curtains, I slipped to the cold floor and padded
through the dimness, dodging furniture, to the window. The glass was thick with frost. I rubbed at it with
the curtain and stared through, onto a seascape of grey.

I couldn't see what was wrong, at first. It was still

dark, the sky a fading blue, stars winking away. I wrestled with the window, and nearly lost it to a whip of wind—but I spotted a uniformed man in the street below.

The constable's whistle wailed and wailed, as if it might bring the whole village down. As my eyes adjusted, I finally made out a strange, lumpy form in the snow near where the constable stood, blowing frantically. I found my shoes—still wet from last night and no more useful in the snow than they'd been six hours earlier—unearthed a dressing gown, and threw myself into the hallway—

Right into Miss Judson. Wordlessly, we sped toward the stairs, nearly mowing down Dawes as we went.

"What the devil is that racket?" Aunt Helena had emerged from a bedroom, an India rubber mask strapped to her face, concealing all her features save her bellowing voice. It took me a moment to recognize it as a sort of horrifying beauty device.

"It's the police!" I cried.

"Well, don't stand about lollygagging, Helena Myrtle!" Aunt Helena's eyes twinkled behind the mask. "Go and see what it's about!"

With that, Miss Judson and I fairly dived out the back door and plunged into the darkness.

The sky was clear and cloudless, and the cold instantly bit into my cheeks and toes. We hastened across the circle, where a motionless form floated adrift in a sea of snow, a single set of footprints leading to—and fro. It was a rug, rolled up and abandoned, like it had just slipped from a removal van.

The policeman who'd discovered it had evidently paused to Investigate. Part of the rug was unrolled, and its contents spilled out: a bare, pale arm, purplish-blue against the starlit snow, two angry red punctures just inside the elbow.

I halted in the street, and Miss Judson bumped into me. This was just like the latest Display at Leighton's. "Cleopatra," I managed, in a strained whisper. Miss Judson grasped my hand and marched me forward. "Who—?" I couldn't finish the question.

Miss Judson was grim. "We'll soon find out."

As we approached the scene, a police carriage rolled up, and Constable Carstairs and another constable hopped out, landing in a puff of snow. They stalked over, like a bulldog and an eager terrier behind him. Constable Carstairs greeted us with a gruff nod, shocking me. I was too cold and numb to nod back. I could hardly stop staring at the rolled-up rug and its grisly contents.

"Get back," Constable Carstairs growled, and Miss Judson took half a pace backward. Her hands were on my shoulders, holding me steady as we watched them work—but whether to keep me upright or to keep me from interfering, it was impossible to say. I didn't even know myself what I would do.

I tried to study the scene before Investigation wiped it all away. There was very little snow atop the carpet, and somewhere in my mind I knew that could tell us when this latest tableau was created. But only the first policeman's tracks led near the body. My brain jangled with the inconsistency. How did someone leave a body in the snow without leaving tracks? It wasn't possible.

Just like it wasn't possible to drop from a hundred-foot building and leave no trace.

"Ready, sir?"

Constable Carstairs had Observed the scene, taken a spatter of notes, and now nodded at the younger constables. "Go ahead. Let's see who's—in there."

Grimly, the two other men, working as gingerly as they could, unrolled the carpet. For a few heartbeats, all I saw was a flash of red and blue Turkish wool, a flutter of fringe . . . then a long gold dress and dark, dark hair.

Cleopatra was Nora Carmichael.

⁊⁊

Miss Judson did not let me linger to watch the policemen. My teeth betrayed me by chattering, and after giving a brief perfunctory statement to Constable Carstairs (amounting to "You know where to find us"), she turned me round and sped me back into the house, whereupon Aunt Helena, who had been Observing the Scene with her lorgnette through her drawing-room windows, bustled us to the kitchen to be fussed over by her cook and kitchen maid, who were entirely out of character for my aunt's household. They must have been new.

The kitchen was compact and tidy, with shiny modern appliances and a glorious hob that would have driven Cook to tears of envy—iron painted red with three oven compartments and a finely sculpted chimney, beside which warmed a pot of cocoa. The new housemaid bade us doff our shoes and arranged us at the table with toast and cocoa and hot bricks wrapped in rugs for our frozen toes. Only Peony could have made the scene more cozy. Peony, and the lack of a dead body lying just outside the door.

The neat worktable was spread with cookery books—some in French—all open to a mysterious-looking sort of pudding shaped like a log.

"*Bûche de Noël?*" Miss Judson inquired.

The new cook turned toward her. "It's very fashionable in France," she Informed us. "The Mistress is expecting French company for Christmas dinner."

"*Est-ce vrai?*" Miss Judson said softly. She turned to me with an unreadable expression, and I was grateful to have something else to look at—some other image in my mind besides Nora Carmichael displayed like Cleopatra delivering herself to Caesar. The killer had mixed up two historical events, however. Cleopatra's death by asp happened years later.

Of course, we didn't *know* that the killer had used

an asp*–where would he get an asp in England in December, anyway? Not to mention a host of other practical complications, not least of which was convincing said snake to deploy itself as you bade it, and not wherever it pleased or, worse, upon yourself. (All things considered, a most unwieldy weapon.) But he'd certainly gone to some lengths to replicate the Egyptian queen's famous death. Just as he'd gone to lengths to stage Professor Leighton's death like Socrates'.

I supposed we knew one thing now, though it was cold comfort. Nora Carmichael wasn't the killer. I stirred my cocoa disconsolately, as Miss Judson idly flipped through the cookery books.

Gradually it dawned on me that the cook and the maid—whose names were Mrs. Hodges and Cora—were still preparing tea and slabs of hot buttered bread, despite having already stuffed me and Miss Judson full as turkeys.

"It's for themselves," Mrs. Hodges said, with a reassuring air of snootiness. "The Mistress said to have them in for a spell."

Upon those words, the back door opened and all three constables stepped carefully inside the threshold, delicately tapping their snowy boots off. Cora expertly relieved them of their helmets. "Don't worry

---

* We don't actually know that Cleopatra used an asp, for that matter, although historians do agree she poisoned herself.

none about that," she said briskly. "Come warm up by the stove."

"Thank you, Miss," said the youngest constable, the one who'd reminded me of a terrier. Now his boyish, freckled face looked drawn and white, despite the cheek-chapping cold.

Soon enough, the efficient cook and maid had the policemen settled round the table with us, clutching cups of tea with a dash of brandy, and staring grimly at their hands. Constable Carstairs downed his in one gulp, but the one who'd found the body and sounded the alarm was looking a bit green.

Mrs. Hodges pushed a plate of biscuits on him. "Gingersnaps," she said authoritatively, like she soothed policemen during homicide investigations every day.* "They'll help."

He nodded weakly.

None of the men seemed to even notice the two barefoot Young Ladies of Quality in their midst, and as the tea and gingersnaps and brandy and warmth went to work on them, their tongues unfroze as well.

"D-----est thing I ever saw," Constable Carstairs swore. I supposed even by Swinburne standards, two murders inside a week was a bit much.

"And it was just like they showed in that shop window? How *horrible*!" Cora shivered with relish. "We

---

* If this had not been one of her qualifications for employment in a Hardcastle household, it ought to have been.

read all about it in the *Tribune*, those stories by Miss Shelley."

"Now Cora," scolded Mrs. Hodges, "let the poor men eat in peace. They've had quite the ordeal this morning, poor things."

"It was pretty awful," Constable Terrier agreed. (It turned out his name was, in fact, Terrence.) "I just kept thinking, how *cold* she must be." He shook his head at the memory.

My own brain was finally thawing, and I realized that Aunt Helena had somehow engineered this whole tableau—her niece and governess at her kitchen table as the constables confided in the staff. Maybe Miss Judson was right, and the urge to Investigate was contagious. Or hereditary. Or whatever reverse-heredity would be, going upward through generations. I bit my lip and clutched my mug tight and tried to listen carefully without interrupting.

"But who killed her?" Cora pressed. "And why leave her here?"

That was an excellent point. The killer, having staged it in the Display beforehand, must have chosen this location deliberately.

Miss Judson and I spoke up together—reminding everyone of our presence. "The Mansion House," she said, just as I said, "The Mayor."

"Eh?" Constable Carstairs looked pointedly at us. At *me*.

"Cleopatra wrapped herself in a carpet and had herself smuggled to Julius Caesar," I explained. She'd been trying to secure the throne of Egypt and the support of the Roman Empire and, like the killer, had a flair for the dramatic.

"I've seen th' paintings," the constable growled. "What's it got to do wiv Mayor Spence'tings?"

"I'm not sure." Nora was planning to meet an admirer after the museum gala—had she had a liaison with her murderer? "But she was staged that way and dropped on the Mayor's doorstep."

"Like Caesar and Cleopatra," Constable Terrence put in eagerly.

Constable Carstairs grunted. It was a noncommittal response, but I could tell we'd got him thinking. He pulled out his notepad and flipped back a few pages. "The shopkeeper died like whosit—Socrates, eh?"

"Yes, sir," I said, trying to decide what else to say. It was the job of the police to solve this crime, after all, and they would need all the evidence to do that. But I still didn't know how Mum was connected, and I didn't want the police rummaging about clumsily in her past.

That was my job.

Miss Judson was clearly considering this as well. After a discreet glance at me, she spoke directly to Constable Carstairs. "We saw Miss Carmichael at the museum gala last night. Myrtle witnessed"—I could tell she regretted *that* choice of words—"Myrtle over-heard a . . . heated conversation between the Mayor and Miss Carmichael."

All the constables' eyes wheeled toward me, and I worked hard at not fidgeting. "I couldn't tell what they were talking about," I lied. "But they both knew Mr. Leighton, from years ago, at the college." There. That was enough for the constable to begin Investigating on his own.

"Olive Blackwell!" breathed Cora, right on cue.

Still, Constable Carstairs seemed uncomfortable at the prospect of interrogating the Mayor. "I reckon we'd better go'n see what Himself has to say," he finally said—looking not at all inclined to depart from Aunt Helena's comfortable kitchen.

But Aunt Helena had an answer to that as well. With timing that could not have been accidental, she strode into the room, clad in a blue walking coat and a huge fur stole (it appeared to be an entire bear), and announced, "Hodges, do you have that fruitcake for the Spence-Hastingses? I thought I'd pay my call on the Mayoress this morning."

Mrs. Hodges, having anticipated this development, handed Aunt Helena a tin and a bottle of wine. "Herself likes a fuss made," she explained to no one in particular.

Tin in hand, bear slung across her neck, and walking stick held like a scepter, Aunt Helena glared impatiently at the constables. "Well, Carstairs," she harrumphed, "aren't you coming?"

⌒

Dear Reader, I should like to report that Miss Judson and I availed ourselves of the opportunity to question the Mayor alongside Aunt Helena and the constable, but sadly, we missed that particular Family Amusement. As we stepped outside, another police carriage rolled up, dispatching Inspector Hardy, looking authoritative and smart in his black uniform and flat cap. I was surprised to see Dr. Munjal with him—shouldn't Dr. Belden still be handling the case? Dr. Munjal must have felt it was important enough to have Swinburne's official Police Surgeon take matters into his own hands.

Unless he was here at the Mayor's bidding.

I felt a spike of traitorous alarm at that thought. Dr. Munjal would never tamper with evidence! Still, he was one of the few people remaining who could possibly know what had become of Olive Blackwell. The survivors were dwindling by the minute. And his motive was the same as whoever had killed Mr. Leighton and Miss Carmichael.

For of course I didn't believe for a moment that there was more than one killer, or that these two murders weren't connected. The sense of theatrics and the selection of victims was obviously not random. Probability argued against the likelihood of two killers, acting independently, with overlapping motives and the same gruesome interpretation of Classical History. The splashy headlines rang in my head. *Olive Blackwell Strikes Again.*

It wasn't possible.

I didn't believe it.

And yet . . . Hadn't I seen the impossible evidence with my own eyes? How a body had simply appeared atop the freshly fallen snow, without leaving any trace of how it was deposited? It was *impossible* for Olive Blackwell to have survived a fall from the Campanile. Just as it was *impossible* for Nora Carmichael's body to have—levitated into position, as if her rug were Aladdin's flying carpet. Olive couldn't be back from the dead to take her revenge. Could she?

Lost in thought, I nearly missed the other significant development at the crime scene. It took two loud *ahem*s from Miss Judson and a neat, polite stomp of my toes before I finally looked up across the dazzling snow—and my vision clouded over again.

Imogen Shelley, snug and smug in a short blue coat and sturdy boots, leaned against the lamppost, scribbling away in her nasty notebook.

"What's *she* doing here?" I hissed. And yes, Dear Reader, sibilants or no, that is exactly the correct word. I was spitting mad, my fur on end. If I'd had a tail, it would have been puffed up, all the way to its white tip.

"She's been here all morning. I spotted her earlier."

"Why didn't you say anything?" Before she could answer, a beautiful, blindingly brilliant thought burst into my brain like sunspots from a solar storm. "She's been awfully quick with *all* of her stories, hasn't she? Reporting on them before we'd barely had a chance to notify the police? And '*Olive Blackwell Lives*'?" I turned to Miss Judson, triumph flashing (I was sure) in my eyes. "*She's* doing this."

Miss Judson hesitated. "Wait—what?"

I couldn't hold back. The ideas tumbled together into a perfect chain, link by link. "She was there last night! She left early to 'meet a source.' She had opportunity. She has motive—"

"Which is what, exactly?"

"Drumming up a good story!"

"By committing murder? Murders? And her means would be . . . ? Oh! Do you suppose she's hiding an asp inside her coat? It must be awfully cold by now, poor thing."

"This isn't funny! She's a perfect suspect. Think about it."

"I'm trying, but you're not letting me reflect on this sensibly. Which is what I would like you—"

She oughtn't have bothered. I was halfway across the circle, marching over the now well-trodden snow. Dr. Munjal and Inspector Hardy were finishing up with the body, wrapping poor Miss Carmichael in a clean white sheet before bearing her away on a stretcher. Miss Shelley looked on, long and satisfied, smiling like an asp.

She spotted me and gave a wave that made me hate her all the more. What in the world had Mr. Blakeney been doing in her company last night? I was relieved to have a murder—two murders . . . maybe three—to solve, instead of having to ponder *that* imponderable mystery.

Gazing steadily at Miss Shelley, I approached Constable Terrence and tugged on his sleeve, trying to look as young and innocent as I could. Perhaps he'd already forgotten my Discourse on Egypto-Roman history over biscuits just now.

"Excuse me, Constable?"

He glanced down at me.

"You told us to let you know if we remembered anything else about Miss Carmichael?" None of the constables had suggested anything of the kind, but they *ought* to have. That is my excuse for what transpired next—and I stand by that testimony, Dear Reader.

"Er—that's right. Yes. Excellent." He scrambled to produce his notebook. "Go ahead then, Miss—?"

I pretended to misunderstand him as I did an Unthinkably Unladylike thing. I wheeled slowly around, leveled my arm, and pointed straight at Miss Shelley. "She was there last night, too. And she was saying all sorts of things about Miss Carmichael."

13

FEMMES FATALES

In remote Alpine regions of Germany, children are visited at Christmastime by Perchta the Disemboweler, who
rewards the obedient with coins and sweets. Her name
suggests what becomes of the naughty.

-H. M. Hardcastle, *A Modern Yuletide*

To say that the Swinburne Constabulary was not
entirely pleased to see me return for the second time
in a week would be something of an understatement.
And to say that Miss Judson was tolerant of the situation would be an outright lie.

Having pointed the finger (literally) at Miss Shelley,
I was labeled a Key Witness, and therefore ushered to
the police station practically alongside Miss Shelley
herself.

"You're lucky they're not holding *you* in custody."
The police did that—witnesses were often reluctant to

appear in court, so they were detained to ensure their participation. I felt fairly certain that Father's status as Prosecuting Solicitor would preclude such a precaution. But given Miss Judson's mood, I could hardly count on her support at the moment. The notion that they might hold Miss Shelley somewhat longer than necessary, however, was particularly cheering.

I had only Observed the initial encounter between Constable Terrence and the reporter, but Miss Shelley had—disappointingly—seemed unshocked. She gave that little wave again as she climbed into the police wagon, and I had a slightly sickish feeling that this was not quite the triumphant checkmate I had intended.

Even so, Miss Shelley *had* produced her stories on the murders rather swiftly. Either she was involved in the crimes—or she had a source among the police. I couldn't decide which of those options I liked least. Neither Dr. Munjal nor Inspector Hardy had returned from the crime scene yet. I tried to tell myself that only meant they were being exceptionally thorough.

Miss Judson gave an audible sigh. I suspect it had something to do with my fidgeting and kicking the legs of the bench.

"She was horrible, and you know it," I said.

Miss Judson took a moment to marshal her Exceptional Forbearance. "Remind me, which crime did you have her arrested for? Was it horribleness, or murder?"

"She wasn't arrested," I snapped back. "They're questioning her as a witness."

We continued in this vein for some moments before Miss Judson chanced to look up—and stopped herself, mid-scold.

"Don't let me interrupt," said a familiar voice, sounding uncharacteristically weary. "Hullo, Stephen, Miss J."

I frowned. "What are you doing here?"

Mr. Blakeney grinned. "I might ask the same thing, but I'd actually be surprised to pop round a neighborhood police station and *not* see the likes of you two! I half suspect you frequent them just for fun."

"And you would not be far wrong." Miss Judson rubbed the bridge of her nose, like she was fighting off a headache. "But what brings you down?"

He shook his brief-bag. "Genie." He sighed. "She's managed to get herself in trouble again."

Miss Judson worked that out before I did. "Gen— oh, Imogen, of course."

Mr. Blakeney looked chagrined. "Yes, *Miss Shelley*," he said, with the same curious emphasis he'd used last night. He didn't seem to like her much, either, which warmed me a bit. But in that case, I really couldn't figure out why he was so much in her company. "I'm here to dig her out of this latest mess." A constable beckoned to him. He tipped his hat to us. "Wish me luck."

"Well, well," Miss Judson said as he disappeared.

"Would you *stop* with that! If you have something to say about them, just say it already." I crossed my arms and slumped down—just as crossly—against the bench.

Her cool eyes shifted sideways toward me. All she said, however, was, "I'm glad to see he's not letting his legal skills get rusty."

Mr. Blakeney's promising career as a law clerk and aspiring solicitor had been cut short with the abrupt end to his employer's practice this summer. We'd called on his help during our last Investigation, and through our adventures together, we'd all grown to be great friends. But I had to admit, I didn't really know all that much about him. That was entirely befitting an acquaintance between a Young Lady of Quality and a professional young man—but it did rather put my Investigative Skills to shame. I determined to be as Observant as Miss Judson from here on out.

I got my chance sooner than I expected. Only a few minutes later, the interrogation room door swung open, and a pleased-looking Miss Shelley emerged, followed by Mr. Blakeney. He'd recovered some of his own ebullience, and raised a cheery hand. But that wasn't enough for Miss Shelley.

"Myrtle!" She swooped down like a bird of prey— and kissed me soundly on the cheek. "Thank you! I hadn't decided *how* I was going to get the police to talk to me. You're brilliant, you." She plopped down beside me—almost in Miss Judson's lap—and whipped out her notebook. "So. Fair's fair, and I owe you. Share and share alike, right, Robbie?"

"Er." Mr. Blakeney had turned alternately pale and scarlet and was regarding us with something like horror.

Miss Shelley popped to her feet again. "You are quite right. This calls for a far less public venue. Let's all have coffee. My treat. Woodstein's is just round the corner."

Dear Reader, I'm really not sure what happened next, except that somehow the four of us found ourselves ensconced in a cozy nook at a nearby tea shop, sharing a steaming pot of coffee (for them) and a cup of tea (for me) and a hearty plate of bread-and-butter and pickles.

Miss Judson had been silent on the journey over, and now she had out her small sketchbook, sketching away, Observing everything. Miss Shelley kept up a lively strain of chatter, while Mr. Blakeney shrank into the corner, until he was little more than curly hair and wrinkled suit.

"Myrtle, Robbie says I was a perfect beast to you last night and I must apologize." Miss Shelley set down her coffee, looking serious. "I said some dreadful things about your mum. I'm sorry. No hard feelings?"

Mr. Blakeney broke in. "I don't know, Genie, I suspect our Stephen is very good at hanging on to hard feelings."

She wheeled on him. "I don't know why you insist on that ridiculous nickname! She's perfectly capable of standing up for herself without having to pretend she's a boy." She gave him a none-too-friendly shove. "I always knew you were a misogynist. Myrtle, don't let him—or anyone—treat you like that. *Never* be ashamed of being female. Never."

Miss Judson finally looked up. "Brava," she murmured—but I felt a little cowed by Miss Shelley's fierceness. Still, she sounded so genuine that I was tempted to believe her.

"What were you doing there so early this morning?"

Mr. Blakeney answered. "She lurks. She's exceptional at it. Fortunately, she's found a way to make a living with it, so I suppose we mustn't complain."

And Miss Shelley, shocking me utterly, stuck her tongue out at him.

They had a *very* curious relationship.

Miss Judson finished her drawing and laid her sketchbook on the table. It was a comical sketch of a young Miss Shelley and Mr. Blakeney—a fair-haired lad sneaking a frog into the bed of a bespectacled girl. With a jolt, I stared at the drawing. I stared at Miss Shelley. I stared at Mr. Blakeney. I stared at them both. He was blond, curly-haired, and blue-eyed; her hair and eyes were brown, and the spectacles hid the resemblance even more. But otherwise I'd been doltishly *Un*observant about her. About them.

"Your second name's not really Shelley, is it?" I said—halting Miss Shelley in mid-bite.

"Well." She set down her bread with a grin. "Took you long enough. And you said she was clever." She slung an easy arm around Mr. Blakeney's shoulders. "Usually it's obvious to everyone. When I started at the *Trib*, he made me change my name so I wouldn't bring down any more shame on the family." Miss Shelley—Miss *Blakeney*, in true—didn't seem the least bit ashamed of anything.

"You're his sister."

Mr. Blakeney hung his head. "Guilty."

"Twins," Miss Shelley declared. "I'm the oldest." She reached around the food to pick up Miss Judson's sketchbook, then let out a clap of laughter as she passed it to her brother.

"Close," he admitted, returning it to Miss Judson.

"But it was usually *me* putting frogs in *his* bed."

"Oh, dear," said Miss Judson. "I imagine the two of you gave your governesses terrors."

Miss Shelley bit her lip. "Poor Miss Kittridge. She still hasn't been released from the asylum."

"She's kidding," Mr. Blakeney said swiftly. "It was a sanatorium, and she's fine now."

And with that, they burst into peals of laughter that

soon had our whole table—even me, Dear Reader—in an uproar.

"People probably called you *Irrepressible*," I posited.

Genie pondered this. "Well, now, I've been called *incorrigible, uncontrollable,* a hellion—"

"Don't forget *irredeemable*," Mr. Blakeney put in. Genie sighed fondly.

"Oh, yes. Miss Simser. Or was that Miss Nisbett?"

"How *did* you know so much about the crimes?" I asked when we'd all finally recovered. "You knew exactly where to be this morning. You have to admit, that was suspicious."

"Or brilliant," she said agreeably. "That was such an odd gathering last night at the museum. I had a feeling things weren't over, especially after 'Olive Blackwell's' latest handiwork at Leighton's Mercantile." She spread jam on bread with nonchalance. "I just put two and two together and figured out who Cleopatra was likely to be."

"Why didn't you warn anyone?" I cried.

"Oh, I did." Miss Shelley wasn't offended. "I strolled right up to Nora Carmichael and said it straight to her face—"

Mr. Blakeney's groan confirmed this audacious statement.

"—And she just laughed it off. So, of course, I assumed she was the killer, or that she'd staged the Cleopatra thing as a publicity stunt."

"So did we! Well, not that last bit. That's pretty clever," I added grudgingly.

"It didn't turn out to be true, though." For the first time, Miss Shelley sobered. I had the sense it wasn't an expression she wore often. "I wish she'd believed me."

I wasn't convinced *I* believed her. "Can you prove you didn't kill her?"

"Myrtle Hardcastle!"

My beleaguered governess went ignored. "I have an alibi. And a witness." Genie hooked her thumb at her brother, who nodded. "I was all the way across town, at the college. For the midnight carillon concert. It was very impressive. You ought to have been there."

"We saw the first one. How did you get there in the terrible weather?"

"A cab, naturally. Anything else?"

"Yes, actually," Miss Judson put in. "Did you notice anything strange at the Campanile?"

"You mean the chairs?" she said with a grin. "There's no chance you drew that, is there, Miss Judson? It would look fantastic with my article."

"I would advise you against that," Mr. Blakeney said, and Genie sighed.

"Always such a lawyer."

"Somebody always needs one," he shot back.

I got us back on track. "Were you able to learn anything from your—time with the police, this morning?"

"Not much," Genie said. "It was definitely poison—something injected into her arm—and she was chloroformed, first."

"Just like Mr. Leighton."

"That does seem to be our killer's modus operandi. First incapacitate her victims with chloroform, then poison them more dramatically."

"*Her*?" I said.

"Olive, of course." Genie polished off a pickle. "Why? Who's your top suspect?"

"The Mayor."

Miss Judson tossed up her hands in exasperation, and I realized I had probably gone too far.

But Genie was nodding. "That man is involved somehow. He has too much riding on this not to be. But I can't get close to him. He keeps fobbing off all my interview requests. He has a daughter about your age, right? You're friends?"

Miss Judson let out a high, sharp laugh.

I issued a faint growl. "Not exactly."

"What about Miss Munjal?"

"What about her?" I said sharply.

"Come on," she coaxed. "Give me the buzz. You're an inside source with the police *and* the courts."

"I'm not a source!" I glared at her. "Besides, you must already have one, right?"

She only shrugged, not answering. Instead, she said, "What I can't figure out is how the killer is getting inside the shop to leave the warnings in the Display. I've been over there twice, and it's locked up so well it's practically watertight."

I wasn't letting her off the hook so easily, but she had a point. "And how did he leave the body this morning? There were no tracks around it—just the constable's who found her."

"Hot air balloon?" Mr. Blakeney suggested.

Genie ignored him. "I can't get around the confounded *physics* of it all."

I nodded thoughtfully. "Just like Olive Blackwell."

"Exactly."

"Do you really think it could be Olive?" I wasn't convinced yet. "How could she have survived the fall? And where did she go?"

Genie's gaze darted around the coffeehouse, like she was concerned someone might be listening in. "I've been working this story since I came to Swinburne, and sometimes I think she really did just vanish into thin air. There's no trace of her."

"Before, even," Mr. Blakeney interposed. "It's a bit of a lifelong obsession with her."

Genie went on as if her brother hadn't spoken. "And there's more. Every *record* of Olive Blackwell's disappearance has disappeared, too. Every newspaper account"—she held up her hands, in an eerie echo of the carillonist's gesture at the Campanile—"vanished from the morgue."

"The newspaper morgue—that's where they keep all the old copies." Mr. Blakeney had noticed my confusion.

"The police reports? Missing."

"Missing!" I cried—but softly. Her suspicion was catching. "How can that be?"

"Some careless clerk must have 'lost' them." Her voice was thick with skepticism.

"But they never solved the case!" I sputtered with indignation, even as I took in the implications of such a fact. Who could access the police records and make the files disappear? I didn't like the answers.

"And that's not all," Genie said. "This isn't Olive Blackwell's first reappearance."

"Here she goes," said Mr. Blakeney.

Her tone grew low and dramatic. "Every few years, since she disappeared, 'Olive' gets in contact with her old friends. And then her friends start to die."

I sat in stunned silence, and Miss Judson lifted one neat governess finger. "Clarify."

"Thirteen years ago, letters in Latin were sent to David Carmichael, claiming to be from Olive Blackwell. Within a few months, he had his tragic 'accident' in the Alps."

"How do *you* know about these letters? What did they say?"

"Then five years ago—" She stopped, blood flooding her face, and fumbled through her notebook.

"Er—and just this year, the Leightons received their own letters supposedly from Olive."

I was no longer listening. "Five years ago, *what*?"

She continued to study her notes in a way that was all too familiar. "Nothing," she said softly. "I misspoke. The Leightons' letters—"

I crossed every boundary of proper behavior and grabbed the notebook from her, flipping frantically back until I found it. 1888. The year Mum died.

"'*Letters sent to Jemima Hardcastle*, née *Bell*'? I never heard about any letters! And my mother died of *cancer*. Nothing mysterious about it."

There wasn't. I knew there wasn't. I remembered every moment, every visit from Dr. Belden, every symptom, every cough and fever and sleepless night, every meal refused or brought back up, every stone, pound, and ounce of weight shed from her slim figure as she faded away. She had known what was killing her, and had grimly studied up on the condition, monitoring for herself the tumor's growth, as it choked off her breath and crushed the life out of her.

I didn't realize I was gripping the notebook so tightly my fingers were shaking, until Mr. Blakeney reached in and gently untwined them.

"She never got any letters," I whispered.

Genie put her hand on her brother's, atop mine. "I

don't know what it all means," she said. "I'm trying to find out what happened. To Olive. And everyone."

After a long moment, Miss Judson spoke up. "Perhaps we ought to pick this up at another time. It's been rather a lot of excitement for one day." The lunch crowd had started to gather and I realized how late it was. Even Miss Judson—always revived by a spirited gathering—looked weary and wilted, and Mr. Blakeney seemed positively outnumbered by Irrepressible, Incorrigible, and Otherwise females.

Genie rose first. "You're quite right. I have a story to file."

"Wait!" I cried. "You can't print anything we've said here. We're—" I was at a loss for words.

"Off the record?" Mr. Blakeney supplied. "Good luck with that."

Miss Judson saved the day again. She sized up Genie Shelley Blakeney with one level, fidget-inspiring gaze, skirt hems to messily knotted hair, and said coolly, "We would appreciate your discretion, Miss Shelley. Investigator to Investigator."

"I'll see what I can find out," I promised her. "Maybe my father remembers the letters. We all want to figure out who killed Olive and the others." I took a deep breath and faced Miss Judson when I added, "Even if it makes Mum look bad. But I want to know first."

"That's fair," Genie said. "I promise to come to you before I print anything."

We glanced to Mr. Blakeney for confirmation. "You can trust her," he said—looking terrified of the consequences if he was wrong.

14

AMANTES IRA

Although Christmas is meant to be a peaceable season, it
is not immune to frayed nerves and short tempers. Indeed,
it is particularly susceptible to displays of high emotion.
Best to steer well clear of fraught topics and the easily
overset until the conclusion of the merriment.

-H. M. Hardcastle, *A Modern Yuletide*

Father and Miss Judson were fighting. I didn't even
have to hide in the water closet (my usual surveillance
post) to listen in; all of Gravesend Close could hear
them, hollering at each other at the tops of their lungs.
And it wasn't just Father scolding me-via-Miss-Judson-
by-proxy, either. This time both sides freely launched
their volleys—and they all seemed to strike home.

They were fighting about *me*, of course. Some
things never change.

I sat at the top of the stairs, Peony in my lap,

although she squirmed to be free, just as concerned as I by the battle below. She finally wrestled from my grip and fled for the safety of my bedroom.

"Coward." I hugged my stockinged knees to my chest instead, and listened.

"Really going too far! Can't let the two of you out of my sight!"

"—your aunt's doorstep! We could hardly avoid—"

"Oh, you certainly *could* have avoided!" Father's voice rattled the plates on the picture-rail. "I doubt a mob of armed ruffians came in the middle of the night and forced you at knife-point to stomp into a crime scene!"

I shuddered—that image was far too apt for comfort, given everything going on.

"And recruiting Aunt Helena into your exploits is simply unforgivable. She's an old woman, for pity's sake."

(Miss Judson wisely did not mention that Aunt Helena had recruited herself.)

"Not to mention that newspaper reporter!" he said. "Was it necessary to drag *her* into this as well, or just your perverse amusement? I'm already getting enough pressure from the Mayor and the magistrate. They're demanding answers and retribution, and I don't even have anyone to put on trial!"

"I don't blame them," Miss Judson returned. "There are far too many murders in Swinburne for my way of thinking. I've been considering relocating somewhere safer. Like back home to Devil's Island!" Her voice reached an unfamiliar pitch on this last statement, and the room fell into shocked silence. I could hardly believe it–Miss Judson scarcely even *joked* about leaving us. The idea of her fleeing for French Guiana's most infamous penal colony was anything but amusing.

Father thought so, too. "Well, now, that's just childish."

Her pause suggested the deadly gaze she'd fixed him in. "I see. Since the *child* of this house is my responsibility, I suppose that's only logical. Now if you'll excuse me, Mr. Hardcastle, I have some childish duties to attend to. Do try and find someone to prosecute. And see if you can't manage for them to be *guilty*, for a change."

With that, she swished out of the parlor–with, disappointingly, no door to slam.

I (Childishly, if not exactly Dutifully) scrambled to my feet and out of sight. Hardly more heroic than Peony, I slipped into my bedroom and closed the door. I could only hope that Miss Judson would burn herself out, somehow, before barging in and turning her wrath on me. The source of Father's ire was clear enough, but I couldn't tell what *she* was so mad about. Except a general and intractable disagreement with Father.

She did not appear, and I cowered on my window

seat, overlooking the cul-de-sac outside. A moment later a homburg-hatted figure appeared below, brief-bag in hand, stalking out of the neighborhood toward the cab stand. Where was Father going, this late in the afternoon?

"Mrow?" Peony put a paw on my foot, eyes large and worried.

"I don't know what to tell you," I said. "I've never seen them this mad before. Not at *each other.*" More often they formed a united front against me.

Miss Judson's door slammed, and I knew she, too, had seen Father storming out of the house. I listened for the sounds of steamer trunks being hauled out, and I could not stop my wild worries tumbling together: Would Miss Judson need a fur-lined cape in Cayenne? What about the embroidered gloves Father had given her for Christmas last year? Or the brolly, her splendid brown brolly with its spoke bent from when she'd once used it to stop a runaway pram from rolling into the path of a carriage?* Would she need a separate ticket for all her luggage? Would they let her bring her easel and all her sketchbooks? Even the ones with our Investigations detailed in them?

I chewed on my thumb, feeling hot and sick and simmery, like milk scalded at the bottom of a pot. Peony propped herself on the windowsill, ears forward

___
* and you thought that reference was hypothetical, Dear Reader!

and eyes alert, watching and waiting for Father to circle back and come home.

But he didn't.

Eventually I decided that he must have turned his attention to the Investigation, and that I might as well do the same. The imagined sounds of Miss Judson packing for French Guiana had sparked an idea.

We didn't have a carriage, so the carriage house was used for storage. Father and Cook between them kept it neat, uncluttered, and blessedly spider-free.* The well-oiled door left an arc through the snow in the drive and stayed open on its own. Peony trotted in, tail high, hopeful for voles or hedgehogs—or dust—and set about her own Investigation.

Hands on my hips, I wondered what I was searching for and where it might be lurking. Obviously not among the rakes and lawn mower leaning against the wall, or with Miss Judson's trunks, still safe beneath a layer of dust and dead moth and the bicycle pump, which we hadn't seen in weeks. I returned it to the hook where it was meant to live, stretching to reach past a box of my old playthings. With a swell of nostalgia (which sounds like an unpleasant medical condition), I wriggled the twine loose and prized free its lid, unearthing old schoolroom papers—my very

---

* I could admire the creatures from afar perfectly well; scientific appreciation did not require them to scurry out of nowhere into my boots or hair.

earliest Latin efforts in oversized, uneven handwriting. Beneath that, I spotted a tuft of velveteen.

"Rufus!" I cried softly, pulling him from the box.

"*Who?*" demanded Peony from the corner, where she was eyeing the carcass of the moth with disappointment, having experimentally tasted it. Twice.

I smoothed my old plush fox's worn nose and bristly ears, and the row of sutures lovingly set along the ridge of his (sawdust) skull. My fingers went to my own hairline, and for a moment I was five years old again, not kneeling in a freezing carriage house, but snuggled up beside Mum while she stitched a scrap of lacy cotton into her crazy quilt. It was from one of my nighties, which I'd been wearing while trying to reach a book in Father's study—the shelves not being designed for my five-year-old stature—and fallen, cracking my head on the corner of the desk.

"Why on earth are you using the bloody bit?" Father had asked. "That's rather gory, isn't it?"

"Not at all," Mum had replied. "Myrtle earned this bloodstain. It's a badge of honor from an adventure."

"A *misadventure*," Father revised.

"An *adventure*. It's my quilt, and I get to remember it however I want."

Mum had tried to interest me in the needlework, but I was more interested in the stitches she'd set in my own skin. She'd made me wear a babyish bonnet for the whole time they were in, because I couldn't stop trying to see and feel them. But to appease me, she'd done minor surgery on my stuffed toy, using her surgical silk and the fascinating single knots of sutures. Those stitches had never been removed, and Rufus V. Vulpe still bore the scar, forever unhealed.

Mine had healed so well I couldn't even find it with my fingers anymore. I stroked Rufus's wound, feeling unaccountably like crying.

A rustle beside me was a welcome distraction. The Mighty Huntress had moved on from dead *Lepidoptera* and was inside the trunk, considering which of the old papers looked most appetizing.

"Stop that," I said, shifting her aside. A folded letter with a wet, chewed corner stopped my hand. It had a postmark and stamp from Egypt. Another note from Nora? What was it doing in *my* things? No—I did remember. Mum had once given it to me as a sort of puzzle, to keep me entertained and quiet trying to untangle the maze of words. She must have felt my young brain would not grasp the significance of the content.

It was an old-fashioned "crossed letter": two letter writers shared the same single sheet of paper, one writing the normal way across the narrower span of the page, the other turning it ninety degrees to place her—his?—own words across and between those, fitting words into the spaces as he scrawled a message overtop the other. It was an obsolete (and rather challenging) way to write a letter, from the days before the cheap penny-post. But postage from Egypt evidently being dear, these two correspondents had revived the tradition.

Now I squinted at it, hoping its meaning would be more clear. The page was a chaos of different inks and handwriting, neither of which was especially legible at the best of times. It was too dim and cold in the carriage house to manage it here, so I tucked it into my pocket and started packing the box back up again.

"Oooh, taking up archæology, I see!"

I whipped around. Father stood in the carriage house doorway, looking falsely jolly. Peony, genuinely jolly (or at least as jolly as the surly creature ever gets), trotted over to see him.

"You weren't gone long," was the first, foolish thing I thought of to say.

Father answered ruefully. "I forgot there was no late tram on Sunday." He came inside and crouched beside me. "What are you looking for?"

I shrugged and resumed shoving my things back in their carton.

He sat down tailor-fashion, long legs angled and gangly like the spiders that *were not present* in this carriage house, that were absolutely not scurrying across the brick floor right now, and reached into the box, drawing out the Latin conjugations. *"Amo amas amat?"*

He turned to me, and in a grave voice, eyes twinkling, said, "*Te amo, Filia.*"

He held out one hand, pinky finger extended—like he hadn't done since I was small. I hooked my own finger in his and tugged gently. "*Te amo, Pater.*"

A moment later, I burst out, "I hate it when you and Miss Judson quarrel!"

"I do, too." He sighed.

"Then you should apologize," I urged. "She's still upstairs. You won't let her leave us, will you?"

He scowled. "Leave us? What—oh. I think she was joking."

I crossed my arms and scowled right back. "It wasn't very funny."

"No, it wasn't." Shoving a hand through his hair, he still looked angry. "And, by the way, *I* don't have anything to apologize for! She—you both—were clearly in the wrong." He looked like a sulky little boy. Now who was being childish?

"You *know* it wasn't our fault Miss Carmichael's body was left there. And we were some of the last people to see her alive. It was our *duty*, as *witnesses*, to come forth!"

"You could have 'come forth' at the police station. Or come forth *home* and told *me*, and I could have made the report. There was no reason you needed to—" He waved his hand in frustration, at an imaginary body lying in the snow. "Why do these things keep happening to you?"

"I don't know," I said in a small voice. I had now known some *four* murder victims, which surely exceeded one's lifetime quota—and I hadn't even begun my proper career yet. For a moment I felt the weight of all of them: Miss Wodehouse, Mrs. Bloom, poor Mr. Leighton, and now Miss Carmichael. Even Olive Blackwell's disappearance seemed to press on me. That was Mum's mystery—but I was the one left behind to solve it.

"I miss her." That came out before I knew it. I was still holding the fox, and Father knew exactly who I meant. Except—I *didn't*, mostly. Mum had been a memory for me now almost as long as she'd been a real person. I think I missed *knowing* her, learning what she was like as I got old enough to understand her. I remembered a smart, silly woman who stuck out her tongue at Father and stitched up my cuts and read to me in Greek. And I remembered the pale, tired, coughing and hollow-eyed woman who'd taken her place, the one we'd had to tiptoe and whisper around. I'd read to *her*. Wherever she was, did she remember that?

Father tousled my hair. He smelled of coffee and lemon and evergreen. "I do, too. I suppose right now more than usual. This—everything—it would have made her so angry. She'd be burning up with the need to find the truth."

"That's exactly how I feel!"

"I know," he said softly. "And that terrifies me. It might not scare you, and it wouldn't have scared her, but . . ." He shook his head. "She's gone, and this can't hurt her, but even so, I can't help thinking . . ."

"What?" I cried when he didn't finish the thought. "Can't help thinking *what*?" That she must have been involved?

And why couldn't either of us say that out loud?

But Father didn't answer, just kept sifting through my old papers as if they were the most gripping documents in England.

I couldn't stand his silence. "Mum never would have stood by and let Miss Carmichael and Mr. Leighton's murderer go free."

Father didn't answer for the longest moment. He did not meet my eyes when he finally spoke. "Your mum was fearless," he agreed. "Nothing scared her. Except leaving you behind. *And* she believed in justice. And I am sorry every day that she is not here to see the young lady you are growing into. She would be proud of you, Myrtle Hardcastle. She really would."

He finally turned, taking up my hand in his. My sallow, ink-stained fingers looked frightfully small in his great pale grip. "But when *I* look at you, all I can think of is how hard it was to lose her—and how I can't bear to go through that again. Don't you understand? Every time something like . . . this morning happens—"

He cut off abruptly, not finishing that sentence. But he rose to his feet and hauled me up to standing, too. "So I need you to promise me that it ends here. This was the last of it. You won't get any more involved in Mr. Leighton's or Miss Carmichael's murders."

I didn't agree with Father's logic, and I could hardly promise that nobody would drop a dead body on my doorstep again (although probability suggested otherwise). I was prepared to say as much—when my eyes went to Miss Judson's trunks. They were too easily accessible should "something like this morning" happen yet again.

I bit my lip. I could object for my own sake—and for Mum's—but I would not put Miss Judson's position at risk. She was all we had. Losing Mum was bad enough, as he'd said. We *couldn't* go through it again.

Still, it gave me no small pang to stand before him and bow my head. I had to trust him. He and Dr. Munjal and the police could figure this out together.

"Yes, sir," I said solemnly. "I promise not to Investigate Mr. Leighton's or Miss Carmichael's murders."

"Er—" Father looked taken aback to have won so easily, so I added a proviso.

"As long as *you* promise to keep us informed on any developments in the case. Either case." I glared at him, fiercely, out of Mum's eyes, until he conceded.

"Yes. Quite. Er—very good. Let's go inside and see

what Cook's done for tea, shall we? It's freezing out here."

And he led me out of the carriage house and closed the door on our sad memories—not at all suspicious that I was still plotting how to keep the case open.

⤙

I took Nora and David's letter, along with Rufus, to my room, and sat in the fading daylight by the window for a long time, trying to decide what to do. There was little danger in deciphering it—but what if it contained secrets with a direct bearing on the case? I would have to turn it over to Father. I chewed my thumb, debating. I didn't think he would sack Miss Judson over something like that. But I couldn't take the chance.

I set the letter aside and tried to focus on anything else. But the stillness in the house was unbearable, and Peony kept pulling the note from where I'd tucked it, chewing its corner. She would eat the evidence before I had a chance to interpret it, and then where would the case be? What if this long-buried letter held the single most important clue to cracking the mystery of Olive's disappearance, or the murders? I couldn't just pretend it didn't exist.

"Mrow." Peony's conviction was catching.

I eyed her sideways. "It's probably nothing."

"No."

"You're incorrigible," I said. "We *just* promised Father we wouldn't Investigate the murders."

"No." She reached for the note again.

"Oh, I see." Although I really didn't. It just made me feel better, talking to Peony, judgmental as she could be. "It's probably just another newsy letter from Mum's friends. It might not have anything to do with the murders." In fact, how could it? It was sent decades before anyone even thought about killing Mr. Leighton. Peony sat watching me, big green eyes patient. "But it *might* have something to do with Olive's disappearance. And that's a *completely different case.*" I hadn't promised Father I wouldn't Investigate something that happened twenty years ago, after all.

Peony gave a warble of complete exasperation and wandered off, but she might have been muttering something about Loopholes and Legal Technicalities.

Feeling only a little guilty, I retired to the schoolroom, which had the best lighting for this sort of task, and set up facing the door, with a big stack of books concealing what I was really working on. I unfolded the letter from Egypt and, notebook at the ready, set about attempting to decode and transcribe it.

It was slow going, as the two sets of handwriting were similar enough, and messy enough, that it was a challenge to figure out what each blob of ink belonged to—the first letter, going crosswise? Or the second, going lengthwise?—let alone what *word* it was supposed to be. After an unsuccessful attempt to read it sensibly, I started at the end, and found signatures. They would have been just as mystifying, if I hadn't been already familiar with Hadrian's Guard and their Classical nicknames. This one was signed *Cleopatra* and *Ptolemy*: Egyptian brother and sister, Nora and David Carmichael.

Nora had written first, so her note was harder to decipher, buried beneath David's untidy scrawl. I pulled my lamp closer, and with the aid of my magnifying lens, painstakingly pieced the note together—or most of it, anyway.

It was from 1875, just a few months after Olive's disappearance, and it wasn't at all what I expected.

Columba, he wrote,

Tell me you've heard from her. I am mad with worry. She never showed up—I now realize you must have helped her make a different (illegible due to handwriting, age, or Peony). You were her dearest friend. She confided in you. She trusted you. I know you would have helped her, if you could. If you won't tell me where she is, at least tell her to get in touch with me. Not here. She knows where. It will reach me. Nora says to give up on her, she betrayed us all. But I never will. I never will. Tell her I still love her. —Ptolemy

Beside his signature was a sketch of an eagle perched on a branch.

Nora's note, by contrast, was gay and carefree—lighthearted chatter about the wonders of Egypt, how she couldn't believe she'd made it at last. Her final comment was that she "had little Olive to thank for it," whatever that meant. *Send her my love; I gave her a leaving token when last we met.* Her message ended with an ouroboros, a snake eating its own tail.

I sat back, stiff-necked and half blind from squinting at Carmichael hieroglyphics. And stunned.

Mum had helped Olive escape.

15

Mum's the Word

"Mumming" is a Christmas tradition curiously apt to inspire unsocial behavior among those with criminal proclivities. The custom of parading about in costume, performing comical sketches, descends into violence with alarming regularity. Our colony in Newfoundland reports that before the practice was banned in the 1860s, mummers there were involved in some twenty-five legal proceedings, including sixteen trials, nine charges of assault and battery, and at least one murder.

–H. M. Hardcastle, *A Modern Yuletide*

Miss Judson finally reappeared, looking not at all as if she'd spent the evening in a pique, a sulk, or a Mood. She poked her head into the schoolroom, bearing a stack of mail, rosy-cheeked and fresh-faced as if she'd merely been out enjoying an Invigorating Evening

Constitutional.* It took all my Exceptional Forbearance not to scold her for quarreling with Father.

"Look—Christmas cards from Clive and Maud!" She handed them to me, and for a happy moment we were lost in news from friends we'd met on holiday last fall. "And I ran into Priscilla as I was fetching the post. She can confirm Genie's alibi—she was indeed at the midnight concert, plying everyone present for interviews about Olive."

"Anything else?"

"Only that—and I quote—'the second performance was frightfully boring,' compared to the first. And everyone seems to think the chairs were arranged as a sort of memorial tribute." The skepticism in her voice said how much credence she afforded that theory. "What have you been up to?" Her eyes skirted the worktable, and I was sorely tempted to bend over the letter in a fruitless effort to shield it from view.

Instead, I fell on my own sword.† I slipped from the stool and faced her. "I've promised Father that we'll stop Investigating Mr. Leighton's and Miss Carmichael's murders." I'd found what I wanted to know, hadn't I? How Mum had been involved? That should be enough. It would have to be.

* an overblown name for a walk taken for no logical purpose

† a metaphor. Plutarch offers excruciating details of Brutus's death by this favored Roman method, which sounds thoroughly impractical.

Miss Judson blinked, exited, went several tele-graph-tapping steps down the hallway—heels clicking even on the thick rug—then returned, eyes narrow. "I'm sorry. I seem to have lost my way. I was looking for Myrtle Hardcastle's schoolroom."

I was in no mood for her jokes. "I *said*, I've promised Father we wouldn't Investigate the murders."

"Ah. Then I suppose you won't want to see this." She held out the parcel so the label faced me: addressed to Stephen Hardcastle, with *Stephen* crossed out and replaced with *Myrtle* in blotchy, unfamiliar handwriting.

"From the Blakeneys?" My hands folded over the letter I'd been transcribing. "What do you suppose it is?"

She set the parcel between us on the workbench. "At a guess, materials pertaining to the case." She nodded at my recent work. "What's that?"

"An old letter of Mum's. Not from Olive—from the Carmichaels." I handed over both letter and transcription.

Her cool eyes swiftly ran down the page. "Good work," she said absently. Then her face relaxed into a smile. "I knew it—your mum was a romantic, helping two young lovers spirit themselves away."

"Except they didn't," I pointed out. "Or else why was David so upset?"

"Hmm. It's a pity he didn't think to include more

details of the plan—how, exactly, the escape was accomplished, for instance."

"Or *why*," I said—entirely against my will. The case was over. I'd cleared Mum's name. Or the Carmichaels had.

Miss Judson allowed me a moment, during which I pretended I was no longer interested in anything to do with Olive Blackwell or Schofield College or Professor Leighton or Miss Carmichael. I carefully folded up the letter and tucked it into a drawer, safely away from Peony, then closed the books I'd been using as a shield and returned them to their shelves. There. Now this was just an ordinary English schoolroom again.

"The Blakeneys will be sorry to hear it. They seemed to be counting on our help." She put a thoughtful hand atop the parcel. "Your father must be a persuasive litigator, to have convinced you to make such a choice."

It wasn't him, I thought, but didn't say it aloud.

"I see your vow did not preclude you from deciphering that letter."

"That's Olive's disappearance," I said to the tabletop. "Not the murders." With Miss Judson and Peony both staring down at me, it was hard to keep my composure. I *had* to learn how they did that! They could break a witness without saying a word.

"Duly noted. A significant distinction, indeed. I

suppose I'll have to mark this 'return to sender,' and ship it all back."

She was *ruthless*. I felt myself reaching for the box before I could think better of it. I gave her my best glower and snatched it from her hands.

"Maybe it's a Christmas present."

Some present, indeed. I peeled open the package, and found a collection of newspaper clippings wrapped in a note: *A peace offering from Genie, from her work on the Olive Blackwell case.* In addition to the clippings, there were handwritten notes, maps, and lists, along with some ephemera from the college: a cartoon from *Punch*, old programs, and song sheets.

"She told us the original things were missing," I said.

Miss Judson regarded the hoard like it was a box of bonbons and she was trying to select the choicest morsel. Finally she plucked out a handful. "She must have found additional copies somewhere. It looks like she's been collecting materials for years."

Headlines announced, LEIGHTON RESIGNS UNDER CLOUD OF SUSPICION and LEIGHTON LEAVES IN SHAME. The *Schofield Daily* bade FAREWELL TO PROFESSOR LEIGHTON with only the most neutral coverage of his academic achievements, a picture of the Saturnalia Chalice, and lukewarm good wishes. The longest article was an exposé from the *Upton Register*, the newspaper of

Swinburne's larger neighbor. Accompanying this were a drawing that made Olive look sweet and innocent and a sketch of blindfolded figures in togas assembled like ghosts around a single flaming candle.

Miss Judson proceeded to read the article aloud.

GIRL STUDENT AT COLLEGE FALLS TO HER DEATH

OR DOES SHE? WHAT HAPPENED TO OLIVE BLACKWELL?

18 December 1874. Last night witnessed one of the most shocking and mystifying events in local memory. The scene was the Campanile belltower at Schofield College in nearby Swinburne, which is notorious across England for admitting female students. Sunday night, according to Witnesses and Police (see Constable Gerald Hardy, pictured), several students had assembled at the Campanile for a pagan ritual of sorts, an initiation to a so-called secret society. The students have had their names withheld for the protection of their families (mostly local Swinburnians of some repute, whom this newspaper does not wish to malign), but for the missing girl, one Miss Olive Blackwell, the nineteen-year-old daughter of the Reverend Vernon Blackwell, professor of Divinity at Schofield College.

Miss Blackwell, witnesses claim, had gathered

with friends in the Campanile's belfry. Shortly before midnight, through disastrous misadventure, Miss Blackwell somehow fell from the open archway and vanished. Despite a thorough search mounted by College officials and the Swinburne Constabulary, no trace of the girl has been found. Anyone with information regarding the whereabouts—or fate—of Miss Blackwell is urged to come forward. The Blackwell family have offered a reward of £100 for any information leading to her safe return.

I tucked my feet under my knees and studied the picture of the figures in their robes and blindfolds. Now that I was no longer concerned about Mum's guilt, I found the scene thrilling, maybe even a bit romantic. Well, until the bit where it caused a scandal.

"Why did they do it?" I said. "Why did Olive want to disappear? And where did she go? Why didn't she ever write to David?" Somehow, knowing she'd really fled, and not simply been murdered, it seemed sadder than ever.

Miss Judson was pondering the article. "A hundred pounds is a lot of money," she mused. "But five people decided their secret was even more valuable. Or at least one of them did." She picked up another of Genie's notes, where she'd written down six names and a notation:

Olive Blackwell
Jemima Bell
Nora Carmichael
David Carmichael
Henry Spence-Hastings
Vikram Munjal
(Six centuriae per cohort = 6 HG members)

"*That's* why there's six!" I exclaimed. A Roman legion was divided into units called cohorts, which in turn were made up of six groups of one hundred soldiers, centurions like our little lead figure.

"Yes, very historical of them," Miss Judson said. "Top marks."

"Do you think they were all in on it?" Genie had listed the same people from the Cornwall expedition—the ones I'd come up with, too. "But Olive never told David where she was going. Or wait—she *did.*" I indicated my transcription of his note. "But something went wrong."

"It brings us back to her reasons for disappearing. What could have provoked such drastic measures?"

"They all went on that archæological dig together. Maybe Olive absconded with some treasure."

"As we well know, that sort of thing is not easily kept secret," she said, referring to one of our previous Investigations. "And why would they conspire to protect a friend who was a thief?"

"Maybe it made them all look bad. Those threatening Latin messages all mentioned a tribunal for corruption and abuses of power."

She eyed me sternly. "This brings us perilously close to breaking your recent vow of obedience."

I growled—and forged ahead anyway. "We know that the killer—that *someone* accused Professor Leighton of corrupting youth. Which youth? Corrupted how?" I partially answered my own question. "Hadrian's Guard."

"Mmm. When people talk about corruption, they're usually referring to things like bribery, extortion, and embezzlement."

"People getting rich through ill-gotten gains."

"Well, that narrows it down," she said.

"But it *does*," I said. "Nora told us all about it. We know exactly how the members of Hadrian's Guard all got so rich and powerful." I found the article, and jammed my finger down upon the image, the very thing we'd all been admiring last night. "The Saturnalia Chalice."

Miss Judson produced her own drawings of the artifact. "Aside from the—questionable decorations, it doesn't look especially suspicious."

I scowled at it. "Miss Blackwell's father taught Divinity—that's religion, right? Maybe she was offended by the carvings?"

The missionaries' daughter let out a clap of laughter.

"That hardly seems reason enough to ruin someone's career. Let alone kill him. *Or* vanish into thin air without ever telling your friends or family what became of you."

I dismissed my own theory. "And why would the college care about that? It must be something else. Ill-gotten gains. Maybe they stole it from the real owners."

"I doubt the Romans are going to press charges."

We both fell silent, returning to the sheaf of clippings. "Oh, this is interesting," she said, a few moments later. "The dates—Olive disappeared on December the seventeenth."

I was reading the caption accompanying the picture of the chalice, and recognized the date's significance immediately. "The beginning of Saturnalia!"

Miss Judson and I regarded each other evenly. "It could be a coincidence."

"*No*," opined Peony, amid a yawn.

I picked up the drawing of the chalice again. "Nora Carmichael credited this with her success."

"And the Mayor's," Miss Judson reminded me.

"And Professor Leighton's downfall?"

She didn't answer that.

కాు

Monday morning, Father headed to work without stopping for breakfast, which meant his disagreement with Miss Judson was not yet resolved, despite my promise to leave his case alone. I'd lain awake for hours, pondering the Saturnalia Chalice, willing it to reveal its deepest, darkest, deadliest secret. Vow to Father or no, I was sure now that the Chalice was somehow at the heart of everything, both Olive's disappearance and the recent murders.

But how to untangle them? And without crossing from one case—the older one, which I had (more or less) parental sanction to Investigate—into the new one, the murders, which I assuredly had not? I'd stared at the photograph of the expedition to Cornwall, counting the dead and gone. Olive—gone. Mum, dead. David and Nora, dead. Professor Leighton, dead. Only the Mayor was left.

He'd been acting suspiciously from the beginning. There was his late-night secret meeting with Dr. Munjal after Mr. Leighton's death (well, evening meeting, eavesdropped on by Nanette Munjal). The ongoing argument with the Leightons, and Mrs. Leighton turning him away from the shop before her husband was murdered. And his clandestine meeting with Nora Carmichael at the museum—right before she turned up dead outside his front door. Even Father would have to find all of that significant. Not that I could tell him any of it.

I already felt thwarted by the time I dragged myself out of bed, and I hadn't even started yet. But I knew what my next move ought to be—and knew just as certainly that it was impossible.

I had to see the Mayor.

I could well imagine Miss Judson's response, should I propose such a mission. Indeed, I had rehearsed the entire conversation before falling into a fitful, frustrated sleep that annoyed Peony so much she stalked off to bunk with Cook, who snores and kicks in her sleep. I shall spare you the imaginary details, Dear Reader, but sum it up in one concise word from the Feline Dictionary: *No*.

I sulked through breakfast (which, admittedly, perplexed Miss Judson, as she had no idea that we'd been quarreling), and sighed through lessons, until an unexpected turn of events changed the course of the day.

An imperious banging on our front door summoned the remaining members of the household to the foyer. It sounded like the entire Swinburne Constabulary, and possibly the Queen's Life Guard (London regiment), had descended upon us. Miss Judson, Cook, Peony, and I exchanged worried glances. A further moment passed, when it seemed like we ought to draw lots to see who got the unhappy duty of answering the door, before Miss Judson took charge and swung it open. It was not the police.

It was not even Her Majesty.

It was, in fact, far worse.

LaRue Spence-Hastings marched in, hair tangled and cheeks aflame. She slammed something down on the secretary. "My *father* got one of your stupid letters! You have to do something."

Against my better judgment, I glanced at the item she'd dropped. Creamy white paper with a deckled edge, folded in half. I had no doubt it would contain two words in blotchy Latin. Frowning, I lifted my eyes to LaRue's—how had she known about the letters?

"Caroline told me," she said impatiently. "She said you know all about who's sending them, and why."

I couldn't decide whether to thank Caroline the next time I saw her—or strangle her.

Then again, how had *Caroline* known? Miss Judson and I were the only ones who'd seen Miss Carmichael's note. And the Mayor, of course. He could have taken the perfect opportunity to throw us off the scent by sending one to himself, too.

Miss Judson, Cook, and Peony had tactfully (or cravenly) withdrawn, leaving me alone with LaRue.

"How many people have handled that?"

"How should I know? Are you going to tell me there might be fingerprints on it, and I've spoiled them for you?"

I glared back at her. "Yes, actually. And you have."

She shook her hair in frustration. Miss Judson would suffer a fit of compassion and let her have her little tantrum. It was all I could do not to pick up the cast-iron planter and add another homicide to the constables' workload.

"I'm sure there are other *clues* you can find, Morbid Myrtle."

"I thought you wanted my help."

"I don't *want* it," she snapped. "But I *need* it, and you have to give it to me. My father's the Mayor, and your father works for the village." The *so there* went unsaid.

"It doesn't work like that," I said—stalling, because I didn't want LaRue to know how very desperately I wanted to snatch that letter from her and dash up to the schoolroom to examine it properly. Did it match the others? Was there some way to trace its origin? "Your father's role is entirely ceremonial, and you know it. Stop putting on airs."

"You first," she snapped.

"Fine." I held the door open for her. "I'll have a look and return it when I'm done."

"I can't leave it here! Father doesn't know I took it. My mother's making arrangements for the Christmas Ball. I have to bring it back before they notice I've gone. Can't you do—whatever you do *now*?"

Not very well with you watching. With a grunt of frustration, I turned my back on LaRue and headed for the schoolroom. A satisfyingly long moment later, she followed. I swallowed my private smile.

It was really too bad I didn't have more morbid things on display up here. I would have to consult Miss

Judson (or Dr. Munjal) about ordering an articulated skeleton. I should like to see how LaRue handled *that*.

Not that I ever planned to have her back again.

"Stand in the corner," I commanded, all at once pleased to have her at my mercy and in my debt. If I hadn't been so concerned about the matter at hand, perhaps I could have figured out how to use the moment to my advantage. I placed the letter on the workbench and looked at it.

"Aren't you going to *do* something? You're just staring at it! I've done that already."

It was a good thing every item in the schoolroom was too precious to throw at someone. "I am performing an initial visual examination." I forced professional patience into my voice. "You might have missed something."

Arms crossed over her chest, she said, "I doubt it. It has a Swinburne postmark, it was mailed yesterday from a High Street postbox, and the writer was obviously a woman." Her voice was smug.

I withheld my sigh. She'd done well, actually. "What about the paper?"

"Cheap."

"Why do you need me, then?"

Exasperated, she said, "To tell me who wrote it, of course!"

I slipped the paper from its (cheap) envelope. "I

don't have a crystal ball."* The ink from the address had bled through onto the page inside. As expected, the two words stood stark and lonely on the creamy paper: *QUÆSTIO REPETUNDARUM*.

"What is that supposed to mean?"

"It's from Roman law," I said. "A court to try government officials for wrongdoings."

"My father hasn't done anything wrong! He hasn't had the job long enough."

I thought she was probably right, at that. "We think this has to do with something he was inv—something that happened when he was at college. The other victims—" I winced. "Mr. Leighton was their professor at Schofield College. Nora Carmichael, your father, my mum . . ."

She was nodding slowly. "Caroline's dad. Go on," she urged. "What else can you tell?"

Unfortunately, there wasn't much. Slowly, I retrieved Nora's letter and compared the two. On the surface, they seemed to be identical. Very well, I'd look below the surface. I removed the cover from the microscope and adjusted the mirror to catch the light. It was like showing the letter to Mum, in a way, and getting her thoughts on the subject. She wasn't here to ask, but her microscope was, and that was a connection.

---

* I did, in fact. Miss Judson and I had attempted to rig a Campbell-Stokes Sunshine Recorder for meteorological study, which met with only limited success.

LaRue was silent as I studied the paper, its grainy texture turning to a mass of intertwined threads beneath the lens, the ink thick and dark and feathered at the edges. I adjusted the focus, falling deeper into the image, trying to focus my thoughts as well.

As I shifted the sample, I Observed areas of uneven coloration to the paper. I carefully withdrew the sheet from the microscope and held it up to the light. Barely discernible, if I tilted the page first one way, then another, was a faint, small watermark. "It's from the college," I said. "Look here." The watermark showed the Campanile inside a circle, like a seal. I held Nora's up for comparison. They were the same.

"So?" LaRue was unimpressed.

"*So* this paper must have been made before Olive Blackwell disappeared. They don't use the Campanile as their watermark anymore." Too much scandal, no doubt. "Now it's just a shield and a lamp."

"Old paper? What does that tell us?"

"I have no idea," I admitted reluctantly.

"Do you really think it could be her? That Blackwell girl, back from the dead?"

"Afraid of ghosts, LaRue?"

"Of course not. I *am* afraid of murderers who lurk about threatening innocent people with silly models and then kill them in public outside my house!"

"Somebody doesn't think your father is all that innocent."

LaRue glared at me from hot, damp eyes. "He's a good man," she insisted. "He *didn't* kill that girl, no matter what that reporter says. I know he didn't."

"What about Mr. Leighton? Or Nora Carmichael?"

"I wouldn't make many more accusations like that, Morbid Myrtle," she said. "Or you'll find out just how ceremonial my father's position really is."

Without awaiting my rebuttal, LaRue left the schoolroom and headed downstairs. "Get your coat. I have a cab."

I scurried after. "Uh—where are we going?"

"To get some answers. I can see I have to do everything myself." And she marched off my front stoop, fairly dragging me along with her.

Some moments later, I had cause to wonder if this wasn't another of LaRue's hilarious pranks, like the time she'd locked me in Dr. Munjal's morgue. Although, I reflected, that had ended up being a singularly effective point in that Investigation. Not that I was going to tell her as much.

I reconsidered her threats in a new light. Was it possible LaRue knew something, some incriminating fact about her father, and was trying to scare me off the Investigation? It seemed unlikely, and yet—

"What?" she snapped, making me realize I'd been staring at her.

"Do you know anything about the Saturnalia Chalice?"

"That old cup thing at the museum?"

"It was a great find," I said. "It helped make your father's reputation." As I said that, though, I began to wonder. Exactly *how* had it done that? Seeing how it had helped Nora was obvious—she'd become a famous Egyptologist. But being Mayor of Swinburne was about as far from an archæological dig as you could get.

LaRue gave an exaggerated sigh. "I know. Mum's always on about it—all the honors he received after the find, the scholarships and whatever. He was first in his class, as I'm sure you know, and immediately got a Civil Service post when he graduated. I think the thing's ghastly—I mean, it isn't even gold—but what can you do?"

That didn't tell me much, and I had no chance to ask more, for we'd arrived at the Munjals' house. Hobbes was outside, fixing more greenery in place, under the direction of Mrs. Munjal. It was as if draping the house in as much Christmas as possible would help keep out the spectre of Olive Blackwell and the scandal her disappearance had brought—and could still bring down—on her family. I felt the urge to run out and reassure her that Miss Judson and I were close to figuring it all out. But of course we weren't, and besides, LaRue didn't give me a chance. She hopped out of the coach and slammed the door in my face.

"Stay here," she snapped—although whether to me or the driver (or possibly even the horse), it was not clear. A moment later, she returned with Caroline in tow. Caroline looked half sick with apprehension.

"I told Myrtle you told me everything," LaRue said. She'd used this tactic before, pitting me and Caroline against each other when we were smaller. It generally worked.

"But I don't know everything," Caroline protested.

"Just where are you taking us?" I asked. That came out sounding like a character in a penny dreadful.

"Don't be so melodramatic," LaRue said. "We're going to see those Blackwell people, to tell them to stop spreading such awful lies about our parents."

16

BOAR'S HEAD
REVISITED

The tradition of serving a boar's head at Christmas dates back to the Middle Ages, with a legendary encounter between an Oxford underclassman, a wild boar, and a volume of Aristotle. The specifics of the incident are gruesome and improbable, but suffice it to say the boar did not come out on top, the student no doubt aced his Greek examinations that quarter, and the Aristotle was retired. Permanently. What this has to do with Christmas, however, is anybody's guess.

–H. M. Hardcastle, A Modern Yuletide

Half an hour later, we disembarked from the cab at the edge of the Schofield College commons. The Reverend Blackwell lived in a flat for retired professors on the college grounds, according to the address provided thoughtfully by the old *Schofield Daily* article.

Inside, the building was musty and old-smelling, with bare stone walls and damp seeping from everything.

A tall, narrow woman, all sharp grey angles, answered our knock, her hair wrenched back into a knot whose sole purpose appeared to be torturing the wearer, like a form of penance.

"We're here to see the Reverend Mr. Blackwell." LaRue fished in her reticule for a card. "I'm Miss Spence-Hastings, and these are Miss Munjal and Miss Hardcastle."

"You may have five minutes in the parlor, and then a cup of tea apiece. He does not care for 'Little Town of Bethlehem,' if you please."

"We're not carolers, ma'am."

"Miss!" she cried, voice sharp and cutting as the rest of her. "I am *Miss* Blackwell, the Reverend's daughter."

Caroline and I exchanged Looks of surprise. Was it this easy? Olive had really just come on along home one day? But no—*this* Miss Blackwell was much older than the Mayor and Dr. Munjal and the rest of Hadrian's Guard. "Olive?" I hazarded anyway.

Her lips thinned to a knife blade. "Of course not. I am Damaris." She turned on her heel and stalked into the flat, disappearing into the kitchen, skirts swishing like the ghost of a wind.

I'd expected the Blackwells' tiny flat to be a spare, prisonlike cell, such as a monk might inhabit. But we found ourselves in a cluttered parlor with a roaring fire, beside which four stockings hung in wait. A towering Christmas tree swallowed up the corner, dwarfing a stack of wrapped presents as tall as I was. Only when I looked closer did I realize they were all faded, their corners torn, the wrapping shabby.

"Like Miss Havisham,"* LaRue muttered, edging me backward into a framed picture, which clunked against the plaster and woke a sleeping crow on a perch. *"Iniquity! The Sinners shall burn!"* it screeched.

"Shut it, Pontius." Another voice croaked out of the shadows, from a bundle of sticks that turned out to be an elderly gentleman under a lap robe. His spiky silver eyebrows looked like they would reach out and grab you at the slightest infraction. A skeletal hand waved us in. "How much do you want?"

"I beg your pardon?"

"You're not students, and you're never carolers, and Damaris hasn't any friends, so you must be collecting for charity. What is it this time? Homeless dogs? Wayward girls? War widows?"

"Um, no, sir. We're not here for a donation . . ." LaRue's voice wound down as she took in the cramped space with its whistling draft and dead Christmas tree. Caroline apparently felt the same, gazing at the

---

* an unflattering allusion to a character from Charles Dickens's *Great Expectations*, 1861, an unhappy old woman lost in her memories. And her wedding gown.

pictures and bric-a-brac of the Blackwells' very own Christmas Display. She approached the tree to peer at the packages wrapped beneath.

"Don't touch those!" Mr. Blackwell cried, and the bird shrilled in echo. "Those are Olive's! She'll want them when she comes home."

Caroline snatched her hand back and stared at me in alarm.

I tried to rescue both Caroline and the interview. "That's what we've come to see you about, sir. Have—have you heard from Olive lately?"

Instantly, the old man's face took on a secretive twist. "Wouldn't *you* like to know, little Miss Munjal and Spence-Hastings! Oh, yes—don't think I didn't hear your names when Damaris let you in." He wheeled on me. "You look familiar, too."

For some reason, this made me bolder. "Perhaps my mum? Jemima Bell?"

The name seemed to mean nothing to him, and I swallowed my disappointment. Perhaps that was a good thing. Maybe he only remembered those who'd wished Olive ill, and this was further proof that Mum had been her friend, that she'd helped her. I pulled the note I'd found in the museum from my satchel, signaling LaRue to hand hers over, too. "Sir, do these look familiar? Could this be Olive's handwriting?"

He took the notes from me with his trembling, clawlike fingers—and tossed them into the fireplace.

LaRue and I let out matching cries, but the damage was done. The notes vanished into cinders and ash. Miss Judson was right—I ought to have turned Nora's over to the police immediately. Now it was gone forever, and it was all my fault. "That was evidence," I said, voice small.

"Bah," he said. "It's rubbish."

I fought for composure. "Was it her handwriting?"

"Are you daft? My daughter is *dead*. How could she send letters to anyone?"

I stared at him. "But—you said—" I waved a helpless hand at the presents and the tree. "Did you write them?"

Olive's father held up his hand, which shook, the fingers curled in on themselves. "Can't write a word, not since the stroke." He looked pleased to have beaten me. Was this how his students had felt, facing him down in a lecture hall or examination? Or even Olive, here at home? Maybe she'd fled simply to get away from this terrifying household.

"Do you know why Olive might have wanted to disappear?"

He didn't answer for the longest time, staring into the fire as it cast devilish shadows across his face. "Olive was special, we knew that from the time she was born. The light of her mother's eye, she was. It all changed when she got older, though. Her mother said it was just high spirits." He breathed a bitter sigh.

"What kind of high spirits?" LaRue broke in.

The flinty look in the old clergyman's eyes had hardened. "It started with that group of lads. And that other girl—what was her name, now?"

"Jemima?"

"What? No—the Carmichael girl, Nora, and that brother of hers. But the whole lot of them were unsavory, for all their money and fancy names. Never managed to make it to chapel on Sunday mornings, always carousing or playing pranks on each other."

"Like that ritual they were performing?"

"Ritual?" he boomed, coming half out of his chair. "Rituals are holy things! That was some pagan nonsense—dressing up like ancient Romans and parading about indecently. If Olive's disappearance hadn't killed my Esther, that alone would have done her in." He grew petulant. "Why are you asking all these questions? Where's Olive?"

Before we could answer, the Campanile's bells began to ring, shuddering the thin glass in the flat's old windows. It acted like a thunderbolt, smiting the old man where he sat. His body went abruptly rigid, arching in his armchair like the victim of a strychnine attack.

The kitchen door slammed. "What have you done!" Damaris dropped her tea tray with a crash and rushed to her father. "Father! Catch your breath. That's it. Everything's fine." She turned to us. "Did you bring up *O-l-i-v-e*?" She mouthed each letter silently.

We all nodded. LaRue's eyes were wide with mute

terror, and the three of us tripped over one another in our crush to back away from the scene we'd caused.

"Should—should I send for my father?" Caroline asked. "He's a doctor."

"He just has these fits. Always has. I'm the only one who can help." Indeed, her presence was calming, and in a few moments Mr. Blackwell was slumped in his seat, asleep or dazed, but at least peaceful.

"Did we kill him?" LaRue asked—and I elbowed her, none too gently, in the side.

After a few dreadfully long minutes of fussing over her father, and then attempting to calm the shrieking bird, Miss Blackwell finally turned to us.

"Had your fun, then? It's bad enough that we live in the shadow of that horrid belltower—especially now. That girl had to go and convince everyone that it would all be so lovely to have the bells ringing again. But we have to contend with folks like you lot coming about, digging up the dead. Why can't you leave well enough alone?"

"Don't you want to know what really happened to your sister?" I said.

"I know what happened. It's all in the past, and we're better off without her."

She paused to straighten the picture I'd bumped. It was a needlework sampler with a dark blob stitched in the middle. I drew closer, trying to make out the image. A Bible verse was stitched around it:

They shall go into the holes of the
rocks and the caves of the earth
for fear of the LORD

Miss Blackwell's sharp fingers touched the stitches. "Olive's work—or it was meant to be. I had to finish it for her, of course. Never had the patience for anything."

The next picture had also been knocked askew: a framed family portrait from happier times, with a cherubic little Olive posed front and center, clutching a doll. Elder sister Damaris was just as recognizable—the younger, feminine version of her father in his stern clerical robes. Their mum looked like Olive, small and round and pretty, and on her lap she held an infant in a heap of white frills.

Caroline couldn't help herself. "Oh, who's that?" she cooed, pointing at the baby. "Do you have a little brother?"

Miss Blackwell's expression did not soften. "After Olive's—after Olive, we decided our youngest would be better off raised by family elsewhere." She looked briefly pensive. "Mother never got over losing two of her children in one blow. Olive was always determined to bring shame down on our family. And she's *still* upsetting things, all these years later." She opened the door, letting in a gust of frigid corridor, and fairly shoved us all out into it. "Good day."

"Well," said LaRue, once we were back outside in

the bright cold air, "it's obviously them. They killed the shopkeeper and that Cleopatra woman and sent those crazy letters, and they're trying to ruin Father's Christmas Ball. Let's go tell the constables."

She sounded precisely like a small version of Aunt Helena. "That's not how it works," I said, knowing it was useless. "We don't have any evidence against them."

"Evidence?" she crowed. "You saw them! How much more obviously murderous could they be? I'll bet the bird was in on it, too."

Caroline and I exchanged worried glances as LaRue marched off toward the waiting cab. Evidence or no, I had a feeling LaRue was probably right.

℘

The cab trundled away from Schofield College, the castlelike buildings fading into the background, even as the haunting notes of the Campanile filled the sky. I tried to spare a thought for the carillonist, merry Leah hammering away at the bells, despite all the chaos and tragedy that belltower had caused.

As we left the college behind, Caroline could not hold her tongue any longer. "Myrtle, you should have told me that Nora Carmichael got one of those notes before she was killed!" she said. "What if the killer is after our fathers, too?"

I swallowed my answer—hadn't Genie told us as much? But Caroline had more to say; she was twisting the end of her braid. "What is it?"

"I didn't tell you this before—I *couldn't*, because—" She waved a distraught hand. "But I do know what our fathers—LaRue's and mine—were talking about that night the Mayor came over." She took a great sniff. "Back when Miss Blackwell disappeared, they arrested Father for it. They held him in custody for three days, until Mr. Spence-Hastings provided an alibi for him. A *false* alibi."

I stared at her, aghast. No wonder her mother was so upset!

"He didn't do anything to her!" Caroline insisted. "He was at home with Mother that night, which wasn't good enough for the police. But when Mr. Spence-Hastings said he could vouch for him, they let him go. They wouldn't believe my father—but they believed *yours*." There was bitterness in her voice.

"Because he was rich and English," I said bluntly. Even LaRue gave a half-hearted acknowledgment.

Caroline nodded tearfully. "Anyway, that's why Mr. Spence-Hastings said Father owes him—because he gave him an alibi all those years ago, and he needed Father to do the same now."

LaRue had turned scarlet to the roots of her hair. "Why would my father possibly need yours to lie for him?"

"He would if he didn't have an alibi for the murders," I said.

LaRue looked like she wanted to kick both of us

out of the cab right then—but our argument was forestalled when the carriage turned a corner onto High Street and slowed to a halt. The street was jammed with carriages and pedestrians, and the odd cyclist.

"What's the holdup?" LaRue banged the carriage ceiling to get the driver's attention. He didn't have a chance to answer her. He didn't need to. Soon enough we could see for ourselves.

The knot of traffic clogging High Street was centered around Leighton's Mercantile.

"Is it another Display?" Caroline's voice wavered, and I craned my neck to see past her. It was impossible to tell what was happening inside the Leightons' shop window—but there was plenty of excitement outside.

Two police wagons were parked there, horses snorting clouds of steam into the cold afternoon air. On the corner, watching intently, was Genie Shelley in her short blue coat. I spotted young Constable Terrence standing rigidly beside the shop door, which swung open. Inspector Hardy and Dr. Munjal came out, escorting a careworn woman in a white cap and apron. Her shocked blue eyes seemed to look straight at me, as the men bundled her into a police carriage. Following behind, red robes swinging, was the Mayor.

I stared at the scene in disbelief, but Caroline found her voice.

"They're arresting Mrs. Leighton!"

17

UPON THE
MIDNIGHT CLEAR

Amid the hustle and bustle of the holiday season, nothing
stirs the mind to contemplation quite like a still, cold, clear
midwinter's night.

–H. M. Hardcastle, *A Modern Yuletide*

I could not believe it. I could not *make* myself believe
that poor Mrs. Leighton had killed her kindly husband—scandal or no—let alone Nora Carmichael.
Father had absented himself to his office in town,
chiefly so he would not have to hear Miss Judson's and
my Idle Speculation on the case.

We gathered in the kitchen, with a bright and
cheery fire in the grate and comforting smells of cinnamon and clove emanating from the hob. Cook had
made eggnog and had served small, nutmeggy cups of

it to each of us. I didn't like the sharp burn of liquor, but Miss Judson had deemed it Medicinally Appropriate— for all of us, like cough syrup after a day in the rain. (Peony got a serving smaller still and minus alcohol.)

"I never should have made that promise to Father." I had lugged all my case notes down and spread them across the table, and nobody complained.

Looking over my shoulder, Miss Judson made an Observation. "I take it this is not the suspect to whom the evidence would have led *your* Investigation?"

"Harrumph," opined Cook, who had known Mrs. Leighton longer than any of us.

"It just doesn't make any sense."

"Murders seldom do," Miss Judson said.

"Of course they do! They always make perfect sense—at least to the killer. There's always a cold and ruthless reason for everything. Or at least a motive! What's Mrs. Leighton's supposed to be?"

Miss Judson paused to consider this too long.

"And even if she was angry with her husband for some reason, that wouldn't explain her killing Nora."

"Maybe she were trying to cover up the first crime," Cook said. "Misdirection. Make everyone think someone were trying to do 'em all in, those Hadrian's Guard folk."

"Cook!" Miss Judson gave her the exasperated look usually reserved for me or Peony. Cook just settled comfortably into her rocking chair, looking like a pleased hen.

"No," I said. "It's too elaborate. Those murders were very public and very—"

"Showy?" Miss Judson filled in.

"Exactly. Mrs. Leighton's not like that at all. If she were going to kill somebody, she wouldn't do something so . . . attention-grabbing."

Once again my thoughts went to Olive—dramatic, center-of-attention Olive Blackwell—and I couldn't help shivering, despite the cozy warmth and the nog. What about the other Miss Blackwell, Damaris? She'd certainly seemed to hate everyone involved in Olive's disappearance—especially Olive.

I turned my attention back to the scene outside Leighton's that afternoon, or, more specifically, the cast of characters who'd been present.

It could have been perfectly natural. Dr. Munjal was the Police Surgeon who'd examined Mr. Leighton, and it was a high-profile crime that had the whole village on edge. Of course the Mayor would want to be on hand to supervise the arrest of the prime suspect, *especially* if a certain newspaper reporter could be there to witness his triumphant success.

Except . . . what if it was more than that? Dr. Munjal and the Mayor were the only members left of Hadrian's Guard—the only people alive to keep their secrets. Caroline's confession had thrown a shadow over their whole relationship, and we could not be certain anything they did together was truly innocent. What if they'd decided to wrap up the case in a tidy little Christmas bow?

I hated that idea. It was hard to believe that Dr. Munjal might be involved in something nefarious. But LaRue's father was another matter.

"It must have been the Mayor," I decided. "He's the only one left, and he has enough influence to convince the police to go after Mrs. Leighton, even without strong evidence."

"I hesitate to take your father's side of this argument," Miss Judson said. "But I must point out that we don't *know* they don't have strong evidence. Perhaps she confessed."

I Looked, Cook *harrumphed*, and Peony said, *"No."*

"All right—unlikely. But they might have been building a case against Mrs. Leighton this whole time," she pointed out. "You saw how her passions were aroused when she spoke about the scandal. Maybe the dedication of the gallery, along with the depiction of the Campanile in the Display, was enough to push her over the edge."

"Fine," I conceded. "But I still think the Mayor is worth Investigating. He has access to all sorts of resources—it would be easy for him to come up with both means and opportunity—and he has a strong motive for killing both the professor and Nora."

"Aye, and how are you going to prove it, then?"
Cook wanted to know.

I kicked the chair legs. "I haven't figured that out
yet."

❧

As Miss Judson tucked me in, my thoughts were still
churning over the long, strange day. The image that
kept leaping to mind was young Olive's ugly sampler,
with the cave and the Bible verse.

"Miss? Do you know any scripture about caves?"

"Very likely," she replied. "Why do you ask?"

I told her about the sampler. "I keep thinking about
it. It was something about people hiding in caves to
protect themselves?" Why was it ringing round in my
head like a song I couldn't quite remember?

"Hmm. Perhaps Isaiah? Let me see." She strode
down the hallway to her own bedroom, and returned
with a copy of the Bible (an English one, not her favorite French volume) and thumbed through it. "Here.
Isaiah 2:19: *And they shall go into the holes of the rocks, and
the caves of the earth, for fear of the LORD, and for the glory
of His majesty, when He ariseth to shake terribly the earth.*"

I let the words sink in, sleepily imagining Roman
soldiers hiding from the wrath of God in tunnels
(although I was mixing my Old and New Testaments;
the Romans came much later), stashing their Cornish
Saturnalia Chalice for safekeeping. It was a dreamy,

vague image—but a moment later it jolted me wide awake with sudden clarity.

"That's it." I sat up, unable to hold still. "Tunnels!" I half leaped from the bed. Complaining, Peony stalked off, and the look on Miss Judson's face was not much keener. "That carillonist at the Campanile—she told us, remember?" It was perfect. It was so perfect, I couldn't believe no one had thought of it before. "The Campanile is built above a network of steam tunnels that run underneath the whole college grounds."

Miss Judson's fingers froze in leafing through the Bible. "Well, now." A slow smile spread across her face, as she read the next verse aloud. *"In that day a man shall cast his idols of silver, and his idols of gold, which they made each one for himself to worship, to the moles and to the bats."*

We grinned at each other. Olive had vanished into the tunnels.

☙

Miss Judson, naturally, would not permit me to launch an expedition that very night, but convinced me (somewhat grudgingly) to postpone it until first light. We breezed past Father as he came down for breakfast.

"Are you two off somewhere? It's not even eight o'clock." He was well to be curious (if not concerned). Many of our most spurious escapades happened before elevenses.

We were, in fact, off to visit the Blakeneys, although it would hardly do to admit as much to Father.

"Just errands," Miss Judson prevaricated smoothly.

It was a good thing we were in a hurry; if we lingered any longer, I'd be forced to fling myself at Father and pester him within an inch of sanity about the case. It was madness to even consider that Mrs. Leighton might have killed her husband, and I knew he wouldn't share any of the evidence against her with us, despite his promise. And he certainly couldn't explain the mystery of the relationship (or collusion) between the Mayor and Dr. Munjal. *If* he even believed it. Father had been working closely with Dr. Munjal on the case. Would he think it suspicious to find the Mayor lurking in the shadows, pulling the strings?

Miss Judson and I cycled into town, keeping close abreast to discuss the particulars of Olive's escape. As much as we both liked the idea that she'd slipped away from the world by disappearing beneath it, it didn't answer everything.

"How did she get from the belfry to the tunnels without everyone seeing her?" Miss Judson said. "They *all* agree that she fell out the open archway."

"Like Cook said. Misdirection," I answered, with a decided lack of specificity. But she was right. We still hadn't solved that essential part of the mystery—how *had* Olive fooled everyone into thinking she'd died? "Maybe we'll find more clues in the tunnels themselves."

Miss Judson's bicycle squeaked to an abrupt halt. "Who said we were going to the tunnels?"

"We have to! How else will we find out what happened to Olive?"

Miss Judson did not exactly answer. She adjusted her hat and gloves, and then the fit of her bloomer cuffs, then her gloves again, and then set off once more, brow creased. Nonplussed, I followed in her wake.

We arrived at the *Swinburne Tribune* offices just as the morning staff was switching over. Sleepy-eyed men staggered out of the building, passing sleepy-eyed men staggering in. Inside, there was no sign of Genie or Mr. Blakeney. I realized they'd never actually told us whether Mr. Blakeney was working for the newspaper now or not, or if he was just following along at Genie's heels, cleaning up her messes—figuratively or literally.

The newspaper office was a splendid, modern affair, full of typewriters (three!), its own telegraph unit clattering in the background, even a telephone. Newspapermen in sleeve garters and visors typed away frantically. No one looked up. There was a reception desk, but the clerk was nowhere to be seen, and a teakettle on a gas jet had boiled itself dry and was making an alarming rattle. Miss Judson coughed politely, which was also overlooked.

As we glanced about for direction, a door at the back of the office swung open, and thence appeared

Genie, in a neat twill frock and a jaunty little felt hat with a turned-up brim. She frowned at a half sheet of newsprint in her hands.

"Mr. Kent, you've misspelled *Parliament* again. This will have to go back." She passed the page off to a strapping fellow with dark hair and glasses and hastened over to us, pushing up her own spectacles.

"This is a surprise! Come in." She swung a little half door in a low wall, admitting us to the bustling heart of the newspaper. The invigorating scents of ink and paper and coffee hung over the room, which hummed with noisy energy. It reminded me of the police station, and I could see exactly why Genie would want to work here.

Miss Judson seemed to agree. She leaned over and whispered to me, "I think it would be fun to run a newspaper."

Genie led us to a desk strewn with papers (no typewriter, sadly), found some extra chairs, and cleared a spot for us to sit. "You must have heard what happened to Mrs. Leighton!" she exclaimed. "We can't keep up with the extras. I had the whole front page last night!" She handed over the smaller evening edition to Miss Judson, with EMILY LEIGHTON ARRESTED FOR HUSBAND'S MURDER splashed across the top.

"Yes, it's hard to believe," Miss Judson said diplomatically.

"It's a complete frame-up! The idea that Mrs.

Leighton suddenly took it into her head to put hemlock in her husband's tea? It's ridiculous!" Genie leaned in, just as she had at the coffeehouse. "You must be on to something with the Mayor, Myrtle. I can't figure any reason *Olive* would want Mrs. Leighton arrested."

"That's actually why we're here," I began eagerly, but Genie interrupted.

"Oh—there's my editor." She jumped up from her desk. "I've been trying to talk to him all morning. Are you in a hurry? Can you give me a moment?"

"Of course," Miss Judson said, adding to her departing back, "Olive's secret has already waited twenty years."

While Genie was gone, I let my gaze rove round her workspace. Copies of her Olive Blackwell stories were pinned to the walls in her corner nook, a reprint of Olive's college photograph front and center, alongside a color poster of the Campanile. Scattered throughout were sloppily scrawled notes—apparently all those governesses she'd terrorized hadn't managed to instill good penmanship.

I moved closer to study her research. Pins and strings led from Olive's picture to Genie's notes: *Which 6?* read one, and *110-foot fall—HOW?* One was merely a series of savage question marks gouged into the paper.

I Observed something familiar tacked behind a faded ticket stub for a theatrical performance: creamy paper with a deckled edge, folded in half. I could see the inked contents through the paper. Heart banging, I nudged it open to what I knew I would find. Two words in Latin: *QUÆSTIO REPETUNDARUM.*

Genie squeaked through the swinging half door again. "Sorry about that," she said, slipping into her chair. I plucked the note from the wall and waved it at her.

"When did this come? Why didn't you tell us?"

Her face took on a closed look, and she snatched it from me. Turning to the wall, she pinned it back in place, smoothing down the ticket stub and neatening the red strings.

"Genie?" Miss Judson prodded gently.

"It's nothing," she mumbled. "Don't worry about it." She flashed us a grin. "I'm not. Now. What did you want to tell me?"

"The killer could be after you next!" I cried.

"I *said*, don't worry about it." She dug through the stacks on her desk, hunting for her notepad and pencil. A packet of letter paper spilled out at my feet, and she lunged for it, hastily sweeping up the loose pages.

"Genie, this is serious," Miss Judson said. "I think you *should* be worried. Have you gone to the police?"

Genie's eyes were full of fire. "You're not my governess, so give it a rest." A moment later she softened. "I'm sorry—you're a sport, Miss J., really. But who would want to kill me? I'm just a reporter."

Miss Judson shot me a quelling look. I could think

of at least one Prosecuting Solicitor who might be glad to see Swinburne down one journalist. But I held my tongue, instead stooping to pick up the last of the fallen papers, fingers catching on its roughened edge.

Genie tugged it from my hand and shoved the whole pile under . . . another pile. "Now. You have news—I can tell by the look in Myrtle's eyes! Spill it." She gave us her easy grin once more.

I explained my deduction (well, hypothesis) about the steam tunnels underneath the Campanile.

"That's brilliant!" I could tell she meant not just my theory, but Olive's escape. "Oh, *so* very clever."

"We haven't figured where she went afterward, or how she got down there with no one noticing, though."

Genie tapped her pencil on the edge of her desk. "David Carmichael," she said thoughtfully.

"Clarify," Miss Judson directed.

But I knew exactly what she meant. "They planned to run off together—that was in his letter to Mum. And he was an expert mountaineer!"

"Until he wasn't," Miss Judson murmured.

"He could have rigged it so that Olive could climb down the side of the Campanile!" I didn't know all that much* about mountaineering, but they could have concealed the equipment for just such an escape, deceiving and distracting the rest of Hadrian's Guard.

* nothing, in fact—not that it stopped me from speculating on the details

While Olive was scaling down one sheer face of the Campanile, no one the wiser, David could have led the group to another opening, to stare down in horror at where she had "fallen." *Misdirection.*

I sat back, eyes wide and heart thumping, like I'd witnessed it myself. Genie was right—it *was* brilliant.

"The killer could be using the same tunnels." Genie scribbled notes.

"But are we right?" I looked to both of them. "How can we prove it?"

Genie thought a moment. "Give me a minute," she said. "I'm going to phone my brother."

18

AD FUNDUM

The mystifying tradition of making merry with an array of intoxicating (note the root word, *toxic*) substances has apparently been going on since the Yule celebrations of our pagan ancestors. Their Roman conquerors likewise toasted the season during Saturnalia.

—H. M. Hardcastle, *A Modern Yuletide*

Thursday afternoon we assembled in the basement morgue of Genie's newspaper. Funny how it had so swiftly become that, Genie's newspaper instead of the *Tribune*. We were a convivial crowd, and I hated to think that the murderer was after her now, too. Or worse: what would happen if Father found out we were aiding and abetting his nemesis.

Even without dissection equipment, I found this morgue enthralling. Tall shelves held bound issues of the newspaper, going back generations, and huge filing cabinets stored notes, clippings, pictures, and more. Study tables marked it as a room designed for research. It was like a library, but somehow all the more thrilling thanks to its hint of scandals and secrets.

With a sound like an entire herd of out-of-work solicitors crashing down the stairs, Mr. Blakeney arrived, arms overflowing with rolls of paper.

"You would not believe what five shillings will get you in the county records office!" he exclaimed, spilling it all across the table—heedless of the stacks of archived newspapers that were already there. "These are plans for Swinburne, going back—well, practically to the Romans."

Miss Judson eyed the bounty skeptically. "How did you come by these? By which I mean, how *exactly* did you persuade the records clerk to part with it all?"

Mr. Blakeney put a stricken hand to his chest. "I assure you, it was completely above board! I merely said I was on official business, and had been directed to have reproductions made, and vowed that I should return the originals posthaste, in pristine condition."

"Silver-tongued," Genie said. "He always could convince our governesses of anything."

"And why was that necessary? *Genie*, I said, *pristine condition*." Mr. Blakeney snatched a pencil from her grasp, before she could make notes on one of the plans. "All right, girls—er, team—what exactly are we looking for?"

Genie and I grabbed opposite ends of a roll and weighted down the corners. "Anything that connects the Campanile with Leighton's Mercantile and the neighborhood near the museum."

"And the Mansion House," I added. "Where Nora's body was found."

"Splendid," Mr. Blakeney said. "Here's the college." He handed one to me, which I toted over to the table where Miss Judson was waiting. Our map was beautiful. Drawn in the 1860s, it showed a prospect of the main buildings, nestled in prettily sketched trees, the Gothic spire of the Campanile poking out like a watchtower. Hand-inked letters read SCHOFIELD COLLEGE QUADRANGLE & CAMPANILE. The rest of the sheet, which was as big as the tabletop, was covered by a tangle of pathways and intersecting lines. It would take some sleuthing to tease them apart—walkway from roadway from sewer line.

"Look," said Miss Judson, "here are the steam tunnels the carillonist mentioned."

I bent my head and traced them from the Campanile across the grounds to a building marked POWER STATION—evidently the site of the boilers powering the heating systems for the college. "How far do they go?"

We examined the schematic, but it seemed to be a closed network. "The tunnels don't leave the college grounds." I shoved the map away in defeat.

"What, Stephen, giving up so soon?" Mr. Blakeney hefted his own roll of papers at me. "Don't forget, our culprits were archæologists."

"Exactly," Genie said. "They could have excavated connections between tunnels."

"She was *one* college student, not an army of engineers. Do you suppose she's been living under the village all this time, like—" I fought for an analogy.

"Grendel's mother?"* Miss Judson suggested.

"Not a bit," Mr. Blakeney said. "Mother Grendel was nowhere near as industrious as a nineteenth-century English girl! We've bred pluck into our girls in the last eight hundred years."

"Robbie, stop while you're ahead." Genie pushed her sleeves back. "I still think Myrtle's tunnel theory has merit. We just haven't found the connections yet. Swinburne has steam tunnels and catacombs† and sewers and things all over. Look here, for instance." She planted a finger down on the map her brother had been studying. "Drainage sewers running right down High Street. Someone could have used an older system or taken advantage of a weak spot between two networks."

"Good." Miss Judson's voice was brisk. "Find the two termini in closest proximity to each other.

---

* A cave-dwelling monster from the eleventh-century poem *Beowulf*. Although the work has historical significance, I found myself impatient with its protagonist's lack of scientific inquiry.

† I am not convinced she was correct about catacombs.

Schofield's tunnels extend . . . about half a mile to the north. Where does that put us?"

"In the middle of Lake Laverne. Try again, Miss J."

She chose another path leading away from the college. "A quarter mile due east?"

"Oh, that's better." Genie waved her hand to get our attention. "That's within spitting distance of the end of the tramlines." There was a glint in her eyes. "Telegraph wires."

"Where do the telegraph wires go?" I was starting to feel eager again. All over England, telegraph wires were buried alongside train tracks, to keep the train signals running correctly.

Mr. Blakeney had the High Street map. "The tramline goes straight down the street. Assuming the lines for the cables are deep enough, you could conceivably get almost anywhere from there. They have to be accessible, to allow for maintenance of the lines."

Miss Judson had come closer, and now bent over the table with great intensity. "There appears to be a sewer outlet right here, in front of the Leightons' shop. And another . . ." She traced a finger across the map, bringing it to a stop near the museum. "Right here near Aunt Helena's. Exactly where we found Miss Carmichael. The museum must be connected to these sewer lines as well."

I stared at it, pulse racing. "That's it, then," I said, forgetting I was looking for Olive. "That's how the killer's been doing it all—through the tunnels. We have to examine them. There might still be evidence."

"Right-o, then," Mr. Blakeney declared. "I'm always up for a little subterranean archæology."

Genie fixed him in a look of such deep skepticism, it was impossible to mistake their familial connection. "You. In a tunnel."

"I beg your pardon." Mr. Blakeney looked outraged. "I'll have you know that in my association with Hardcastle and Judson, I have survived gunshots, explosions, and the collapse of a seaside Pier. I hardly think a steam tunnel is beyond my ken."

"I think not." Miss Judson's voice was crisp and final.

"But we *have* to! What if the killer strikes again?"

"Remind me, why do we have police constables?" Miss Judson said.

"They're not going to do this! Besides, we promised Father we wouldn't get involved in the current murders. If we notify the police, you *know* what will happen." Word would, eventually, get to Father.

"Exactly."

"What is that supposed to mean?"

"It means I have no intention of granting my approval for such an expedition. I am satisfied that our Investigation may safely—and successfully—be accomplished aboveground, in the open air, in the spirit of open and—"

"Miss J., you're babbling." Genie's voice was gentle—but it broke into Miss Judson's train of speech.

"Babbling?" Miss Judson's eyes grew narrow. "I am not aware that I ever *babble*."

But she had gone even more than usually still, her celebrated composure now less implacable calm, and more rigid—*dread*? For a moment I could only stare at her, slack-jawed, until I remembered to shut my mouth and sit down, like a Young Lady of Quality. This turned my whole orderly world upside down. Miss Judson wasn't afraid of *anything*.

For a moment we all just sat there, no one saying anything. Finally, Mr. Blakeney spoke up. "I believe I have a suggestion." We turned to him, expectantly. "Rather than taking the tunnels from the Campanile into town, wouldn't it be more"—searching for a word, he came up with one guaranteed to woo Miss Judson—"efficient, to start at the destination and work backward?"

I realized what he meant. "Of course! We just need to look for tunnel *exits* near the crime scenes—at Leighton's, and in the square near the Mansion House."

"And wherever Olive Blackwell got to," Genie added.

Miss Judson gradually thawed. "Very well." I could tell she still wasn't enthusiastic about the plan—but she also didn't want it to proceed without her. "We might as well get this over with."

Genie demurred. "I can't today. Deadline on the latest Mrs. Leighton nonsense. Don't worry," she put in hastily. "I won't say anything about this. No tunnel talk at all. I promise." She mimed turning a key at her lips. "But I can wriggle away this weekend. Robbie?"

"Footloose and fancy free," he said. "I'll be there."

❧

We had succeeded in figuring out how Olive Blackwell might have disappeared, but we were no closer to knowing why. As we emerged from the newspaper morgue into the brisk afternoon, Miss Judson and I regarded each other grimly.

"Now what?" I said, flinging my mittened hands aloft. "I feel like we haven't done anything."

This would have been an ideal time to pay a comforting (and inquisitive) call on Mrs. Leighton—but of course she was not at the shop to answer our questions. I sank down upon the newspaper offices' low brick windowsill to sulk, thinking about the workshop underneath all those fascinating Wonders of the Empire.

"Wonders of the Empire," I said softly.

"Hmm?"

I slipped off the ledge. "Can we go to the museum? I want another look at the Saturnalia Chalice." It was the key to everything, that Wonder of the Roman Empire, and we hadn't really examined it properly.

Miss Judson looked relieved by this proposed

expedition, so we set off for the grim brick edifice. In bright daylight, it was not much cheerier than when we last had visited. We chained our bicycles to the iron railing and rattled up the steps to the main doors. The cavernous great hall was hushed and empty, and our footfalls on the marble stairs echoed overloud. The festive greenery had been removed, and the objects looked lonely and bored. And wrong.

"Miss! It's gone!"

The glass case that had held the Saturnalia Chalice was empty. I whirled about in a panic—had they been robbed?

"The plot thickens," Miss Judson murmured. "Let's find out where it's got to."

It did not take long to track down one of the museum fellows, the gentleman who had introduced Miss Carmichael at the gala.

"Well, well," he said. "What can I do for you two ladies?"

"What has become of the Roman chalice? We saw it here the other evening, and were hoping to have another look."

The fellow's face took on a bright and ruddy smile. "You're in luck!" he exclaimed. "It's being moved to the new Leighton Gallery, so we're doing more testing on it. Come—you can see it up close while it's out of its case."

A little thrill went through me, and I couldn't resist

saying, "My mother was on the Expedition that discovered it."

Now he was practically beaming. "Is that right? One of Professor Leighton's students? You'd be a grandstudent, then!" He laughed at his own joke. "In that case, you certainly deserve to see it for yourself. Follow me."

He led us down wide, marble-clad corridors to an ordinary, businesslike door—but behind which, I suspected, lurked all sorts of fabulous secrets. It was almost as exciting as gaining entry to an Egyptian tomb. We followed him into a workshop not unlike our schoolroom at home, with cabinets and paraphernalia and tall windows letting in lots of light. A slight fellow with a stoop and side-whiskers bent over a long workbench, and in his hands he held the Saturnalia Chalice.

"Mr. Smithson is one of the keepers here," our fellow said, handing us off. "Smithson, I have some notable guests who've come to see the Chalice."

Up close—or at least no longer behind glass—the Chalice was even stranger and more wondrous than ever. The aged bronze glowed with warmth, and the figures on its surface seemed almost ready to come alive.

"It's extraordinary," Miss Judson breathed. "Truly remarkable. And to think it sat buried for centuries under a farm field in Cornwall."

"I think it was actually near a tin mine," said Mr. Smithson. "But yes. It's a miracle they even found it."

"Is it heavy?" What must it have been like to see its buried face peeking out from the soil, then the excitement of unearthing it, watching the curves and edges emerge into the world once more? I couldn't help myself, and reached a hand out to touch it. ·

The keeper grinned. "Go ahead," he said. "Bronze is sturdy. You can't hurt it." He handed me the goblet, and it was much lighter than I'd expected—perfectly poised to lift to the mouth in a celebratory toast. I felt strange and tingly, holding it, touching what Mum had touched.

"Beautiful," Miss Judson said. I lifted it to her, and as she accepted it from my hands, I caught a glimpse of its base. Markings were inscribed inside the hollow of the goblet's circular foot.

"What's that?" I asked, pointing them out to the keeper.

"We don't know," he said. "One of the Chalice's many mysteries. They've never been deciphered, but we assume they're some sort of maker's mark. Here— have a look." He rummaged about the workbench for a magnifying lens, to which Miss Judson politely said, "She has her own."

I accepted his, however, and we tipped the Chalice upside down, so it sat on its uppermost rim, and I peered inside the base with the magnifier. Shapes leaped out at me, crudely inscribed lines, begrimed with age and filled with tarnish. But—I tried to wipe away a smudge that someone had missed. Those symbols couldn't be what they looked like. I took a sharp intake of breath, and stared—*stared*—at Miss Judson.

Anxiously, I handed her the magnifying glass, and just as anxiously, she looked for herself, a long, long, very long moment.

"Oh, dear," she said.

Our gazes met. I couldn't speak. I didn't dare. But inside the foot of the ancient Roman Saturnalia Chalice was a symbol I recognized all too well: a tiny dove. And next to that, an ouroboros—a snake swallowing its own tail. Heart in my throat, I followed the symbols around the edge, to an eagle, a laurel wreath, back to the dove. The symbols—the *signatures*—of Jemima, Nora, David, and the rest of Hadrian's Guard.

The Chalice wasn't ancient at all.

19
LORD OF MISRULE

If your holidays seem to pass all too quickly, consider that
at one time, the Christmas season lasted from All Saints'
Day (1 November) to Candlemas (2 February). Certainly
enough of an argument to convince stubborn parents to
let you stay up an extra hour on Twelfth Night.

-H. M. Hardcastle, *A Modern Yuletide*

We couldn't stand there staring at each other in alarm
for very long; the museum keeper would wonder what
was wrong with us. Miss Judson forced herself to smile
and gently but firmly set the goblet down once more
upon the bench. What could we say? What should
we *do*?

"It does take one's breath away, doesn't it?" said
the oblivious Mr. Smithson.

Miss Judson's face was a study in reserved emotions. She held her features perfectly still, but I saw

the passage of worry, consternation, disquiet, and half a dozen similar reactions shift across her cool eyes, before she finally decided how to proceed. "How is the age of an object like that determined?"

Mr. Smithson was busy with his beloved artifact once more, and did not notice our concern. "A number of ways," he said. "First is from the artistic style— it's definitely consistent with other Roman British artifacts of the fourth century. Secondly, from stratigraphic dating—we know how old an object, like a fossil or an archæological artifact, is by the layers of soil it's found in. The Law of Superposition, you know."

Miss Judson and I had briefly studied stratigraphy, how geologists were hard at work across the globe, dating the layers of sediment, rocks, and minerals in the earth. And I understood it as a basic tenet of archæology as well: objects found closer to the surface were necessarily younger than those found below. (Rather like a heap of dirty laundry.) We nodded attentively.

Mr. Smithson continued. "And thirdly, from provenance and provenience."

I frowned at this—provenance I knew from Miss Judson. It meant the history of a work of art or an antique, everyone who had ever owned it and everywhere it had been since its creation. Provenience sounded similar, but I didn't know what it meant.*

* Subsequent consultation with a dictionary revealed that they share the same French origin: *provenir*, "to come from."

"Provenience?" said Miss Judson.

"Ah—it's a word used by archæologists," he explained. "It means the exact details of an artifact's discovery, its location within the dig site, what other items were around it. It's how we understand the context of the find. That's why it's so important not to just yank things out of the ground willy-nilly as was done in the past, but to record every detail of how they were found."

I glanced at Miss Judson. I was afraid I understood the context of *this* discovery all too well. If it was not the ancient artifact Professor Leighton and the others had always claimed, there were so many implications, tumbling up through the strata of years, that I could barely count them all. But they started with Olive Blackwell's disappearance, and ended with Henry Spence-Hastings as Mayor of Swinburne—with at least two murders in the layers between.

Running my finger along the edge of the wooden workbench, I said, "Do you have any more information on the Chalice and its discovery? Maybe the professor made some—erm, notes about these symbols?"

"Unfortunately, no." Mr. Smithson looked up with an apologetic smile. "My understanding was that the professor intended to donate his personal archives before he died, but there's been some—" He made a vague motion with his hand, suggestive of the current

upheaval in Mrs. Leighton's life. "It's a real disappointment—we would love to have all of the documentation
here along with the artifact, of course."

"I see, yes, such a shame," Miss Judson said
smoothly. "Well, thank you anyway."

Somehow we managed to extricate ourselves from
the museum's laboratory without explaining our discovery or giving ourselves away.

"Although we *have* to tell someone," I insisted. We
were huddled beside the diorama of Hadrian's Wall
again, staring down at the tiny soldiers and their
model garrison. It seemed so obvious now. Professor
Leighton had made *all* of these Roman objects—what
was one more, a life-sized one? My thoughts rattled
loose, and I tried to keep my voice hushed, lest these
awful truths echo from the marble walls, before we
quite knew what to say or who to tell it to.

"Nora told me that they never expected to make
a big find in Cornwall. Experts all said there was no
real Roman presence there." I wanted desperately to
pace, but didn't dare move from Miss Judson's side.
For her part, she was frozen in place, hands locked
together at her waist. "They were running out of time.
The Chalice saved Professor Leighton's career."

". . . Until it didn't," she murmured.

My mind reeled. All those things Nora had said,
about how archæology was full of frauds before
Professor Leighton, when *she* was a fraud all along!

I had another thought. "Could they have made it *for* him? To save him? And then slipped it into the dig for him to find?"

Miss Judson's face was set. "That seems a terrible way to repay a beloved mentor. And surely he'd have seen through the ruse?"

I gnashed my teeth (or I wanted to; I wasn't certain how it was accomplished, but it sounded entirely appropriate for the circumstances). "Do you suppose Mrs. Leighton simply didn't have time to turn over the professor's papers, given everything that's happened—or that she didn't *want* to turn them over?"

"I'm afraid we must consider the possibility that she wished to guard this secret just as keenly as her husband had. Perhaps with the dedication of the gallery coming up, he'd decided to come clean, and she put a stop to having their name dragged through the mud again."

"I won't believe it," I said fiercely. I was still stuck on the older mystery. "Olive must have known—or found out—that they'd forged the Chalice, and threatened to expose them all."

"Or she blackmailed everyone, then ran off with the booty."

She was full of horrible thoughts today.

I turned to face her. "The Mayor knows. We *have* to talk to him."

Miss Judson shook her head—and I braced myself

to argue, but she said, "It's premature. We need proof to confront him."

"But it's *obviously* a fake—"

"And it was so obvious that it took twenty years and two amateur Young Ladies of Quality to figure it out? No. They'll never believe us, and the Mayor will have all sorts of plausible explanations. He's had years to come up with them. No one will be able to refute him."

"Because everyone else is *dead*," I muttered.

She fixed me with a chilling look. "Exactly."

❧

That night Father was late for dinner. Again.

I sat alone at the table long after everyone else (even Peony) had left, fiddling with the remains of my meal whilst I pondered the case. What had begun as a straightforward mystery had tightened into a knot of suspects and motives as tangled as the network of tunnels under the town. I glared at my water goblet and absently slid the tall silver saltshaker next to it. A forged Roman chalice had somehow led to Olive's disappearance at the Campanile. And then what? Olive had come back twenty years later to send threatening letters (I tossed my napkin to the tabletop) to Professor Leighton and the Mayor and a young reporter at the local newspaper (the knife rest) who had barely been out of the nursery when she vanished? None of it made any sense.

And what about Mrs. Leighton? I moved over one of the dainty crystal candlesticks with the fluted base. Maybe Miss Judson—and Father, *and* Inspector Hardy, *and* Constable Carstairs, *and* Dr. Munjal were right, and she really was just that desperate to keep her husband's past from becoming a scandal once again.

If so, she'd failed rather spectacularly.

I stared miserably at the objects before me, assembled in an absolutely meaningless tableau. It took all my Exceptional Forbearance to keep from sweeping them off the table in frustration.

"Ho-ho-ho," said a soft voice from the hall. I turned round to see Father in the doorway, face drawn, still in his overcoat and hat, brief-bag in hand. "Is that the remains of Stansberry Pie I see?"

I hopped up. "I'll ring Cook."

Father waved me back down. "Don't bother," he said. "I think I'm too tired to eat."

"*No*," said Peony with alarm, appearing from nowhere. She trotted off to the kitchen, announcing to the household that the master had returned and Second Dinner was required forthwith.

Father came in and sank into the chair next to mine, not even doffing his hat. "What's all this?"

"Nothing," I mumbled.

"Ah. Well, it looks a bit like my desk at work at the moment." He picked up the saltshaker. "Who's this represent, Mrs. Leighton?"

I shot him a look. "No, she's the candlestick. That's the Campanile."

"What's the mustard pot for?"

"Mustard." I pushed it out of the way.

We both regarded the strange Display glumly. "It's a tough one, isn't it, Detective?" he said.

"Do you really think Mrs. Leighton is guilty?"

Father was silent so long I thought he might have fallen asleep, but he finally said, "I can't ignore the evidence, Myrtle."

"*What* evidence?" I demanded. "*You* promised."

"So I did." He sighed and rubbed his whiskers. "Emily Leighton has means and opportunity. She had access to the shop—and, more to the point, the display window—and she could have acquired the hemlock from any chemist. Or any roadside ditch, for that matter."

Not in December, as had been pointed out already. In which case the crime was very much premeditated. "But you don't know that she did."

"No," Father admitted. "We haven't traced the murder weapon to her yet."

I kicked my chair legs and stared long and hard at the stand-in for the Chalice. I should tell Father our theory about the forgery—but I hardly wanted to give him *more* material to hang poor Mrs. Leighton with. "What about motive? Was there insurance money? An inheritance? Did she have a—a gentleman friend?" Father and I both winced at that.

"Not that we know of."

"And Miss Carmichael?"

Father loosened his collar. "Nora Carmichael was last seen entering the basement of the Antiquities Museum. Presumably she was killed there sometime overnight, although the killer left no clues behind that we could find and the exact site has not been identified."

"Mrs. Leighton wasn't at the gala," I reminded him. He had no answer for this. I frowned and pressed on. "You don't think Mrs. Leighton has been sending all those threatening letters, do you? They were written by a woman, but Mrs. Leighton doesn't speak Latin." I hated to think it, but I supposed that wouldn't preclude someone determined enough from copying out a threatening phrase.

Father's sleepy expression had sharpened. "What do you mean 'all' the letters?"

I blinked at him. "The ones that Dr. Munjal and the Mayor and—others got."

He sat up straighter. "How do you know this?"

"From Caroline and LaRue. Didn't they"—I meant the Mayor and the Police Surgeon—"tell you?"

Father regarded the tableau of table settings grimly. "No, they did not."

Which meant the Mayor and Dr. Munjal were still hiding something.

I could not help asking the one question I knew

Father least wished to answer. "Do you think anyone else is in danger? What if—someone else gets a letter?"

"Like who?"

I looked at the tablecloth. "I don't know," I mumbled. "Like you, maybe." Or Genie.

Father tried to be reassuring. "Well, when did the letters arrive?"

"Before you arrested Mrs. Leighton."

"*I* didn't—never mind. The point is, we have a suspect in custody, and no further threats have been made, either by post or in the shop window. I won't say we have all the answers yet, but we are very close to closing this case." He spoke in his most authoritative courtroom voice, like he was giving a statement to a skeptical press.

On those words, Cook arrived with a plate of roast and peas for Father and a second helping of Stansberry Pie for me. As we dug in, I could only wish I shared Father's confidence.

20
SHOP AROUND
THE CORNER

The holiday season is best spent in convivial celebrations
and shared activities with friends.

–H. M. Hardcastle, *A Modern Yuletide*

Saturday morning, we set off as a collective, the three
Investigators: Miss Judson and I–and Peony, who had
refused to be left behind. She followed us to the tram
stand, hopping aboard to the amusement of the con-
ductor, who waived all our fares.

Peony would be insufferable after that.

The Blakeneys were waiting at the High Street
stop. Genie had a pack slung over one shoulder of her
nubby blue jacket (I imagined it stuffed full with ropes
and chalk and pickaxes, just like Olive's must have

been), and Mr. Blakeney had found a magnificent leather miner's helmet with a candle on.

Peony nearly wriggled out of her skin to reach him.

"I see you've brought another associate," Genie said. "May I be introduced?" She held tentative fingers down to Peony, who sniffed at her skirts.

Peony regarded her with wary eyes, then said (predictably), "*No.*"

"Well, hello to you, too," Genie said, breaking into a laugh. Affronted, Peony stalked off in the other direction.

"She took your measure, sis," Mr. Blakeney said.

"Quite right, too," Genie said. "Well, what now? I was thinking Robbie and I could take the college, and you two could explore here in town."

Miss Judson was nodding. "Exactly what I had in mind. Shall we meet back here at—say, half ten?"

"Unless our paths cross before that!" Genie's voice rang with anticipation. I felt it, too, rising in me like steam.

Miss Judson took a final moment to gather us all together and speak to us firmly, like schoolchildren. No one seemed offended. "Now, be *careful*," she said. "There's no telling the condition these tunnels might be in, and it's possible they've claimed lives before."

"And there could be a murderer lurking in them," I put in.

"And that," Miss Judson said.

"*Now* you tell us," said Mr. Blakeney.

"I've brought whistles for each of us." She handed them out, lovely brass things on long leather cords. "Be sure to use them if you run into trouble. Carry a light apiece, and take notes. Blakeneys"—here her voice got especially stern—"your steam tunnels might be dangerously hot. Don't touch any pipes you see, and proceed with caution. I don't fancy explaining to your parents that I lost the both of you in a caving expedition."

"They wouldn't be surprised," Genie said, but she was looking soberly at her whistle. "Thanks, Miss J., this is capital." As she and Mr. Blakeney made their way to the tram, I heard her say, "Miss Kittridge would never have taken us exploring tunnels for murderers."

I watched them go, anticipation ripening to anxiety. We were letting Genie venture into the tunnels, armed only with a whistle, even knowing that the killer (who was using said tunnels to strike silently at her victims) had threatened her. Genie might be unconcerned, but she was taking an awful chance.

The next item Miss Judson produced from her supplies was a sturdy key on a tasseled fob. I thought I recognized it.

"You have a key to the Leightons' shop?"

"Evidently," Miss Judson replied, strolling down High Street to let us in.

"But—?" I knew my next question would have no

answer, but I asked it anyway. "Why didn't you say something? Why do you have it?"

"I promised I'd look after things while Emily was—indisposed," she said. "She gave it to me when we visited last. It seemed prudent."

"It didn't seem prudent before when we wanted to go through her husband's papers?"

Here she looked sheepish. "It might have slipped my mind in the excitement."

I tossed up my hands, hitched my bag higher on my shoulder, and hiked after her.

Leighton's was shadowy and freezing, not at all the warm and welcoming space we'd always known. Peony promptly disappeared behind the counter, no doubt looking for a neglected tin of pilchards. Miss Judson doffed her gloves, then thought better of it and put them on once more.

"Everything seems in order," she Observed. Indeed, the shop was as neat and orderly as it would be on any morning, crocks and tins arranged, labels-out, on every shelf; the Christmas tree in the window still fragrant. Spotting that, Miss Judson was spurred to action, and went to fetch some water for its base, lest Mrs. Leighton return to a wilted tree and dead needles everywhere. I took a moment to Examine the Display window—just in case—but the figurine of Cleopatra still lay in the snow behind the closed baize curtains. I stared down at it; it was like seeing the real Nora Carmichael dead once more, and I fought an irrational urge to cover her up with a hankie.

One sensible thing accomplished, Miss Judson set the pitcher aside and proposed we begin our search in the cellar. Although she did not seem especially enthusiastic about the prospect, and I felt a small disloyal pang that Genie was not on our crew.

We lit every lamp we could find in the workshop—the better to locate any secret passages. I am sorry to report, Dear Reader, that they did not immediately leap out at us, declaring their existence via scrapes on the floor or cracks in the brick walls. Or neatly lettered notices announcing SECRET TUNNEL ENTRANCE: AUTHORIZED KILLERS ONLY. Miss Judson carried a lantern along every wall, shining it behind shelves, as I did the same.

After some twenty minutes of thorough study, we turned to each other once more, faces bearing mirrored expressions of defeat.

"I can't believe it," I said. "It *has* to be here!"

"Your theory was most sound," Miss Judson conceded. "But without proof, I'm not sure what to do next."

"Well, keep looking," I said. "Peony!" Where was that cursedly inquisitive cat when you needed her?

Miss Judson turned her attention to the cartons stored on the shelves. "Perhaps we'll find something among the professor's papers," she said, without tremendous enthusiasm.

I had experienced that side of police work on a previous case, and while I do enjoy research, digging through someone's old records is a thankless task—the very drudgery of Investigation. Not wishing to leave Miss Judson in the lurch, I went to grab a box of my own. But my hand stopped in midair, as I realized something was amiss. Or, more precisely, *missing.*

"Those racks were full of boxes when we were here before," I said. "And there was a footlocker under that shelf." My pulse skipped. "Did Mrs. Leighton get rid of her husband's archives?"

She was frowning now in earnest. "Mrs. Leighton— or someone else."

"The police?" I whispered. "The Mayor! He knew she'd have the only evidence that Hadrian's Guard fabricated the Saturnalia Chalice! He must have cleared everything out when they arrested her." I groaned, knowing that all of the proof was now probably at the bottom of a sewage canal, or feeding the Mansion House boiler.

"Maybe they missed something." It did not seem promising, but Miss Judson was determined to double-check their work, and if they'd been at all negligent, her sharp schoolmistress's eye would find any undotted *i* or uncrossed *t.*

"You keep looking," she said. "I'll make short work of this. The Blakeneys are probably halfway here by now—perhaps *they'll* find *us*."

That was a cheering thought, and I allowed it to bolster me upstairs to check on Peony. I could hear her scratching the floorboards even from down here; returning her shop to her with claw marks in the varnish would be a poor way to repay Mrs. Leighton.

Peony was still behind the counter, where evidently the fish juice had dribbled into the microscopic crack between counter and floorboards. Only it wasn't so microscopic. That was the same spot where the photograph from Cornwall had been jammed. I knelt by Peony, dug my fingers into the panel, and fell back in shock as it popped off easily, tumbling me onto my backside.

"Brrb?"

"Miss . . ." I'm not sure I said that aloud, as I was staring breathlessly into a cavity in the wall—a great gaping hole that had simply had the wooden panel fitted in to cover it. What was it for? Did mercantile shops generally need escape hatches? It must be for storage, or maintenance in the crawl space, for pipes, or plumbing, or mousetraps—although Leighton's had a proper cellar, so this seemed extraneous. I scrambled to recover my lantern, heart thumping loudly in my ears.

I glanced to Peony first. "Mousetraps?" I hazarded.

"*No*," she said scornfully—and I stuck half my body in, lantern first.

It was . . . dark.

The lantern made a warm but largely useless circle of brightness around my arm, and offered little more illumination (literally or figuratively) beyond that. I could not tell if the tunnel went down or outward, or even up. I was about to discover for myself, through the practical experiment of crawling inside, when hands grabbed me by the skirts.

I let out a shriek and dropped the light, which clattered into darkness (down, and at something of a leftward angle) and disappeared, the flame blowing out.

"What in the name of sanity are you doing?" Miss Judson had hauled me out, and the look on her face was well past anger, though she fought for composure.

"I—I found the tunnel?" I said hopefully. "Look!"

"I can see that." Her color was returning to normal, blood warming her face once more. She set about brushing off my clothes with a ferocity that made me think she would really like to give me a proper punitive swat or two. "Remind me, what is hanging about your neck at this moment?"

I put a hand up to find the forgotten whistle. "Oh."

"Indeed. Were you attending to my preparatory remarks at all?"

"But look," I said again. "I found it!"

Miss Judson gazed ceilingward for a long moment—I

think she was mentally counting to thirty in French. Or perhaps sixty. Or seventy-five. At long last, she dropped to a crouch beside me, as if none of the previous moments had come to pass. "Well," she acknowledged, "that is extraordinary." Her fingers came out and brushed the edges of the wooden cabinetry where the panel went. "I wonder if Emily knows this is here."

We test-fitted the panel back in place. Were it not for Peony's ministrations, it would have been easy to overlook the fact that it was removable at all.

"She might not have. But the killer obviously did." I chanced a careful glance at my governess, who seemed fully recovered. "We must have a proper look. We'll need another light."

"Which you shall fetch." Clearly she suspected I would topple headlong into the gap the moment her back was turned. Penitently, I retrieved the second lantern, and together we leaned into the space, from a safe, land-bound distance.

"An experienced mountaineer would have no difficulty with that passage," Miss Judson judged, "although it doesn't seem designed for human traffic."

From what we could see, it was a smallish, iron-clad chute whose purpose was not immediately apparent. A ring of rivets revealed where two sections had been sealed together. "Laundry?" I posited. "Coal? Flour? Empty tins and rubbish?" I submitted it to a robust sniff, but no odors of refuse greeted me. Just cold and damp and a pervasive sort of rusty age.

"Wait—go back, shine the light on the right side there again. What is that?"

That, Dear Reader, was a fleck of something that did not match the rest of the iron-and-darkness interior of the mysterious chute, caught in one of the rivets.

"I think I can reach it."

Miss Judson bit her lip until all color vanished, but ultimately nodded. With the hem of my coat in a talonlike grip, she half lowered me into the passage. I had no trouble reaching my fingers down to the scrap we'd seen.

"Got it," I called, and felt Miss Judson pull me out. I sat back and held our discovery up to the light.

It was a bit of blue wool, like from a nubby jacket.

Genie Shelley's jacket.

"*No!*" Peony cried mournfully.

21
Dux Femina Facti

Much of the work of readying the home and family for Christmas celebrations seems to fall on the women of the house. Perhaps this is why our Italian neighbors have held on to their ancient goddess Strenia, who comes now in the form of La Befana, to sweep the house clean at Christmastime.

–H. M. Hardcastle, *A Modern Yuletide*

We sat and stared at each other for an endless moment, neither of us knowing what to make of the discovery. It seemed so improbable, and yet–

"I told you." The words bubbled out of me, sticking in my throat. "I *said* it was her. All along, she's known far too much about what's been happening. Facts only the killer would know."

And not just facts. It flashed back to me now, belatedly. She also had *paper* only the killer would have—Genie hadn't received a threatening letter. She'd been sending them! No wonder she wasn't worried about it. A hot, sick feeling spread through me, and I felt it creeping up my neck and face. I couldn't believe how I'd been taken in by her.

Miss Judson put a hand on my sleeve. "Genie is Mr. Blakeney's sister," she said with disbelief. "There *must* be another explanation."

"Good," I said. "What is it, then?"

But she was at a loss.

Slowly, with Peony's encouragement, we dragged ourselves to our feet, replacing the wooden panel over the hidden passageway. I felt dizzy. What were we going to say when we met up with the Blakeneys in a few minutes? Ordinarily, I would have confronted my suspect with the evidence against her—but I couldn't do that, not right in front of Mr. Blakeney.

To my surprise, Genie was not at the rendezvous. Miss Judson gripped my hand fiercely as we approached the tram stand, but Mr. Blakeney raised his arm in salute. He was still wearing the miner's helmet.

"Genie's had to run back to the office. Some sort of new lead on the Mayor," he said. "Did you have any luck?" He rubbed his hands together eagerly, blowing puffs of steam from his ruddy cheeks.

Miss Judson and I glanced at each other. "Er—you go first," I invited.

He scratched his blond curls under the helmet's brim. "Well, we didn't get as far as we'd hoped, unfortunately. It turns out the steam tunnels are well known, and until recently were well traveled. They've been locked up to discourage trespassers. We couldn't get past the gate."

"Oh," I said, not sure whether to be relieved or disappointed. Or skeptical—perhaps Genie had known all along that the tunnels were locked at the Campanile entrance. They snaked all over town, after all, and she could have entered the network from any one of the other entrances.

"And what about you, Stephen? How'd you make out?"

Miss Judson—the traitor—let me take this one. "We did find the opening that the—er, that the killer likely used to enter the shop." I described the hatch and the metal chute we'd discovered.

"About so wide, you say?" He held his hands in an approximately-body-sized circle, then snapped his fingers. "I'll bet it's an old pneumatic postal tube!"

"Like in Paris?" Father had witnessed this technological marvel on his visit last fall: a splendid system of pressurized tubes that shot messages across the city along air-powered underground lines. "We have those in Swinburne?"

"I don't think it was ever finished," Mr. Blakeney said. "Too expensive. Even the one in London was abandoned. But they started to lay lines for them in places all over England. We had some of the old contracts back at Ambrose and Belgrave." That was the law firm he'd worked at—Father's old firm, before he became Prosecuting Solicitor. "Decades ago, folks thought they'd be the wave of the future—pneumatic subways, pneumatic streetcars. There were a lot more of them built than you'd think, still lurking about here and there."

"But a person couldn't *hide* in them," Miss Judson said. "You'd suffocate."

"Not necessarily." Mr. Blakeney was warming to a subject I'd had no idea interested him. "The systems use a blast of air, not a vacuum, and there were all sorts of designs proposed—everything from tiny ones just for telegrams, to some large enough for human travel."

Peony was looking skeptical, so he added, "I even heard they once sent a live cat through a network, with no ill effects."

"No." She apparently did not find this evidence convincing.

Seeing Miss Judson and me staring at him, Mr. Blakeney shrugged. "I thought about going into engineering. Somehow the law seemed less dangerous." He tapped the mining helmet.

Olive's escape was seeming more probable—and hazardous—by the moment. "What *happened* to her, though? Where did she go? Why didn't she ever contact anybody? Why didn't she meet up with David?"

"We might never know," Miss Judson said gently.

Well, not without a *thorough* Investigation of the entire tunnel system to look for clues, we wouldn't. But I only grumbled that privately to myself. "Her family might know something," I said—without much hope. My chances of getting helpful answers from the terrifying Blackwells were even smaller than my chances of getting a proper look inside the tunnels, especially now that Miss Judson had *Asphyxia by Pneumatic Misadventure* to add to her list of inherent tunnel hazards.

Mr. Blakeney looked sympathetic. "Genie hasn't had much luck with them, either."

Miss Judson and I shared the same Telepathic revelation. We turned to each other—and then to Mr. Blakeney.

His blue eyes darted between us. "Stephen, I've seen that look on Genie's face too many times. I'm about to be recruited, aren't I?"

"Olive's father might talk to you," I said eagerly. "You're a man, for one thing—he seems very skeptical of Young Ladies of Quality who step out of line. Plus, you're not a reporter or from the police, and you have a name he won't recognize!"

"Er, what'll I tell him? Who will I say I am?"

"With your silver tongue," Miss Judson said, "you'll have no trouble at all."

Trying not to look deflated, Mr. Blakeney said, "Is there anything else?"

"Nothing now. I have to return Myrtle before Mr. Hardcastle gets suspicious." She made that sound like I was a key she'd swiped for some nefarious purpose, no one the wiser. "We'll be in touch," she finished, vaguely.

"Oh. Are you sure?" He looked disappointed. "I've got the whole afternoon free, you know. And the week." His habitual merry tone seemed to falter, and I felt doubly sorry for him. He'd already lost one job to a murderer, and now his sister was a killer, too? The least we could do was give him something useful to do.

"Maybe he could look into the Chalice for us," I suggested. I began to wonder if we ought to keep him on retainer—how much would an Investigative Researcher charge? I probably didn't get enough allowance.

"Good idea," Miss Judson said. "Did you tell him what we'd discovered?"

He held up a hand. "You'd better not," he said. "You know what Genie's like. Solicitor-client privilege can't stand up to an inquisitive twin sister on a story."

Miss Judson and I considered this, but she said, "I think everyone will know soon enough. Tell him."

I took a deep breath, and said the words aloud. "The Saturnalia Chalice is a fake."

I half expected the sky to tumble down atop us all, the way Olive's and Mr. Leighton's worlds had collapsed, but nothing happened. The details tumbled out instead, along with all our speculation about the motive behind Olive's disappearance and the murders. Except–I stopped myself before I could put voice to our new theory of the crime, the one where his sister was busy killing all the members of Hadrian's Guard, for reasons nobody had figured out yet. Even without that part, Mr. Blakeney's blue eyes grew wider and wider, until he gave a long, clear whistle.

"How did the museum take the news? Ah," he said, understanding instantly. "I'll be discreet, then, shall I?" He touched the side of his nose with his index finger. "Very well, I accept the mission. How shall I reveal my findings to you?"

Before Miss Judson could answer, I jumped in. "We could meet at that coffeehouse to compare notes. The day after tomorrow?" It seemed like an eternity, but we had to give Mr. Blakeney time to produce some results. And it would give us forty-eight hours to figure out how to explain Genie's involvement to him, before we had her arrested. Again.

"That will suffice," Miss Judson said. "And Mr. Blakeney—"

He waited, attentive. "Yes?"

"You be careful, too."

∽

That night Miss Judson, Peony, and I sat together in the schoolroom, simmering with disbelief and consternation. And arguing, a bit, about what to do next. I studied the blue wool under Mum's microscope, but beyond an intriguing glimpse at the minute qualities of the fibers (hairy, porous, and squiggly, in a tweedy weave of beige, blue, and grey), it could offer no explanation for its presence in the tunnel underneath Leighton's Display window.

Other than the obvious one.

I was again cursing my carelessness with the *QUÆS-TIO REPETUNDARUM* letters; if only we'd had those, we could compare the handwriting to the samples we had of Genie's penmanship and be certain she was our culprit. Although I shouldn't have been surprised—who else would have old Schofield College letter paper? She had every other souvenir from the year Olive disappeared.

"We should turn the wool fragment over to your father," was Miss Judson's take on the scenario: wash our hands of it, and let Father and the police deal with Genie.

"What about the Mayor?" I said.

"What about him?"

"And Olive? We still didn't figure out what happened to her." I shoved away from the microscope, feeling like we'd failed. Somehow, I'd imagined we'd get to the end of things and all the pieces would fall neatly into place, like the orderly green-brick rectangular cells of a plant. Instead all we had was a hairy blob, tangled up and pointing every which way—except the one we wanted.

Miss Judson came and sat beside me. "You've come closer than anyone has before. You can give her family some closure. Olive ran away, and in all probability it was because she'd discovered the truth about the forged Chalice, and the rest of Hadrian's Guard were threatening her."

"That's all just supposition," I argued. "We don't have any evidence of what really happened." There were still pieces missing. I couldn't just sit here and do nothing. I knew there was still more to learn. The Mayor, at least, could give us the last pieces of the puzzle, if only I could talk to him. Or if I could get into the tunnels myself—both of which seemed nigh on impossible.

༄

As it happened, the opportunity I could not manufacture arrived on its own, in the evening post, in the form of engraved vellum, heavily scented with orange and clove, and delivered with some ceremony right to Father's office by Cook. She'd even unearthed a silver tray (freshly polished) and a pair of white gloves for the occasion.

Miss Judson and I lurked in the hallway as she passed, mouths agape. Well, mine was, and might have stayed thus if Miss Judson hadn't coughed politely.

"The Worshipful Mayor of Swinburne, Mr. Henry Spence-Hastings, requests the honor of your reply, Mr. 'ardcastle," she said.

Father looked up from his work. "Well, well. Bring that on in, then."

"Is that what we all think it is, Cook?" Miss Judson inquired.

Cook stood at the ready, eyes alight as the letter knife was procured and drawn across the wax seal to free it from the thick envelope. For a moment I felt a belated stab of panic—what if the letter was a short note in blotchy Latin? Would Genie come after *us* next?

Father was silent too long. I thought I would burst from the suspense, and Peony uttered a *mrow!* of agonized impatience.

Finally, with nearly as much ceremony as Cook had shown, he held it up for us to see: a small card, one-sided, lavishly printed and embossed, with Father's name handwritten in:

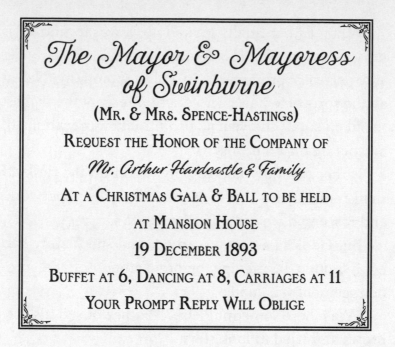

*The Mayor & Mayoress
of Swinburne*

(MR. & MRS. SPENCE-HASTINGS)

REQUEST THE HONOR OF THE COMPANY OF

Mr. Arthur Hardcastle & Family

AT A CHRISTMAS GALA & BALL TO BE HELD

AT MANSION HOUSE

19 DECEMBER 1893

BUFFET AT 6, DANCING AT 8, CARRIAGES AT 11

YOUR PROMPT REPLY WILL OBLIGE

A small cheer went up, although I couldn't say exactly who issued it. I let all my breath out—here at last was my opportunity to question the Mayor.

Assuming Father would let me come.

"And family?" I turned pleading eyes to him. Cook and Miss Judson did the same.

Peony, from her perch in the letter tray, gave a hopeful warble.

Father deigned to speak only to her. Bending to scratch her neck, "I don't believe the invitation extends to felines," he said, with great apology.

Unconvinced, Peony demanded a closer look for herself.

When Father finally looked up, it was to find Miss Judson and me waiting demurely, irresistibly ladylike and perfectly presentable in Polite Company. Not at all the sorts of females who might interrupt the biggest social Event of the year with impolitic accusations of murder against our host.

Father carefully laid the invitation on the desk. "I shall reply forthwith." He returned to his paperwork, and it seemed we were all dismissed.

But Cook's feet were planted, and she plainly had no intention of moving before Father's official pronouncement was made.

"Was there something else?" Father raised his eyebrows and tried to look stern.

"As a matter o' fact, sir, an' I ordinarily wouldn't interrupt your work, but I meant to ask if I might have the night of the twentieth off. Molly Carter—she as is housekeeper at Mansion House—were looking to bring in extra help for the event."

Father clapped a hand to his chest. "But however shall we survive without you for a whole evening? That will mean no stewing chicken, no fillet of sole, no Stansberry pie . . ."

Cook turned red and fought off a smile. "Get on with you, sir."

He relented. "Very well, yes, of course, enjoy your evening with the Mayor."

"An' what about yourselves? Do I need to lay by dinner before?"

"Mr. Hardcastle, if you would kindly put us all out of our misery," Miss Judson interjected.

Father stood up, yawned elaborately, and finally said, "Well, if we won't be fed here, I suppose we'll have to find other arrangements. Yes, we'll all go. I'd better see if my evening suit still fits."

And he wandered off to his room, whistling "Greensleeves," as Miss Judson and I realized that he'd successfully circumvented any potential discussion of the case. He was getting nearly as good at this as we were.

⁊

The merry weather did not last. Monday morning at breakfast, Miss Judson and I were greeted by a sudden winter storm.

"Oh, my god!" came the thunderclap, reverberating through the dining room and rattling the glass in the sideboard. Father was reading—or, rather, scorching with the heat of his glare—the *Tribune*, which had a huge black headline:

MYSTERY OF OLIVE BLACKWELL SOLVED!

MAYOR IMPLICATED IN FRAUD, CONSPIRACY & MURDER

I sat down with a commanding thud, which Father under ordinary circumstances could not fail to notice. Miss Judson's graceful slide into her seat was more than normally subdued.

We did not dare to interrupt. Neither did I dare glance at Miss Judson. My mind was spinning and I felt cold all over. I did not think I could feel any more betrayed, but Genie had surprised me, yet again.

"Mr. Hardcastle?" Miss Judson's voice was at its most tentative and surgically precise.

Father didn't answer. He merely gathered up the newspaper, threw it into the fireplace, and stormed from the room.

In one swift, athletic motion, Miss Judson leaped to her feet to rescue the newspaper. But as with Nora's note at the Blackwells', she was too late. The paper had gone up in flames. Jaw set, she said, "We'll get another copy when we go see Mr. Blakeney." I could tell she was nearly as angry as Father.

"Maybe it didn't say anything about us?" If it had, surely Father would have lingered long enough to immolate us, too.

"We can hope," she said. "But we'd best make ourselves scarce, all the same."

⁓

A surprise was waiting at Woodstein's Coffeehouse. A bespectacled, brown-haired, blue-coated lady journalist had commandeered a booth big enough for a grand jury and made herself at home, with notebooks, newspapers, and the remnants of a meal. She waved us over. Mr. Blakeney sat slumped guiltily across from her.

"Did you see my story?" she cried, before we even made it to the table. "Isn't it perfect?"

"Stephen—" Mr. Blakeney tried to begin, but Miss Judson spoke first.

"*Perfect* may not be the word I'd use."

Genie eyed her, head cocked. "I'd not have pegged you for such a stick in the mud, Miss J."

"Why would you write such a thing?" I cried. "You promised!"

"Can't blame a girl for reporting what she hears." At this, Mr. Blakeney looked even more miserable. We should have taken his advice about not confiding in him.

Genie gave a slimy little shrug. "It worked, though—just see if it doesn't. It'll get the whole town talking, and sooner or later, somebody will slip up and say something. And I *didn't* break my promise," she added. "The story doesn't mention you or your mother by name. Not once." She handed me a fresh copy of the paper, which I flung down unread.

"My father was right about you," I said.

She didn't look wounded at all. "Probably. Now sit down, and let's talk sensibly. I want to know what *you* found out!"

"Actually, you may not." Miss Judson had seldom sounded so cold.

"Genie, what did you do?" There was an edge to Mr. Blakeney's voice.

She shot him a look. "Well, I don't know, little brother. Let's hear what the detectives mean to accuse me of."

I slid into the booth, Miss Judson beside me, so we wouldn't be overheard. Mr. Blakeney deserved that, at least. I dug in my satchel and withdrew the scrap of blue wool, safely preserved in a specimen jar. I had brought it along as a sort of talisman, hoping I would not need to show it to Mr. Blakeney. But his sister's actions had stripped away all my sympathy.

She peered at it with great appreciation, holding it to the light. "What is it?"

"*That*," I said, "is what we found in the tunnel beneath the Leightons' shop window."

"You found evidence? Why didn't you say any-thing—I could have put it in my story. Myrtle, that's splendid!"

"Not so splendid," Miss Judson said.

"That came from *your* coat." As Genie held the jar, I could see how obviously it matched her jacket.

If I'd expected her to give herself away so easily—patting down her sleeves and hem, looking for the tear—I was disappointed. "I don't think so." She set the vial down on the table between us. "There must be hundreds of blue wool coats—or skirts, or scarves, or blankets—in Swinburne. *You* have one," she pointed out.

"Not this color."

"Well, I've never been in the tunnels—Robbie can tell you that."

Mr. Blakeney was looking at his sister with dismay. "Not really."

"Is that all?" Genie sounded wary.

"We know you wrote the threatening letters in Latin. I saw the paper on your desk."

Now her lips spread in a slow, lopsided smile. "There's the clever Myrtle Hardcastle I've heard so much about."

"You admit it?"

"I'll always take the credit," she said. "I work too hard on my writing not to. The chairs at the Campanile were me, too."

Mr. Blakeney, taking this all in, had turned pasty white. He grabbed her by the (blue, wool) shoulder. "Imogen Shelley Blakeney, what have you done?"

She pulled away, nonchalant. "Stirred the pot, little brother, that's all. Kicked the anthill."

"Hit the hornet's nest with a stick? Oh, Genie."

She glared at him. "And why not? All the little ants are scrambling to cover their tracks. It's obvious I'm making everyone nervous."

I was starting to understand—only I wasn't, not

really. "You made them so nervous they arrested Mrs. Leighton!"

Here she looked briefly chagrined. "Those charges will never stick. Especially not when we expose the real culprit."

"You might have gotten Nora Carmichael killed. Or killed her yourself."

She leaned over the table. "No. I sent those silly notes, just to see how they'd all react, but I *didn't* monkey with the shop displays. That was all the killer's doing."

"Maybe you're in on it together."

Her bark of laughter was cut short. "You're serious, aren't you? You think I was involved in the murders?"

"Genie, don't you ever learn? This is what got you kicked out of Elmhurst!" I had never seen Mr. Blakeney so angry. His face was flushed so red even his hair seemed aflame. "You have gone too far this time! What were you thinking!"

"Robbie! You can't believe I'd actually kill somebody for a story!"

"I don't know," he said. "I didn't believe you'd string Headmistress Peabody's Sunday petticoat up the flagpole, or whatever that stunt with the donkey on the hockey field was, either, but here we are."

She rose to her feet. "This is not the same. I'll prove it to you." She dug in her pockets and withdrew a pair of folding scissors on a watch fob. Before our very eyes, she turned up the hem of her coat and snipped out a slice of the cloth. "There. Compare it. Test it. Do whatever you want. You'll see I was never in that tunnel. And I didn't kill anybody."

She gathered up all her things in a messy armload, blinking furiously. Her cheeks were burning and she wouldn't look at the rest of us. But as she shoved away from the table, the last thing she said was, "But I'll find out who did. You can count on it."

22

ADVERSE
CONSEQUENCE

*The selection of Christmas gifts for friends and loved ones
must be undertaken with the utmost care, and if at all possible, planned throughout the year. Waiting until the last
minute is a fatal mistake.*

—H. M. Hardcastle, *A Modern Yuletide*

We sat in numb silence for some time afterward, Mr.
Blakeney staring at the spot that, a moment before,
his sister had occupied. Finally he came back to life,
rubbing furiously at his ruddy face. "I'm really sorry,
Stephen, Miss J. I should have known even I couldn't
trust her."

"Should you go after her?" Miss Judson said.

"Not in that mood," he said. "I'm no fool. Well,
not a complete one, anyway. How much time before

you tell the police—or Mr. Hardcastle—what you've learned?"

"Wait." I was confused. "How come you're not protesting her innocence? Defending her honor, or something?"

"Ah. Therein lies a tale, indeed. But the short version is, I'm all tapped out."

Something in his voice restrained me. Or perhaps that was Miss Judson's hand on my arm. She looked at him gravely and said, "Perhaps you'd better tell us."

I felt sorry for Mr. Blakeney. "Unless it violates solicitor-client privilege." I didn't want him to compromise himself, simply to satisfy our curiosity.

"I'm not aware that she's done anything that would require my discretion," he said stiffly. I didn't know if that made me feel better or not. "But I guess this whole thing started when we were kids. Genie's always been fascinated by the Olive Blackwell story. She saw her as a kindred spirit—a mischievous prankster who met a mysterious fate. When she was expelled from her last school, she set about trying to solve the mystery."

He waved to the server to bring another pot of tea. I had a feeling we were all going to need it. "When she got the job at the *Tribune*, my folks were thrilled that I'd be here to look after her. But when she moved in—" He shook his head. "I couldn't believe how obsessed she'd become. All those clippings we sent you? They don't even scratch the surface. The walls of her room are *papered* with them. William Morris* has nothing on Imogen Blakeney. I didn't know what to think—and then the shopkeeper died, and her stories took off. But I swear I never thought there was any connection. I still don't. There can't be." He turned his stricken gaze to us. "Can there?"

How could we answer that?

Mr. Blakeney dragged himself to his feet. "Well, there must be a fire I should be putting out somewhere. She usually leaves a burning trail in her wake. As you've seen."

Miss Judson's frown deepened. "I hope she doesn't mean to do anything drastic."

His smile returned fleetingly, before vanishing again. "Genie?" he said in mock disbelief. "What in the world would make you think that?" He rummaged in his pockets for some coins to pay for the tea, and found a slip of paper. "Oh, Stephen—I don't know if this is any use anymore, but I did go to the museum to ask around about the Chalice. The curator told me that it was the third time somebody had asked about it in recent weeks."

"Well, one was *us*," I said. "Who was the other?"

"All he could recall was that it was a young woman." Mr. Blakeney looked toward the coffeehouse door,

* the author, artist, and purveyor of arsenic-infused wallpaper

where his sister had stormed off, with a rueful sigh. "I suppose now we can guess who that was."

෴

Miss Judson, Peony, and I spent the evening in the schoolroom, staring at the vial of wool and the sample Genie had given us, sitting untouched on the workbench. Somehow, despite having the evidence and equipment at hand, I could not bring myself to examine it.

"What if it's not the result we want?" I asked Miss Judson.

"Which is what, exactly?"

"Well, that she's not guilty, of course . . ."

Elbows on the counter, Miss Judson said, "Are you asking me, or telling me?"

"Miss!" I wailed. "I don't *want* her to be guilty. But if we look at this, and it turns out that she is—" I flailed a hand. "We'll have to tell Mr. Blakeney, and it'll be our fault."

She eyed me steadily. "You know that's not true."

I nodded. "But it still *feels* like it is."

She put out a hand to meet mine. "I know exactly what you mean. Get out the microscope and let's find out the truth. We don't hide from the evidence—good news or bad."

Moments later, I took a deep breath and slid Genie's sample under the lens, saying a silent prayer to Mum. I'm not even sure what I asked her—something entirely unscientific, no doubt. Without waiting for her reply, I plunged down to the eyepiece.

I gazed through it silently for so long that Miss Judson started to fidget. "Well?" she demanded. "What's the verdict?"

I stared and studied the wool fibers from Genie's blue nubby coat. Like the sample we'd found in the tunnel, it was wiry and kinked, fibers pointing every which way. These strands all looked alike, a deep, even, solid blue, dyed before spinning and woven from the same yarn.* The sample from the tunnel had been tweedy—a mix of colors.

"*You* look," I said, moving aside. I wanted independent confirmation of my findings. Genie's coat had looked the same to the naked eye, but the microscope told the truth.

"Similar," Miss Judson said judiciously. "But not identical."

I let out all my breath. "It wasn't hers."

Miss Judson was less relieved. "Whose was it, then?"

❧

The next day, there was no further story by Imogen Shelley in the *Swinburne Tribune*. Nor did we hear from Mr. Blakeney. It ought to have been a reprieve (Father

---

* Miss Judson's expert artistic determination was that the exact shade was called "Stirwaters blue," although frankly I think she got that from a fairy tale.

certainly took it that way), but I could not help feeling a certain foreboding disquiet.

Father was determined to be in a good mood, however. With the Mayor's party tonight, he came home early, then swooped down on me after lunch.

"I have to pick up my suit from the tailor's," he said (Miss Judson and Cook having demurred from this particular task—the alterations, not the fetching). "I thought we could go into town together. Make an afternoon of it." His eyes kept darting down the mistletoe-strung hallway to Miss Judson's door.

"You haven't got her a present yet, have you?"

Father shook his head. "No, have you?"

I matched his mournful expression.

"That settles it," he said. "This is definitely a matter for two superior Hardcastle intellects. Or one superior intellect, and one solicitor with a wallet."

Happy for the diversion, I ran for my coat, with Miss Judson calling after us, "Be back by teatime! We don't want to be late!"

We headed into town on the crowded tram. The holiday atmosphere had thickened like fog, and three of our travelmates were attempting to outdo each other in a merry medley of semi-identifiable carols. They exhorted us to join, and Father, to my intense embarrassment, obeyed. With gusto. I sank into my coat and pretended not to be related to him.

And fretted. Every blue coat on the tram and in the

street reminded me of Genie and of the killer who'd left the scrap behind in the passageway. Although we'd exonerated Genie from our suspect pool, the way she'd stormed off felt ominous. She'd kicked the Mayor's anthill, as she'd said, and there was no telling what he meant to do next. He'd already arranged to have Mrs. Leighton arrested to keep his own crimes from becoming public. Would he do worse? *Had* he? Shivering in the overheated tram, I was afraid I already knew the answer to that.

I was thus engaged in a roiling circuit of unpleasant and unproductive thoughts, set to the disturbing rhythm of "The Boar's Head Carol," when the tram clanged to a stop on High Street, depositing everyone in a convivial heap in the blustery afternoon air.

"Ah," Father said, clapping his arms round himself. "Bracing!"

I shook myself back to the moment. "Miss Judson doesn't care for the cold," I Observed. It came from being born in the tropics.

"You're right. Perhaps she'd like a nice woolly jumper?"

And thus we embarked upon the Great Quest. With Leighton's still closed, we had to choose from several other Purveyors of Fine Goods from Across the Empire, and we spent a diverting, silly, and increasingly frustrating two hours ducking in and out of various shops. We Considered and Rejected a monogrammed silver card case (too late to have the engraving done); a repoussé desk set (too expensive, despite my lobbying hard on its behalf—I quite fancied the inkwell, which was shaped like a rabbit); and the woolly jumper (too woolly). Also rejected were a globe (too practical), a velvet hat (too *impractical*), and a gothic romance so ridiculous each of us set the book down without comment.

At long last, another shop window caught my eye. Arrayed on a bed of lush velvet were ladies' toilet items: powder jars, hatpins and hairpins, hair receivers, and the other assorted bric-a-brac that littered a dressing table and contributed to the well-turned-out appearance of a Young Lady of Quality. I halted. Father halted beside me.

"Is that ivory?" he Inquired.

"Celluloid." I indicated the sign advertising French Ivorine. "No elephants involved. We studied it last summer, remember?"

Father's moustache twitched. "I seem to recall an ill-fated experiment and a lot of fumes."*

"That's the one!" I tugged on his sleeve. "It's perfect."

"Well, it's better than that hat," he agreed, and hauled open the shop door.

Twenty minutes later we emerged victorious. Or

---

* It turns out that guncotton and camphor are not as easy to homogenize in a kitchen laboratory as one might wish.

at least Father did, having ultimately selected a pair of celluloid combs in a tortoiseshell pattern of mottled brown and amber, guaranteed to reflect the rich dark shades of Miss Judson's hair (and signal to Miss Judson that Father *thought* about her hair, at least occasionally).

"You should give them to her tonight," I said firmly. "So she can wear them to the ball."

He frowned at this. "Then what do I give her on Christmas?"

The shopkeeper had a suggestion for this as well. "The matching hairbrush, of course," she said with a smile, taking more of Father's money.

I had not had Father's luck with Miss Judson's gift (having given him my best idea), but I refused to let that dim my enthusiasm for his choice. The combs were the ideal combination of practicality, beauty, and technology, with an understated elegance that suited Miss Judson perfectly.

I should simply have to keep Pondering. Inspiration would be forthcoming. It had to.

Father consulted his watch. "We have some time yet. Shall we stop for a cocoa?"

While we'd been shopping, the bracing air had turned damp and gloomy, dull grey clouds draping the roofs and chimney pots of the High Street buildings. But I nodded happily, and as we turned toward the teashop, I spotted a familiar figure strolling our way, her fringed cape swishing in the snow.

"That's the carillonist from the college!" I waved heartily. The young woman lifted a vague hand—but recognized me a moment later.

"Why, if it isn't Myrtle! We do seem to keep running into each other."

"We told Father how splendid your recital was," I said—which was patently untrue. Miss Judson and I had, in fact, left out most of the pertinent bits. Like Genie's prank.

"You're too kind," Leah said. "The midnight program was even more thrilling. Even without our duet!" Her merry laugh matched her bells—bells ringing, everywhere she went—until I realized she wore them on the fringe of her cloak, miniature silver sleigh bells, jingling with her every movement. "It was a singular performance, if I do say so myself."

I felt Father waiting for me with mild reproof, and remembered manners. "May I introduce my father, Mr. Hardcastle? Father, this is the carillonist I was telling you about, Miss—" I broke off with a mortified realization. "I'm very sorry, but I don't know your last name."

"How rude of me," Leah said, offering her hand to Father. "I'm Miss Blackwell."

For a stupefied moment I just stared at her, as Leah Blackwell shook my father's hand, my brain skittering back over everything she'd told us. *My father taught Divinity, my mother played the carillon, Olive ran away to a happier life.* Of course. I was embarrassed not to have recognized the family connection.

She and Father chatted easily, and Father made no sign that he was bowled over by the revelation of her identity. Well, why shouldn't Olive have had another sister? We'd seen baby Leah in the family photo, after all. And what possible reason would poor Miss Blackwell have had to confess her identity to the two people who had rudely descended (well, ascended) upon her private sanctuary out of morbid curiosity over her sister's fate? No, I realized—of course she hadn't fully introduced herself.

They were talking about the Mayor's ball. ". . . playing the pianoforte there tonight! I was so honored to be asked," Leah was saying. "Mr. Spence-Hastings was one of my father's favorite students. Father can't attend, of course, but I'll be there for the family. You'll have another chance to admire my work, Mr. Hardcastle!"

"I'm looking forward to it," he said, and I put in: "Miss Judson will be there as well."

"Perfect," she said. "It's certain to be an unforgettable evening! Happy Christmas!"

"Merry Christmas," Father said.

With a final wave, Leah drifted away into the mist, cape tinkling.

Father watched her thoughtfully, no doubt thinking there went the sort of Young Lady of Quality who would never consort with scandal-mongering newspaper reporters and accuse the Mayor of murder. I sighed, but Father didn't notice, merely hooked his arm in mine and steered me toward the hot cocoa.

We never made it.

A fellow was stalking across High Street, forging ahead like an oncoming pneumatic railcar. There was a cacophony of shouting and neighing as a carriage narrowly missed mowing him down. The coachman yanked the horses out of the way at the last moment with a jangle of harness and neighs, which did not quite cover the shouted invectives.

"I say, there's no call for that language," grumbled Father, trying to shield my ears. I shook him off.

"Father, it's Mr. Blakeney!" I broke away and dashed into the street myself—looking both ways in case further carriages threatened. "Mr. Blakeney! Mr. Blakeney!" It was Not Done for a Young Lady of Quality to run after a young man in public, shouting his name, certainly not in such close proximity to her father, but it could hardly be helped. In his current state, there was no telling what misadventure Mr. Blakeney might fall prey to.

"Stephen? Where'd you come from?" he said when I caught him. He looked like he'd been running all over town. His overcoat was unbuttoned, his collar and tie askew—and he'd lost his hat. Again. "Oh, you're

with your father. Good afternoon, Mr. Hardcastle."
He didn't sound like he thought it was very good.

"Young man, are you quite all right?" Father took
in Mr. Blakeney's disheveled appearance and red face
with concern.

"No, not really, sir," he said. "It's Genie—my sister.
She didn't come home last night."

23
NON VERBIS, SED REBUS

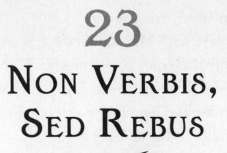

On the subject of gifts, in general most people do not enjoy overly practical items, and it should hardly be necessary to note that while fruit is marginally acceptable (oranges yes, raisins no), new underthings and socks are *never* a welcome thing to find under the tree and should in no wise be considered "gifts."

–H. M. Hardcastle, *A Modern Yuletide*

I did not think I could take more surprises. And certainly Mr. Blakeney was not taking this one particularly well. He shoved and shoved his hand through his hair, red-faced and jaw set. I could practically see the steam coming out his ears. An ugly, wet, spitting snow had started, stinging my forehead, but Mr. Blakeney didn't seem to notice.

"Steady on, lad," said Father. "Explain what's happened. Your sister, you say?"

"Yes, sorry, sir." Mr. Blakeney forced himself to speak calmly. "Genie—Imogen—and I share rooms. We both work here in town, but I haven't seen her since yesterday, and her employers say she never bothered to come in today at all."

Father immediately jumped to the most dreadful conclusion. "Have you notified the police?"

"I don't think she's done anything wrong," I said uncertainly.

Father looked at me oddly. "Something might have *happened* to her."

I fought the urge to grasp Father by the arm. Not too many months ago, a situation chillingly similar to this one had played out, very near here. But then, it was me telling Mr. Blakeney that Father hadn't come home.

"I doubt that, sir. I'm more concerned about what she might have got herself into."

I took charge. "Do you have any idea where she might be? Where were you going, just now?"

Mr. Blakeney gestured vaguely down the street. "I thought I'd try Leighton's, on the off chance she's gone there."

"Good idea," I said. "We'll come too."

Father frowned, obviously wondering who this wayward girl was who would be frequenting a closed shop. "Do you know this . . . Imogene, Myrtle?"

"Imogen," I corrected unthinkingly. Was this the moment to tell Father I'd been fraternizing with the enemy? But Mr. Blakeney struck off, dodging shoppers and moving at such a pace we were hard pressed to carry on any sort of conversation—let alone one so fraught with self-incrimination. I held my tongue.

We soon assembled before the dark and shaded shop. Miss Judson still had her key, and there was no sign that Genie had broken in (although I would not put that past her—picking locks seemed just like something she'd know how to do). I checked to see whether the hatch over the pneumatic tunnel had been opened.

But my gaze stopped at the Display itself, and held there. "Oh, no."

"Stephen, please tell me you didn't just say, 'Oh, no.'"

"I'm with him," Father said, as they joined me at the window. The three of us looked down together, into the model streets of Swinburne, and at the newly rearranged tableau of miniatures.

"Oh, no," so said we all.

In the shadow of the olives and the wishing well, a figure was awkwardly laid out on the stone steps of the Town Hall, surrounded by lead Roman soldiers. A red cloak spread down the steps beneath him like a pool of blood, a tiny dagger nearby, blade bathed in red. All across the figurine's body were slashes of red paint—stab wounds. I didn't need to count them, but I did anyway. They were all there, in ghastly miniature perfection.

"Twenty-three," I said, cold and sick to the very bone.

"What?" Father's head jerked up.

"Julius Caesar was stabbed twenty-three times," I said woodenly. "Caesar, the red robes, the Town Hall . . ." I almost couldn't get the words out. "She's going to kill the Mayor."

Their eyes swung toward me. "Or he," I back-tracked. I was staring at the olives and the well.

Father caught me by the shoulders. "*Who's* going to kill the Mayor, Myrtle?" Unspoken behind that, but brimming sadly in his blue eyes, were the words, *You promised. You promised me.*

"I didn't mean to," I said, voice barely a whisper.

"Er—sir, I think she might mean my sister."

"What? Why should your sister want to kill the Mayor?" Father had a hand to his forehead, looking headachy.

"She doesn't!" I cried.

"She wouldn't," Mr. Blakeney said. But now that he was staring at the figure of Caesar, bleeding out on the steps of the Town Hall, he didn't seem at all certain.

"Will someone *please* explain what's going on!" Father was clutching the garment bag with his suit like it might shield him from danger.

For the first time in my life, I didn't know what to say. I stared at Father, then at the Display. Despite everything—even finding Mum's letter and mapping the tunnels—I hadn't *really* believed that Olive Blackwell could have come back to Swinburne to kill Mr. Leighton and Miss Carmichael. The Mayor just made more sense. Or the Mayor, somehow making it look like Olive. Or even Mrs. Leighton.

But this latest tableau shook all other theories to ruins. We'd cleared Genie with the wool. Mrs. Leighton was in jail. And the Mayor was the next target.

That only left Olive.

Mr. Blakeney recovered first. "It'll take too long, sir. Time is of the essence, if we mean to save the Mayor. The other Displays occurred shortly before the victims' deaths."

Father rubbed his whiskers. "Very well. Let's bring the police in."

"Shouldn't someone warn the Mayor? Everyone in Swinburne will be at his house soon!" I certainly did *not* say, *including the murderer*—but Father heard it anyway.

For a moment, he stood locked in indecision, gaze darting from the Display to the police station up the street, to the direction of the Mayor's nearby Mansion House residence. I seized the moment.

"I'll go." I launched myself onward before anyone could stop me. "You summon the constables!"

I heard them behind me—a low grumble that was Father protesting, and then Mr. Blakeney coming to my rescue. Or perhaps Father's. "I'll go with her, sir. Tell the police about my sister, too. Imogen Shelley's her name."

I was fortunate enough to be out of earshot before Father could respond to that.

℘

Mr. Blakeney huffed to catch up, but I was small and spry and motivated to keep some distance between us. Eventually, though, his longer limbs got the better of me.

"Whoa, there, Stephen."

I slowed down enough for him to fall in beside me. We trotted awhile in silence before my mortification broke through. "I didn't want your sister to be a murderer." I explained how her jacket had exonerated her. "I'm glad it's not her."

His laugh shouldn't have surprised me, after all this time. "Believe it or not, that's one of the nicer things she's been accused of." He shook his head. "She brought this on herself. Don't let it bother you."

How could I not? "She's missing, maybe doing something mad, and it's my fault."

Mr. Blakeney stopped in his tracks, catching me by the arm. "No, Stephen. Whatever Genie's got herself into this time, it was not your doing. She's responsible for her own actions. If she'd only owned up—" He broke off, ruffling his hair. "I sound like our father, talking to *me*. And now I'm giving you the same lecture. Guess the old man must have been right all those times. Funny, that."

It didn't sound funny, and Mr. Blakeney only seemed sad.

"We'll find her," I vowed—although it sounded as hollow and chilling as the Campanile bells. "Where could she be? After, erm—kicking the hornet's nest? Did the hornets get her?" Had she gone after Olive, only to— I couldn't finish that thought.

A cloud flitted over Mr. Blakeney's face, but he shook it away. "Genie?" he said heartily. "Hardly. Wherever she is, I'm sure she's having a laugh."

I eyed him sidelong. He *sounded* sure.

The snow was growing thicker and wetter, slick over the cold pavement and brick streets. Heads bent against the wind, we sped the rest of the way to the Mayor's house.

We rounded the corner right into a crush of delivery wagons and carriages and servants making last-minute adjustments to the decorations—greenery and flocked ribbons and shiny silver bells bedecked every surface of the Mansion House. The poor building looked ashamed of itself, showing off before its stately, well-behaved neighbors.

Mr. Blakeney and I clattered through a pair of maids fruitlessly brushing fresh snow from the stairs, who stopped and bobbed to us. Mr. Blakeney gave the brass knocker several furious raps.

The door swung open, revealing LaRue Spence-Hastings in a red velvet ball gown—bare shouldered, hair half up and cascading down her neck in holly-hung curls.

"You're not supposed to be here until the dancing starts."

"I don't care about your stupid party. The killer is going after your father next."

She stepped back, arms folded across her chest, crushing the swags on her dress. "You're just trying to scare me. We saw them arrest the killer last week."

"I'm afraid she's right, Miss—" I didn't give Mr. Blakeney time to finish.

"Yes, I'm trying to scare you! The *killer* is trying to scare you. She's already struck twice. First Socrates, then Cleopatra—and now Caesar!"

"You're delirious." LaRue started to shut the door in our faces.

"And you're a stupid, stuck-up cow!" Agreed, Dear Reader. That might not have been my crowning achievement in persuasive rhetoric.

Fortunately, we'd drawn attention. Faces appeared in the hallway behind LaRue—I spotted Mrs. Spence-Hastings, dressed as a sort of Snow Queen, in glittering white and silver, and a couple of anxious servants.

"Here, now, what's all this? LaRue, darling, you

shouldn't be answering the door; that's the butler's—
Oh." Mayor Spence-Hastings found his way to the
threshold. "Dear me, it's young Miss Hardcastle, isn't
it? And who are you?"

"Blakeney, Mr. Mayor."

"You two look like you've had a fright. Best come
in and get warm."

"Father!" LaRue screeched.

"Henry!" echoed her mother.

"Mr. Mayor, you need police protection, and you
should probably call off the ball."

"Impossible! Deerborn, send them away before
our guests see them."

"Don't be foolish, Eva." Mayor Spence-Hastings
stepped out onto the stoop, getting snow on his freshly
waxed floor, and his freshly shined shoes, and drew
us inside.

I was temporarily overpowered by the attack of
Christmas from all sides. The greenery outside was only
a starter course, and if there was a pine forest anywhere
in England that had not been sacrificed utterly for this
affair, it should surprise me greatly. The evergreen scent
was suffocating, and Mr. Blakeney had to duck beneath
a branch to get inside, dislodging at least one pine
cone. At least before Olive could reach Mayor Spence-
Hastings, she'd have to risk being smothered or stabbed
or buried with a stake of holly through her heart.

"Now, you'd better start from the beginning."

I bit my lip and looked at the crowd of spectators. "You might not want anyone else to hear this, sir."

"We're not going anywhere." Mrs. Spence-Hastings glared at me. "Whatever you have to report, do so immediately."

"Eva, please. Take LaRue and make sure that the musicians know the menu."

That directive made no sense, and in his distraction the Mayor didn't seem to realize it—but his wife certainly realized she was being dismissed. She and LaRue turned and marched out, like a pair of ruffled turtledoves. The Mayor led us into a side room heavy with the scent of old fires and stuffy chairs.

"Please, tell me what's happening." He seemed anxious, face drawn and damp. I looked to Mr. Blakeney for support.

"Sir, there's been another scene in Leighton's display window. The assassination of Julius Caesar."

The Mayor—pale already—went downright ashen. *"Et tu, Brute?"* The words were barely a whisper.

It was so hot in here I felt feverish, my previously frozen skin prickling. "You *know*," I whispered. "You know who's killing everyone!"

"Shh! No, not really. It's impossible . . ." His colorless eyes darted nervously about the room, and I almost felt sorry for him. He really did look like all he wanted to do was escape from everything—from the killer, from the post as Mayor, from his wife and daughter, and from his past. He unfastened his robes and slumped into the armchair. "It's some dreadful person, playing a horrible prank."

"Murder isn't a *prank*."

"No, no, of course not," he said. "I mean, pretending to be Olive. She's been gone for twenty years now. She *must* be dead. She must be!"

"Perhaps you should tell us what you know, sir." Mr. Blakeney had stationed himself before the great door. I was not certain his lanky frame would be enough protection against the killer, if it came to that, but I was glad to have him at our backs.

"Why is Olive Blackwell after you?" I pressed. "Because of the Saturnalia Chalice? We know it was a forgery."

He glanced up sharply.

"We saw your signature," I said. "From Hadrian's Guard."

"Ah. This whole sorry business has gone too far."

"Olive threatened to expose you."

The Mayor nodded. "She'd already written to the board of governors. They would take her seriously— her father was a respected faculty member."

"So you had to get rid of her?" said Mr. Blakeney.

"It was Nora's idea," the Mayor said. "But we were all to blame. We just wanted to scare her—let her know the *Cohortis* weren't to be trifled with, that she'd have to defy all of us if she went forward with her accusations."

"How did you get her up to the tower?" Mr. Blakeney was asking all the sensible questions this afternoon.

"Told her we'd make her a full member, privy to all the secrets and privileges of membership in the Guard. It really was the key to success in those days, you know. Guard members went on to great careers. My own father—" He cut short his reminiscence with a shake of his head. "We thought we could bribe her, appeal to her loyalty."

"So what happened?"

He stared into the fireplace, face sweaty.

"Mr. Mayor, you have to tell us," I said. He wasn't under any legal obligation to make a confession to the Prosecuting Solicitor's daughter and an out-of-work legal clerk, but I was hoping to appeal to his decency. And his long-simmering guilt. He must have wanted to unload these crimes to someone.

"I don't know," he said. "And that is the God's honest truth. We put the blindfold on her, we were chanting, and then—she was gone. I—I always thought Nora must have pushed her, somehow. But where did she go? When we didn't find her body, I didn't know whether to be relieved or scared."

Mr. Blakeney appealed to *my* sense of decency. "You'd better tell him, Stephen."

The Mayor's head jerked up. "Tell me what?"

"We think Olive escaped. Through the steam tunnels."

For a moment he looked wildly relieved—but a shadow crumpled his features. "Oh, heavens. It's really true, then—she's coming for me?"

Mr. Blakeney nodded. "It appears so, sir."

"All right, let's think this through." The Mayor rose, patting his thinning hair with a nervous hand. He looked older than the rest of them, I realized; tired and worn down and ready for this all to be over. Although not, I supposed, with his murder. "We're safe for now."

"She can get *anywhere*," I said. "She's been using the tunnels under the town. There's a hatch inside Leighton's for some kind of pneumatic tube—"

"Pneumatic tube, you say? Of course! Oh, clever girl." His mouth twisted in an expression that was half smile, half grimace. I didn't think he meant me.

"You know about it?" Mr. Blakeney seemed surprised.

"Know about them? Why, I designed them!" He managed a small laugh. "Thought I'd be one of the great engineers of the age. I convinced my father to invest in a trial system for a pneumatic railway of sorts—a way to deliver not just messages, but parcels. In fact," he said thoughtfully, "the line terminates in this very house. Father's business partner lived here then. Thought it was a good idea. It never did quite work, however. Couldn't get the pressure right; the seals kept breaking. Pity."

"That's how she's going to get in!" I cried, but the Mayor was shaking his head.

"Impossible," he said. "It's too small. The aperture here would never fit an adult. She'd have to find another way in. And we're surrounded by constables now, thanks to you."

Indeed, we'd heard the clanging of the bells on the police wagons as they approached.

"That must be Father!" I said with relief.

A clattering of hoofbeats and the eerie jingle of sleigh bells cut through the falling twilight. At the same moment an obsequious butler rapped on the study door. "The guests are arriving, Mr. Mayor."

"Ah, thank you, Deerborn." Turning to me, Mr. Spence-Hastings said, "It seems our time has run out."

"You can't mean to go out there," I said.

He shrugged on his Mayoral robes. "What choice do I have?"

Wildly, I groped for ideas. "Someone else can wear the robes—Mr. Blakeney! Smuggle you out in disguise!"

"Stephen?"

The Mayor looked sad and amused at the same

time. "Something out of a penny dreadful,* I'd say. No, I can't put anyone else in danger." He clapped Mr. Blakeney's shoulder. "Wouldn't want our killer to mistake someone else for me."

I was touched, and surprised. "That's quite noble of you." I doubted very much LaRue or Mrs. Spence-Hastings would be as selfless.

"Not at all," he said, drawing himself up stoutly. "There are a number of police constables and officials here tonight; I am in their capable hands, and Miss Blackwell—if indeed that is who she is—will not strike tonight."

"But—" I was torn with indecision.

"I would like *you* to do something for me, if you will. Please get LaRue to safety."

I groaned inwardly, but when I was a police Investigator, I would have to take disagreeable assignments all the time. I stood up smartly at attention. "Of course, Mr. Mayor. But where can we go?" Outside, the snow was falling thicker than ever. Soon it would be too dark and treacherous to leave on foot without risk of freezing, and the street was too crowded to get away by carriage.

The Mayor had come to the same conclusion. He sized me up with one careful look—and, Dear Reader,

* **Billy Garrett No. 4:** *The Counterfeit Queen*

that turned out to be exactly the right expression. It seemed that Henry Fairbush Spence-Hastings still had some radical engineering ideas bouncing around in that balding head.

"An *adult* won't fit in the pneumatic tunnel," he said. "But you would."

24

Un Flambeau, Jeannette, Isabelle

Should you find yourself short on gift ideas, the following items are appreciated by nearly everyone: Camera equipment, books (the thicker the better), ~~a subscription to *The Strand*~~, a typewriter, fountain pens, fine writing paper, anatomical models, or a telephone. Biscuits and chocolate are also acceptable.

–H. M. Hardcastle, *A Modern Yuletide*

Dear Reader, I shall spare you the whining and protestations set forth by LaRue Spence-Hastings in the wake of her father's suggestion that she not only miss the greatest social triumph in her family's history, but that she do so in the company of Morbid Myrtle Hardcastle, and on such an inconceivable expedition as crawling through a tiny subterranean passageway.

We had gathered in the already crowded kitchens, where the bustling staff (including Cook) stopped to regard us with no little surprise. The hatch for the pneumatic tube was in the butler's pantry, a brass-bound circular window like a ship's porthole. It was much smaller than the passageway we'd seen at Leighton's. The killer would have to find another way in. The pneumatic tube was not the Mansion House's only Technological Marvel: I also Observed an array of household signal bells and the speakers for an internal message service. It was so unfair that LaRue should live here; she had no appreciation for the devices' mechanics.

The Look she was giving her father and me now made it plain that her resentment for them would last a lifetime. I hesitated, hoping another alternative would present itself.

Mr. Blakeney seemed to be thinking the same. "Are you sure, sir? This all seems a bit drastic."

"Nonsense, it's perfectly safe. This line goes due west to the Town Hall. Just a hop, skip, and a jump from the police station."

I glanced at Mr. Blakeney—neither of us wished to note that the death of Caesar had been staged on the steps of the model Town Hall. I could only hope the lack of a figure representing Julia Caesaria meant that LaRue was not among Olive's targets. There was no telling how far her revenge would spread.

Mrs. Spence-Hastings was livid. "Really, Henry, this is too much!" she fumed. "We have *guests*—the Bishop is here from Upton! And you're sending our daughter into the sewer? Have you lost your mind?"

He squeezed her by the shoulders. "I am, and I have not. I'm thinking more clearly now than I have in some time. If I thought you'd fit, I'd shove you down there as well. I've explained the situation. These girls have pluck, and they'll be quite safe. Unless you'd rather they toddle off in a snowstorm?"

"I'd rather you come to your senses!" She might have convinced him, if at that moment their argument had not been upstaged by a disturbance from the kitchens.

Frantic banging shook the back door, so loud we could hear it in the next room. Mrs. Spence-Hastings let out a ladylike little scream, and the Mayor bundled LaRue to his chest. She didn't even object. Cook bustled to the door—but it flew open in her face, and a white-faced figure plunged inside, snowy wind blowing all around.

"I—I saw her!" gasped the young woman, fair hair piled atop her head, eyes wide as dinner plates. Leah Blackwell hugged a battered music case to the breast of her long blue cloak. "My sister—it's her. It's really her. Olive."

Cook slammed the door soundly, bracing herself against it like she'd been hired for extra security, and

Mr. Blakeney helped Leah to a chair. "It's all right, Miss. The police are on their way."

She nodded faintly, still trembling.

The Mayor stood by the portal, gripping the door-frame to the butler's pantry. What little color he'd had drained from his face, and his red robes stood out stark and gruesome. "She's here?" He shook himself. "She's here. Miss Hardcastle, please. Go now. Take LaRue. LaRue, *don't argue.* I could not bear it if something happened to you because of me."

"But–" She faltered, but something in her father's expression seemed to communicate our urgency. She reached into a cabinet and withdrew two bull's-eye lanterns and lit them. "Don't drop yours," she snapped, and climbed headfirst–red velvet gown and all–into the iron tunnel.

With a gulp and a silent apology to Miss Judson, I followed.

Dear Reader, the thrill of crawling through a pneumatic parcel tube is short-lived. Perhaps it was the company, but we had barely made it ten feet before LaRue's complaints had worn thin.

"Where's your taste for adventure?" I muttered– and I'm not sure who I was talking to.

The passageway was dark, freezing, narrow, and surprisingly smooth–I supposed it would have to be, to carry parcels swiftly along a gust of air. The Mayor had been correct: no full-grown human could have squeezed through. There was barely room for LaRue's dress.

"This . . . gown . . . cost . . . fifteen . . . guineas," she grunted. "I . . . will . . . bill* . . . you." But she gripped her lamp and crawled, one-handed, steadily forward. I could see nothing but her backside and heels, and the waver of her lamp, like the tail of a glowworm. Mine bit into my fingers as I inched along, wriggling down ironworks that hadn't seen the light of day in—well, ever.

"How far is it?" LaRue called back. The close surroundings swallowed up her voice, giving it back in a muffled hush.

A hop and a skip? Had we gone a full jump yet? "Not far now. Just keep going."

"How will we know when we're there?"

I didn't answer, but LaRue kept talking. "What if we get lost? Or suffocate?"

Asphyxiate, I corrected silently—we'd die breathing our own carbon dioxide. For all the difference it would make.

"We *won't*." Although she raised excellent points I myself was trying not to consider. "Your father said the tunnel goes straight there."

"Why is this even here?" she wailed. "Why is this happening to me?"

---

* At least, I *think* she said "bill."

Because your father participated in a dastardly crime in college and has been covering it up for twenty years and his victim is back for revenge. I credit the exertion of crawling and holding the lamp and trying not to burn myself, and of being grateful that I could not strangle LaRue from my current position, for not saying that aloud.

It was very much like snaking through an iron catacomb, and I tried not to think about what Olive must have gone through, doing this after scaling down from a tower window. The Town Hall had to be close now—and if we just hung on, we'd be there soon.

Finally, after breathless and endless minutes, hours, or weeks, I heard LaRue's sob of relief. She pushed her light forward, and I thought—I hoped—I Observed a faint widening of the glow.

"I see it!" she cried. "There's an opening!" She scrambled to gain speed—no mean feat—and within moments her crawl had become a crouch, and she peeled herself half to standing in the mouth of a much larger tunnel. "I have to jump down," she said, and did just that.

My own exit was not quite so graceful, and I landed on LaRue's velvet train. She made no response. My light had gone out when I fell, but LaRue held hers aloft, and I could not see her face. I did not need to, to know it bore an expression of dismay.

We were not, by all evidence, at the Town Hall.

The iron tube had dropped us into a network of

other tunnels, with corridors branching off in several directions.

"What happened?" LaRue said. "Where's the rest of it?"

I stared at the orifice we'd come down from, a bare circle of metal hanging overhead, jutting out of the brickwork. "Your father said they never finished the system . . ." My words trailed off uselessly. Were we stranded down here?

LaRue took a sharp breath. "Which way do we go?" she whispered.

"West?" I said.

She turned to me. "Which way is *that*?"

I was trying not to let her anxiety infect me. I fumbled with my lantern while I fought for an idea. "I should have brought the map."

"You have a *map*?" LaRue's voice rang from the bricks.

"I've *seen* a map," I admitted. "And it wasn't very helpful." If we couldn't fix our position and navigate, we might wander for miles under the city. *Think, Myrtle.* There had to be some way to figure this out.

I had matches in my specimen kit, so I dug in my satchel, searching. LaRue hugged herself with her free arm. Her bare arms and neck and shoulders must've been half frozen. Above us, anything could be happening. Was Olive really at the Mansion House? Would Father and the police stop her in time? By the time we emerged at the Town Hall, our fathers would be there waiting for us, Olive arrested and everyone else safe and sound. And Miss Judson and Mr. Blakeney. And Cook. With blankets and cocoa.

The thought was cheering.

If only I believed it.

LaRue's teeth were chattering, and I had an urge to doff my coat and drape her in it, chivalrously. But she'd locked me in a morgue, so I kept it to myself.

Then I heard Miss Judson's phantom voice chiding me.

"Do you want my coat?" I mumbled—and her murderous expression was all the answer I needed.

"Now what?" she demanded. "You must have some idea."

"Of course," I lied. "Be quiet a minute while I think."

We could not be *that* far underground—how thick was a street? I recalled that the pathways at the college had been clear of snow thanks to the heat from the steam tunnels below them. Perhaps that could help us now. Was one direction *warmer*? Where had we decided that the steam tunnels connected with the sewers? That must be nearby. A wisp of icy air zipping overhead suggested that one of the sewer grates was not far off.

"I think I hear something," she whispered. "Above us? Traffic?"

I strained to listen, and she was correct—there was the faintest rumble overhead. "It's the tram!" I cried. "Oh, *brilliant*, LaRue! The tram runs straight down High Street. We just need to follow the line, and it will take us somewhere we can get out. There's a hatch at Leighton's."

She regarded me silently for a long moment. "The killer used that?"

I nodded.

She squared her shoulders. "Fair enough," she said. "Which way?"

I got my light relit, and together we searched the tunnel ceiling for signs of the tram tracks above. "I don't see anything."

"Then *listen*." We trained our ears to the faint rumble—which was getting louder.

"It's coming closer!" My voice was eager. "There!" As the rumble reached its peak right above our heads, we could trace its route over the central corridor. "That way!" I nudged LaRue, and with a cry of relief, she stumbled forward.

It was not that easy, however. Trams ran infrequently at night, and we would not have another one to guide us. "We need to make sure we don't get lost."

"Do you have a spool of thread? Like Ariadne?"*

* the mythical Cretan princess who—along with her thread—helped Theseus find his way to the center of the Labyrinth to kill her half brother, the Minotaur, and escape safely once again

Did I *look* like I had thread? "I have chalk. We can mark the tunnel walls so we don't accidentally backtrack." If we survived this, I would make certain Miss Judson never learned that one of her dastardly sewing implements might have saved us sooner.

It was easier going than the pneumatic tube had been. The tunnel was large enough to stand in, for one thing. But a slick of ice ran down the center of the passage, and in places it had filled up with drifting snow. I tried to consider this a hopeful sign—there was an aperture to the surface, somewhere. We just had to find it. I shone my light against the wall, making marks with my chalk every thirty paces—nice big *M*s and arrows pointing in the direction we'd headed. So some archæological team a hundred years from now could trace our path and find our bones.

I stumbled into LaRue, who squeaked with annoyance.

"Sorry," I mumbled. "What's wrong?"

"There's another fork." She held up her light, and again we were faced with the awful choice. The tunnel spread out in two branches, left and right. Wherever we'd been going, following the High Street tramline, we'd come to the end of that road.

This time, LaRue didn't bother trying. She just flung herself to a seat at the junction—right in the patch of ice—and said, "That's it. I give up. You go on, I'll wait here."

For a moment I didn't argue with her. I'd been running about outside all day—first with Father, then with Mr. Blakeney, and now with LaRue. I'd never got my cocoa with Father, and I'd missed teatime, and Cook wasn't even at home to make my supper. I wanted to sit down with LaRue and cry.

But professional Investigators do not give up, and they do not (generally) cry in the middle of Investigations. I had to forge onward—and hang it all, LaRue was relying on me. I didn't particularly *want* to save her, but I had to.

"Not so fast." I reached out a hand, which she took unwillingly, and hauled her to standing. "We're safer together. And *smarter*," I added grudgingly. She'd thought of marking our path, and she'd heard the traffic overhead. "Now, listen again. What can we hear?"

This time, there was nothing overhead. Had we gone lower underground? Or beneath buildings? I glanced about for signs that the temperature was increasing and we were nearing the college steam tunnels.

Instead, what we heard was a faint and distant whimper.

LaRue grabbed me with clawlike fingers. I was slow to shake her off. "What was that?" she gasped.

"Probably just rats," I said—not realizing how LaRue would take this. Well, not *immediately*. I might have known by the time I actually said it out loud—but there is no way of proving that, Dear Reader.

"Rats!" She gripped me harder, and I tried to pry her hand from my coat sleeve.

"Calm down. They're just hungry."

I know what you're thinking, Dear Reader, and I'll admit it. I was enjoying myself, just a very little bit. Every condemned prisoner gets a last wish, after all.

"Maybe it's Olive," I said, in a spooky voice.

She released her grip. "You," she said coldly, "are not funny." Snatching up her lantern, she stalked off down one of the tunnels, totally at random.

Almost at once, it was plain that LaRue had chosen poorly. The wide, modern, bricked-in tunnels narrowed and aged; the path crumbled into awkward dips and turns. "What is this?" she said. "It's not the sewer anymore, is it?"

"Maybe where they abandoned the pneumatic tube?" Mr. Blakeney could probably tell us.

"I don't think this is the right way," LaRue said doubtfully. She held up the lamp and took a few tentative steps forward, to where the tunnel abruptly curved into darkness. "Oh," she said. "I think I see something."

I was close on her heels. She had found another tight, twisty passage that could not have been on any map, and her light barely penetrated the gloom. A tangle of roots and ivy had grown through the masonry, evidence that we'd gone under a lawn or some wooded area. I tried to think where that might be, as LaRue continued forward, shoving roots away from her face. "It's a door!" she cried—an aged wooden hatch set into a packed-earth wall. "Is this a root cellar?"

She pulled on the ancient wood, but it wouldn't budge. "Help me!"

I reached in, and together we tugged and pried and wrenched, and eventually were rewarded with a faint groan. Gritting our teeth, we gave the door an almighty yank, and it cracked apart, spilling us backward.

And not just us.

LaRue gave an almighty shriek.

25

SOLVITUR AMBULANDO

Before considering a so-called *qaq* gift, be absolutely certain the recipient shares your sense of humor. How unpleasant to be anticipating a box of chocolates or a lovely new storybook, only to open the box to find . . . something else indeed.

–H. M. Hardcastle, *A Modern Yuletide*

Somehow we both managed to drop our lamps, which clattered out, leaving us in darkness. LaRue threw her arms around me, crushing my larynx.

"What is *that*? What *is* it?"

I'd caught scarcely a glimpse before the shock caused us to blind ourselves. I groped about in the darkness for the lanterns. "Let me find the—*yech*." I recoiled. That wasn't the warm smooth edge of brass I was hoping for. It was clammy and mossy and papery all at once, with a mouth-filling scent of age and dirt.

And something else. I put a hand out again, this time with scientific curiosity. Yes, was that—could it possibly be what I thought it was?

I wasn't entirely sure I wanted to know.

LaRue had found one of the lights and fumbled it into my hands. We crouched in each other's laps in the narrow passage, crumbs of earth and splinters of wood spilling around us. Together we managed to find my matches and get the lantern relit—and the bloom of light revealed that we were not alone. Not anymore.

Olive Blackwell was right here, too.

Or what was left of her.

She'd never made it out of the tunnels after all.

To her credit, LaRue just stared, fingers to her own lips. *Of course her own lips*, I thought a little wildly—*Olive doesn't have any anymore.* I twisted the lamp from her fingers for a better look. Olive's skeletal remains had tumbled partially through the wooden door when we'd broken it apart—her skull, part of her shoulder, a bit of arm and rib cage. Still recognizable, in tattered, mouse-eaten shreds, were the clothes she'd died in: what must have been a dark dress, and red-trimmed white wool. A toga.

"What—what happened to him?"

"Her," I said softly. "It's Olive Blackwell, the missing girl."

"The *murderer*? The one who's trying to kill my father?"

She had me there. "I guess not," I said slowly. "How did she die?"

I held the lamp closer to poor Olive's lonely form, feeling a pang of sorrow. "What happened?" I asked her. "Did you get lost, like us?"

"Myrtle!"

These were no conditions for a proper autopsy, although the cold tunnels of Olive's final resting place had preserved her remains somewhat. I glanced past the body into the chamber where she'd been hidden, all these years. An old lantern, a haversack, a reel of rope. She'd been so well prepared. I crept as close as I could, crawling over LaRue, hoping Olive might still be able to tell me how her story had ended. I hated to think she'd come this far, only to fail.

"Are you crying?" LaRue's voice was unexpectedly gentle. She reached out and squeezed my fingers. "Merciful Savior, we give thanks that it hath pleased Thee to deliver this our sister out of the miseries of this world. Through Jesus Christ our Lord, amen."

"Amen," I echoed. It didn't seem strange at all, LaRue Spence-Hastings saying a prayer over the skeleton of Olive Blackwell. "Can you light the other lamp? I want to see what happened to her, if I can."

A moment later, the deed was accomplished, and the two of us gave Olive Blackwell our best postmortem examination. LaRue was silent as I ran my fingers along the skull and mandible (taking care not to dislodge it), searching for injury. Had she hit her head? Broken her ankle? Starved? Suffocated? Died of boredom?

Something in the folds of her rotten toga caught the lamplight in a frail flicker. "What's that?" I leaned in closer, gently shifting the cloth out of the way. Shreds of it disintegrated at my touch, dust to dust. But underneath I found the source of the sparkle. On Olive's left arm, midway up her ulna and radius, she wore a gold bracelet.

"Is that a snake?"

"An asp," I said, heart stuck in my throat. An ouroboros, the signature of a member of Hadrian's Guard. *I gave her a leaving token when last we met.* Was it true? Gingerly, not at all certain what I was dealing with, I passed my fingers beneath the cold curve of the serpent's neck and found a clasp. It fell open like it had been waiting for me. I lifted it into the light—a circle of gold formed a striking snake, fangs out to deliver the killing bite. I turned it over, where a tiny glass vial nestled inside the metal cavity. Empty now, thank goodness, or Nora Carmichael might have claimed yet another victim.

"I think this was it." I showed it to LaRue, flexing the hinge on the bangle, demonstrating how the movement would cause the hollow fangs to retract and extend, drawing fluid from the vial.

"That's diabolical." I thought I heard appreciation

in her voice. "I've heard of poison rings, but never a poison bracelet."

I wondered how it had all come about. Had Nora followed Olive into the tunnels to strike her here, after she thought she was safe? Or had she given her the bracelet before, perhaps even in the Campanile, and all the time Olive thought she was heading to her new life, her old one was being sapped from her? Had she suffered much? Or had the passing been more gentle? Poisons were seldom as peaceful as most people supposed,* but some acted more quickly and less violently than others. Hemlock, for instance—which made me shudder. Would there still be traces in the vial to identify the poison?

And did it even matter anymore? Olive was dead— she'd *been* dead, all this time. And Nora was dead. David was dead. Mum was dead. I sank against the tunnel wall, dejected. After all that, I wanted to sit here and give up, too.

"Her family will finally know the truth," LaRue said. I couldn't tell if she'd read my mind or simply shared my thoughts. Or perhaps she was being Swinburne's First Daughter, moved by civic duty.

She was peering past Olive into the chamber. "She sure had a lot of candles," she Observed.

---

* certainly not the bite of the Egyptian cobra, which causes gastrointestinal distress, blistering, convulsions, paralysis, and tissue necrosis—no matter what Cleopatra may have claimed

"What?" I jerked myself back to an Investigative posture and looked where LaRue was pointing. Olive's recent little tumble had disturbed her resting place somewhat, but beyond the spot where her body must have sat, with her carefully set-down belongings, was a ring of fat pillar candles, the kind from church. They'd been lit, although how recently it was impossible to know.

"But if Olive lit them when she was dying, they'd have burned to the ground." My hammering heartbeat almost tripped up my tongue, but I got the next thought out. "Somebody *blew these out.*"

LaRue turned to me with a look of horror. "Someone knew she was here?"

Hastily, I wrapped the bracelet in my handkerchief and shoved it to the bottom of my satchel. We had to bring some evidence back, and the path we'd chalked along the tunnels would lead the police to Olive's body.

"We have to go," I said, tugging LaRue to her feet.

"Ow! What's the hurry?"

"You said it," I said. "Someone knows she's here." All at once, all the thoughts clamored together. Olive was dead. Olive wasn't the killer. Someone else had been here before us—and decided to exact revenge on Hadrian's Guard. Someone else knew about the tunnels. Someone obsessed with Olive Blackwell. *Someone else, someone else, someone else . . .* The words rang in my head as I scrambled from the narrow passage, dragging LaRue behind me. We shoved past the roots and ivy and back out into the space where the sewers forked.

Once again, we heard the muffled cry.

It wasn't rats.

This time I grabbed LaRue to me. "Back the way we came," I said, low in her ear.

"There's no way *out* that way. And the killer—"

"Is not at your house."

LaRue didn't listen. Haughty as always, she twisted from my grasp and headed straight down the other corridor—the one whence emanated the sounds of life. I stood for a moment, mentally reciting every Inappropriate Word I knew. Everything in me yelled to run the opposite direction, but I flung myself after LaRue. The two of us could probably fend off a murderer with hemlock, surely? And chloroform?

Now I had a headache. I stumbled along the tunnel, a proper branch of the sewer network, broad and open, refuse pipes rattling overhead.

"I think I see something," LaRue called back, rounding a corner.

I followed, and ran smack into her when she stopped short.

In a perplexed voice, she said, "It's *you.*"

"So it would seem. Myrtle, it took you long enough!" In the darkness and gloom, I recognized the voice.

Genie Shelley was waiting for us.

I banged backward, alarm choking off my breath.

"Myrtle, wait!" Her voice was hoarse.

Against my better judgment, my feet obeyed her. I stood frozen in the passage behind LaRue.

"What are you doing down here?" I croaked. I tried to take in the scene, though my brain flailed like a frightened rabbit, sending up desperate urges to flee. I'd been right all along. And now we were trapped down here with her.

"I think she's hurt. Myrtle, for heaven's sake, get over here."

LaRue shone her light on Genie, who was not lunging for us with a chloroform-soaked rag. Slumped against the curved brick wall, she lifted a hand in a weak wave. The first sensible thing I noticed was that she'd lost her spectacles. And evidently any light she'd brought. It didn't seem to be a very well planned ambush.

LaRue crouched beside her. In the flickering lamp-light, Genie's face was drawn and white, her hair a fright, and she had scratches on her hands and chin. She'd taken a bad fall.

"I think my ankle's broken." She coughed, and now I saw the rip in her skirt. "I've been here for hours, screaming my head off. I knew you'd come. Or Robbie. Somebody. But somehow, I hoped it would be you."

"*Why* are you here?" I said, still wary.

"I told you, I came to find out who killed Leighton and Nora. But as usual, nothing quite goes as Genie plans it. Is Robbie all right? I'm afraid we had quite the barney. Is it still Monday?"

"Tuesday night," I said. "You've been down here since yesterday?"

"You're lucky you didn't freeze," LaRue said.

"Did you find any evidence?" I hadn't decided whether to trust her. She certainly seemed injured in true—but it was just too coincidental, finding her down here. Wasn't it? But if she'd been here overnight, that meant she'd come down *before* the Caesar tableau appeared in the Display.

"I hate to be a bother," Genie said, "but my ankle really hurts, and I'm dying for a cup of tea. Can we talk about this later?" Face scrunched, she tried to make something out. "You're the Mayor's daughter, aren't you?" She struggled to sit up, letting out a whimpering gasp. "Has something happened? Blast it, I've lost my pencil."

"You can interview her later," I said. "We'll have to send for help."

"Nothing doing," Genie said. "I'm not waiting here another minute. We're all strapping girls. We can get out of this together."

I had finally inched closer, and there was no denying that something was wrong with Genie's right ankle. She could not be faking the impossible angle at which her toes pointed. The skeleton of Olive Blackwell had not made me squeamish, but my stomach turned at the sight of Genie's injured foot. I gulped, but came forward. Perhaps we could fashion her a splint from something—the rotted wood from the door to Olive's burial chamber and the strings to LaRue's corset?

Genie was eyeing me stoically. "I'm fine," she said. "I just need a little help."

"We found her," I said abruptly. "Olive. She's down here. She died," I added, softly.

Genie's keen expression clouded over, and she crossed herself. "There but for the grace of Myrtle Hardcastle," she murmured. "An accident?"

"Murder." I fished in my satchel for the bracelet.

Genie squinted at it, holding it close to her face, and sighed. "Nora? It's almost poetic, then. I want to see her."

"You can't even walk," I pointed out. "*Or* see."

She held my gaze. "I've been searching for Olive Blackwell since I was your age," she said. "I will *crawl* there, if I have to."

"Wait." LaRue interrupted us. "If Olive's not the killer, and *you're* not the killer—then who is after my father?"

Genie and I shared a belated, and at least on her part blurry, look.

"We've eliminated all the suspects," I said.

"Or, more to the point, the killer has," replied

Genie. She tried to shift into a more comfortable position. "Oof," she said. "This stupid thing. I was trying to reach for it when I fell. I never even saw what it was."

She was holding out a small, shiny, round object, and I was surprised she hadn't *heard* what it was—but she must have squashed it and lost or damaged the clapper. Giving it a little shake, I heard a faint, dull rattle, not a cheery jingle.

"It's a bell?" Genie said. "Where did that come from?"

But I knew. And the force of the realization sent me straight to my feet, nearly banging my head against the low ceiling of Genie's chamber.

"Myrtle! What is it?"

"We have to go. The killer is at your house."

LaRue wailed, "You just said she *wasn't*!"

"I was wrong," I said. "I've been wrong all along. It's not Olive at all. It's Leah." The scrap of wool, the bells—both from Leah's long blue cloak.

They both just stared at me. "Who's Leah?" LaRue asked.

Genie seemed to search her memory. "Wait—the carillon player? She's—" I watched the pieces come together for her. "Leah *Blackwell*. The baby sister. How did I miss that?" She gave her forehead a gentle smack. "She's at the Campanile every day. She knows all about the steam tunnels. She must have gone exploring once, and found her sister's body."

"The candles!" LaRue exclaimed. "Like a shrine."

"All this time, she thought Olive had run away." I could imagine the disappointment—the disillusionment she must have felt when she discovered her hopes so cruelly dashed. Had she realized Olive had been murdered, and not merely met with some mischance? Would that even matter?

"But—no," Genie said. "She can't have done it. She was playing the carillon when Nora was murdered. I was there. I *heard* her."

And, like that, the gears clicked into motion, and the whole program played out before me, in all its splendid, sinister orchestration. "The bells are automated! Like a music box—if Leah could arrange for them to chime the hour automatically, she must have figured out how to set it up to play her Christmas music, too." I glanced at the tunnel ceiling with a sigh, thinking we'd all be better off if Schofield College produced fewer brilliant engineers.

"Making us all her alibi," said Genie. "She's terribly clever."

"She's after my father!" LaRue cried. "We might already be too late!"

"Get me up," Genie commanded. "We'll find a way out of here. The map's in my coat pocket. My blue, *not*-a-murderer's-coat pocket," she added with a weak grin.

LaRue looked like she wanted to kiss Genie. "You have a map," she said, and it came out a sort of blissful sigh.

"I came prepared." LaRue helped Genie to a position where she could reach into her pocket, and out came a folded paper—and a long leather cord holding a brass whistle. "Oh," she said faintly.

"Give me that." I snatched it from her. "Miss Judson warned you what could happen."

"Incorrigible," Genie said. "I told you."

"I hate you both," LaRue said.

26
SEMPER FERIANS

Above all else, Christmas is a time of good cheer.

-H. M. Hardcastle, *A Modern Yuletide*

There was no rushing Genie, no matter how LaRue complained, cajoled, and exhorted. She was game and hardly protested, but a broken ankle is no trifling thing. We'd recovered her glasses, at least. When we passed the corridor where Olive Blackwell had waited so long for someone to find her, Genie issued a wistful sigh, but gripped LaRue all the harder and nodded her onward.

A slow, painful progress is not conducive to rational thought. My imagination ran away, down the tunnels and back up to the Mansion House. Was the Mayor still alive? Was Leah even now innocently playing the pianoforte, waiting for the moment she'd pull a dagger from her music case and slice him to ribbons? If only I hadn't made that promise to Father, we might have solved the case sooner, and not been duped when sweet frantic Leah burst on the scene, sobbing about her sister. What would we find when we finally emerged from our catacombs? I didn't dare speculate, but I couldn't help worrying.

Genie's hand on my shoulder tightened, and I bucked up. LaRue, taller than I, had the brunt of Genie's weight, so I held the light. We had to make frequent stops to navigate and let Genie catch her breath, but eventually we made it back to the cavern under the tramlines.

"This is where we got lost before," LaRue pointed out. She shrugged Genie into a more comfortable position, as Genie panted and I studied the map.

Genie coughed. "I think I hear someone."

"Maybe it's help!" LaRue cried.

"Maybe it's the killer," I said.

"At this point, I'll take either one," replied Genie. "Blow the whistle, Myrtle."

With only brief hesitation, I obeyed. It was a proper police whistle, and it pealed out gloriously, reverberating from the bricks and ironworks, bouncing down along the tunnels. I gave it several hearty blasts, and I'll admit it—by the last couple, it was for pure enjoyment's sake alone.

When the last cold high pitch faded away, we heard a distant but very distinct, "*No.*"

"Wait," said Genie. "I'd know that scornful meow anywhere."

Peony? "Peony!" In my relief and excitement, I waved the lantern, wreathing us in plumes of smoke.

"Hulloooooo . . ." A man's voice echoed down the tunnels, and I tweeted the whistle once again. A return blast answered me. LaRue and Genie cried out, Genie a bit raspily.

"Help! Hello! We're down here! She's hurt!"

We saw the bobbing of lanterns before we saw our rescuers, but they gradually sorted themselves into a cluster of black-clad constables and a few other figures that weren't immediately recognizable.

"Father?" LaRue's voice was tentative. "Is my father all right?"

"LaRue?" A small figure broke through the knot to dash down the icy sewer and swing LaRue into a desperate embrace. Mayor Spence-Hastings had lost his red robes but seemed otherwise unharmed.

"You must help Miss Shelley." LaRue found a hint of her old imperiousness, and her father waved the policemen over. Genie was propped awkwardly against a curve of tunnel wall, and twining about her injured ankle, bumping her hard black head into it, was Peony. Genie gritted her teeth and made not a sound, although her eyes rolled with agony.

"Myrtle!"

I whirled about to see Father and Miss Judson running down the tunnel toward me.

Father looked much as I'd seen him last, but Miss Judson—where had she come from?

"What—?" I waved the lantern at her, casting a wide bright glow against a skirt, jacket, and face caked in—what was that? Plaster? Paint? I could not identify the *color*, let alone the substance . . . s. But I thought I smelled Christmas dinner: beef, custard, brandy, nutmeg. Olfactory hallucinations brought on by shock, clearly. A cherry rolled down her skirt and plopped onto the tunnel floor.

"You're not wearing your party dress," I managed.

She held up a weary finger—likewise sticky. "Don't ask."

"Where did you come from?" I demanded. "And what about Leah?"

Father caught me up in an embrace as fierce as the Mayor's, momentarily silencing all my questions. "That's my brave girl," he said.

I held on until I ran out of breath—then promptly resumed my report. "Leah is the killer! We found her bell—"

Father's hands were on my shoulders. "We know."

"You know? How?"

Father held a hand out to Miss Judson, inviting her to take the floor. She sighed. "There must be a more convivial place to have this conversation—"

"No!" My voice rang, shrill as the whistle. "Tell me *now!*" I stomped a foot. Behind us, Mr. Blakeney had scrambled through the mob, along with two constables, one of whom toted an armload of blankets.

"Stephen!" He lifted his arm in an expansive wave.

"I found Genie," I volunteered, and he grinned.

"I saved the Mayor," he said. "Or, well, Miss J. did. But I helped."

"You were quite the gallant, Mr. Blakeney."

"Is *nobody* going to tell me what happened?"

Peony had abandoned her torment of Genie. She sat smugly, tail curled. *"No."*

⁓

Eventually, with as much excruciating slowness as the journey with Genie, the details all came to light. The police and Mr. Blakeney took Genie off to hospital to have her leg mended, the Mayor took LaRue home, and the rest of us found our way back to the surface, to assemble where we'd begun—in Leighton's Mercantile. It began with Miss Judson's accounting of herself.

"While you and your father were gone, I took another look at Miss Shelley's clippings," she explained. "It seems she'd solved the case already—although she hadn't realized it." In among them was a retrospective piece we'd overlooked, from the *Upton Register* on the tenth anniversary of Olive's disappearance. "It featured another family portrait—with the two remaining sisters. Then Cook mentioned that a young woman from the college had been hired as the musical entertainment for the Mayor's ball—and as Genie would say, I put two and two together. So I dashed over to warn everyone."

"With Peony," I said. "In a snowstorm."

"Naturally."

Father took over the account. "By this point I'd summoned the police to the Mayor's house. I arrived . . . at about the same time Miss Judson was wrestling Leah on the buffet table."

Miss Judson wiped a smear of something from her bodice and looked at it sadly. "Cook's trifle," she said. "Pity."

Their narrative was improbable in the extreme, yet I could not discount the evidence before my very eyes. I closed my mind to the image of Miss Judson and Leah Blackwell locked in a Greco-Roman bout over a flaming Christmas pudding, and focused instead on the legal practicalities. "What about Leah? Did she say anything?"

"Just a lot of vitriolic raving." Father shook his head. "Bringing a dagger to the Mayor's Christmas Ball? I'm going to recommend a psychiatric commitment."

I sighed, and Peony snuggled deeper into my lap. It was all so sad. "Now the Blackwells have lost two daughters." Sometimes there was too much awfulness to go around.

"I think Leah was always lost to them," Miss Judson said. "Living in the shadow of Olive's disappearance, shuffled away, she never got to have her own proper childhood."

"A proper childhood," Father mused. "What would that look like, I wonder?"

Miss Judson eyed me sidelong. "It would have fewer sewer expeditions," she conjectured.

"Well, happily," I said, stroking Peony's neck, "we'll never know."

⁓

Christmas morning arrived amid a flurry of activity. I forced myself to stay abed until I heard Cook rattling about the kitchen, then scrambled into clothes and down the stairs.

Several days had passed since the Mayor's Christmas party came to such an ignominious end, and the village was still coming to terms with all of the revelations from that night. Genie had kept everyone entertained and informed from her hospital bed, reporting with vigor on every stage of the unraveling story. Leah had taken Mrs. Leighton's place in jail, and the other Blackwells held a small private funeral for Olive. The Campanile was silent.

Genie made the most of her own part of the adventure (taking particular delight in the most gruesome details of her experiences at the Royal Swinburne Hospital), even writing a splendid article casting me and LaRue as her rescuers. The Mayor might have given us medals—if he hadn't resigned.

Father, mug of steaming cider in one hand, watched me bypass the parlor with its laden Christmas tree, ignore the dining room with its enticing Christmas breakfast (it took a considerable share of my Exceptional Forbearance to forgo the gingerbread, sending off its wafts of clovey steam), and slip out the door.

"Father Christmas comes down the chimney," he informed me.

"I'm waiting for Caroline. She has Miss Judson's present!" Inspiration had *finally* struck, in the midst of the week's excitement. And I was hoping she might bring other news as well—the things that Genie had tactfully left out of the public version.

Indeed she did. She bustled up the front walk, braid swinging. "I can't stay long. Mother's organized us to go caroling at the hospital." She handed over a small, flat parcel, already wrapped. "It looks splendid. Nanette did good work."

And *fast*, thank goodness. "She got the gravy out?"

"Most of it."

I grinned. That was even better. "What about your dad? Have you heard anything?"

"He talked to Inspector Hardy for *hours* the other day." She looked pensive. "Mr. Spence-Hastings is going to take a post in Canada. The Northwest Territories."

I felt a surge of something unfamiliar. "Poor LaRue."

"Anyway, you were right. Father had all of the papers from Mrs. Leighton's, and he's turned them over to the Inspector, along with everything he had in his DECAPITATED? file. He'd saved it all, going back twenty years. Even the early police reports from Olive's disappearance."

"Then they weren't missing," I said.

She shook her head. "They were at our house the whole time! Can you believe it? He was worried something might happen to them. He wanted to make sure the whole story was preserved, good and bad."

Thinking about Genie and her suspicions, I had to approve.

"He didn't do anything wrong," I said. Mayor—Mr. Spence-Hastings had cleared him of any involvement in the plot against Olive or the forgery of the Chalice. It was still on display, by the way—now clearly labeled as a replica constructed and donated by Hadrian's Guard. I couldn't decide how I felt about that.

"Neither did your mum."

We regarded each other solemnly. Maybe so, but they'd both lost a good friend—several good friends— in a horrible way. "Tell him I'm sorry that she didn't escape, like Mum hoped."

She gave me a quick, fierce hug. "He told *me* to thank you for putting it all to rest." With a little wave, she scurried back across the snowy park, already filling up with families and merrymakers and boys engaged in a battle with snowballs, and looking every bit the sort of scene Mr. Leighton would have wanted to build in his display. Perhaps Mrs. Leighton, now that she was free again, would fix it up instead.

Inside, Father, Miss Judson, Cook, and Peony were waiting. A stack of presents was waiting. Cocoa and gingerbread and biscuits were waiting—and somewhere across town, Aunt Helena was waiting with her *Bûche de Noël.* But first, the Hardcastles of No. 14 Gravesend Close had Serious Business.

Once the crackers were snapped and the paper crowns distributed, we sorted through the gifts. One of Miss Judson's beautiful combs had broken in all the commotion, and Father never got the chance to present them to her, but the new hairbrush was some consolation. She flicked a finger across the boar bristles with satisfaction.

"Now you," she said, handing me a parcel. "From the Blakeneys."

It was a rigid, lumpy, untidily wrapped, mysterious-shaped package that rattled ever so slightly with my experimental shake. Peony subjected it to her own Inspection as I peeled away the tissue paper then held it up, wonderingly.

"I didn't know you could have a miner's helmet engraved," Observed Father.

I traced the letters inscribed on the candle's metal bracket:

to S M: *Stay Incorrigible.* —G&R B

Peony claimed it, with a long, approving swipe of her whiskers, and gave a contented burble. Unless that was me.

Finally, the moment arrived to present Miss Judson with her gift. Miss Judson, as you might predict, was a methodical and meticulous gift-unwrapper, painstakingly unsealing each flap and slipping the wrapping off untorn, in a process an Observer might find maddening. But at long last, she removed the lid from the box, unfolded the tissue, and held the contents up for us all to admire.

It was a crazy-patchwork dresser scarf—or the beginnings of one—pieced together from her ruined skirt, scraps of Genie's blue coat, one of Father's old waistcoats, an apron from Cook, a snippet of fungus-colored wool from an Anonymous Donor, and a lacy blue frock I'd destroyed last summer. Embroidered on the stained brown wool from her skirt were a sprig of olives, a wishing well, and a whistle, along with *1893* in fine stitchery.

Miss Judson took a long time to react, stroking the

stitches and the stain with graceful, thoughtful, artistic fingers. "That," she finally declared, eyes very bright, "is a work of magnificence."

"Nanette Munjal made it," I said. "But it was my idea. She's going to teach me how to embroider a lily for the tea gown." To commemorate Miss Judson's and my first Investigation.

Father met my gaze with a smile. *"Bene factum, Filia."*

After each scrap of cloth was identified, every stitch examined and admired, Miss Judson rose and draped the scarf in pride of place across the mantelpiece, where the plump stockings hung.

"What's this I see?" she Inquired, prodding at the one that read *Helena.* (Despite years of pleading, this had never been redacted.)

I considered the evidence. "The round bulge at the toe is the approximate size and shape of *Citrus sinensis*, the sweet orange. The other item is hard and cylindrical, but it is unlikely to be a spyglass, as I already possess one. Therefore, I deduce—it is a rolled-up magazine."

In triumph, I pulled it out: December's issue of *The Strand*, with its light-blue cover and illustrated London street scene. At once I unfurled it and commandeered the settee, eager to settle in, at long last, with the much-anticipated Sherlock Holmes mystery.

"That will have to wait." Miss Judson plucked it

from my hands and returned it to the stocking. "I promised the Blakeneys we'd visit Genie before dinner with Aunt Helena, and Priscilla's asked us over for tea this afternoon."

I hopped up, magazine forgotten. "The hospital has an anatomy theater that's open to the public. Maybe they'll let us watch a procedure!" Then I caught the look of dismay on Father's face. "Well, maybe not on Christmas."

Father gave a sigh of relief. "Yes," he said drily, "let's save *that* Family Amusement for another time."

The Investigation Will Continue
in
In Myrtle Peril

A NOTE FROM THE AUTHOR

The term *cold case* did not enter the criminology lexicon until the 1970s, although long before anyone thought up the fitting and catchy phrase we use today, many cases went unsolved and lingered in their investigators' imaginations. One of the most famous cold cases of all time is the still-unsolved murder of five women in London's Whitechapel area in the fall of 1888.

The December 1893 issue of *The Strand* contained the last Sherlock Holmes story to be published in the nineteenth century. "The Adventure of the Final Problem" concerns the ill-fated confrontation between Holmes and a newly introduced archenemy, Professor Moriarty. Fans at the time were shocked, outraged, and dismayed by what they saw as an ignominious end to a literary folk hero. As is the case with Mrs. Blakeney, the opinion of this Learned Reader is not suitable for print. Sir Arthur Conan Doyle eventually returned to writing Holmes mysteries, with *The Hound of the Baskervilles*, serialized by *The Strand* from 1901 to 1902. Anyone looking for a truly worthy Sherlockian villain should reach for "The Adventure of Charles Augustus Milverton," which Myrtle will not get to read for another eleven years.

Scholars have debated the meaning of Socrates's cryptic last words (as quoted by Plato) for millennia. Proposed explanations have covered everything from a simple appeal to the god of healing, to a rude joke. Classicist Colin Wells takes an investigative approach, systematically examining the crime scene, so to speak, for clues to the dying philosopher's last request. Those interested in his conclusions can learn more at www.colinwellsauthor.com/articles.

Europeans have been fascinated by archaeological artifacts since the dawn of civilization, but the modern discipline of archaeology was still in its infancy in the 1870s, when Myrtle's mother and her classmates were students. Forgeries and hoaxes plagued early archaeology, and some well-known artifacts are now thought to have questionable origins. Sometimes these fakeries supported prejudiced agendas. Hoaxsters tried to discredit scientists or give a particular region what they believed was a more distinguished history (such as a greater Roman presence in parts of ancient Britain, as with Professor Leighton's Saturnalia Chalice; or the prehistoric settlement of North America by a "lost race" of Europeans with the so-called Davenport Tablets in the 1870s). Advances in scientific methods and stringent excavation practices gradually turned relic hunters and tomb raiders into scholars and scientists. Archaeology is practiced as a field of anthropology in the United States, while in England and Europe it's considered a branch of history. In the years since I earned my anthropology degree, archaeology has undergone even further ethical and scientific advances.

Schofield College's Campanile was inspired by the Iowa State University Campanile in my hometown of Ames, Iowa (where, to my knowledge, no one has ever fallen to her death . . . or not). I am grateful to Doris Aman, carillonist at the University of Rochester's Hopeman Memorial Carillon, for answering my carillon questions, as well as her haunting and magical depiction of carillon acoustics. I hope I've done her lovely instrument justice.

My thanks, as always, to Myrtle's incredible cohort at Algonquin Young Readers: editor Elise Howard, Ashley Mason, Sarah Alpert, Brett Helquist, Carla Weise, and Laura Williams, for making the books wonderful to behold. Thanks to Kelly Doyle, Megan Harley, and Caitlin Rubinstein for spreading the word about Myrtle far and wide. Exceptional thanks go to copyeditor *ne plus ultra* Sue Wilkins (who will no doubt have something to say about this sentence). Thanks to Scott McKuen for consultation on nineteenth-century physics, maths, and chemistry. And to my partner in crime in all things, C.J. Bunce.